on the shore

Cottonwood Cove ~ Book 3

laura pavlov

To all the women in my life who inspire me to write fierce heroines…I'm thankful for YOU.

"Beauty is being the best possible version of yourself, inside and out. "
Audrey Hepburn

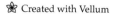

one

· · ·

Brinkley

THE SUN WAS SHINING, and a light breeze bustled around us. It was a beautiful day to be outside.

"So, the moral of the story is… when life gives you lemons, make lemonade," I said.

"Ohhh. I love lemonade, Auntie!" Gracie clapped her hands together and bounced up and down. My niece was turning five years old soon, and now that I was living in Cottonwood Cove, I was able to spend lots of time with her. I'd picked her up from pre-K and brought her to my place to have lunch and do some gardening with me.

"Well, I do have lemonade. Let's take a break and go inside, okay?" I dropped the hand shovel on the ground and swiped at the sweat rolling down my forehead. I glanced around to see the fresh dirt covering the four planter boxes I'd built over the last two weeks.

Two weeks. That was how long I'd been home.

That was how long I'd been unemployed.

Well, technically, I was working for myself. I was currently a freelance sports reporter, and I'd already submitted an article covering the truths behind the arrogance of professional athletes. But I'd had one particular athlete in mind when I'd written the article.

I thought it was my best work. I'd already heard back from *Football Live* magazine, and though they'd loved the article, they felt it was too obvious that I was speaking of one specific athlete.

Lincoln. Mother. Freaking. Hendrix.

I guess calling him out as the GOAT of the NFL in the article was a dead giveaway.

They didn't know that the man had gotten me fired from my last job because he'd had a childish meltdown on a public stage. Most people weren't aware that I'd lost my job; they'd thought I'd just been kicked out of a press conference.

So, *Football Live* requested that I make some tweaks. Make it sound more general.

Don't reference anyone in particular.

Maybe *tone down my anger*.

Their words, not mine.

I was just fine with my anger.

I'd put that article on the back burner because the truth was, I couldn't write it without pointing out that man in particular.

As much as I wanted to prove that I could make it as a freelance writer, I wasn't at a point in my career where I could financially pull this off for very long. I wasn't well known at all, and I'd been working for a horrible man at a small press, trying to make a name for myself over the last few years.

I needed to focus on one strong story that would be easy to sell and land me a position at a large publication.

One where people would actually read my work.

Football Live suggested I write an article on the trials and tribulations of professional football players.

I reached for two glasses and opened the refrigerator, pulling out the pitcher of lemonade.

My mind wandered to thoughts of Lincoln Hendrix.

Trials and tribulations, my ass.

That bastard was the highest-paid football player in the league. What did he have to be upset about?

The damn golden boy of football.

"You looks kind of angry, Auntie." Gracie sat in the chair at my kitchen table, and her chubby little hands were folded together. We wore matching overalls, as she'd loved mine last week, so I'd gotten her a pair of her own so we could be twins today.

I'd rolled two bandanas and tied one around my head and then did the same to hers. Two little space buns with oodles of curls sat on top of her head, where the pink fabric gathered in a knot and the ends stuck straight up like rabbit ears.

She was adorable.

"I'm not angry, baby girl. I'm just thinking about something that bothered me." I set her glass down and took the seat beside her.

"What's you thinking about?"

"Well, remember I told you I moved back home because someone did something that wasn't very nice to me?" I shrugged. My family was sick of me cursing the bastard's name, so if a four-year-old wanted to hear about my woes, I had no shame in my game.

"Yep. And that's why you're living in Bossman and Auntie Georgie's house, right?" Her voice was my favorite sound in the whole world. She spoke with almost a southern accent, which we all found hilarious seeing as we lived in a small town in northern California. It was all sweetness and innocence, and Gracie Reynolds was probably my favorite person on the planet.

She was my oldest brother's little girl. Cage was raising her on his own, so in a way, she was all of ours.

"Yep. I'm living in their house and starting a new job, working for myself until I find the right magazine to work for this time. The last one wasn't a good fit anyway. It was time for a change."

"And you're going to grows all your own foods, right, Auntie? And you make the magic boards now." She looked around the small space. Piles of seeds and a few potted plants sat on the counter, while two canvas boards with magazine clippings and a bottle of Mod Podge sat on the coffee table.

What can I say? I wasn't used to having this much time on my hands. I was trying to figure out what I wanted to do with my life.

So, I'd grow my own food.

Spend time on my vision boards and decide what my dream job looked like now that I had the time to do so.

Originally, when I'd been hired by *Athlete Central* right out of college, I'd been thrilled. But working for a complete asshole had been uninspiring.

And being fired by him had been humiliating.

"Yep. They aren't magic boards; they are vision boards. They hold all my dreams," I said with a chuckle.

"I love my dreams. You knows what my teacher says? Mrs. Appleton's a real smart lady." She smacked her lips together after she took a big sip of lemonade and smiled at me. "This is so yummy."

"It is good, isn't it? Soon, we'll be making it with our own lemons from the garden." I had no idea how long that would take. Hell, I'd never planted anything in my life. But right now, I was going to enjoy this time away from the long hours and do things I'd never had time to do. I was channeling my inner Martha Stewart. Tapping into a new side of myself. "Tell me what your really smart teacher says."

She pushed back in her chair and moved to her feet before holding her arms up for me to lift her onto my lap. Gracie lived with my brother, who was a self-admitted grump, yet he'd managed to raise the absolute sweetest kid on the planet.

Her hands found each side of my face as she settled on my thighs.

"Nobody's perfects. If they say sorry, just give them a hug."

Riveting advice, Mrs. Appleton. Perhaps you've never been publicly humiliated.

"Hmmm… that's great. But what if the person did something really mean to you?" I asked, looking down at her giant chocolate-brown eyes that studied me like this was the most serious conversation she'd ever had.

"She said you give hugs, Auntie. Nobody's perfects. All the peoples makes mistakes."

Was her teacher seriously quoting a Hannah Montana song? I swear I'd heard lyrics that said something very similar to this before. I called bullshit on Mrs. Appleton, but I wouldn't burst Gracie's bubble.

"Well, I'll think about it. But in the meantime, we'll keep planting and hanging out, and next week, I'll help you make your own vision board, okay?"

"Yay. My own dreams board."

"Yes. Never stop dreaming, baby girl."

"I loves the dreams," she sang out.

I laughed and kissed the top of her head just as the knock on the door had us both pushing to our feet.

"Daddy's here!" she shouted and ran to the door.

Cage walked in and scooped her up, glancing around the house with wide eyes.

"Wow. I thought you were going to take a break. You've already submitted one article and planted multiple boxes full of fruits and vegetables, and do I even want to know what those boards are for?" He pointed at my craft area a few feet away.

"Don't you worry about it. I'm a woman of many talents." I shrugged.

He kissed Gracie's cheek and told her to go wash her

hands and grab her book bag while I moved to the kitchen and poured him a glass of lemonade.

"What's going on?" he asked, watching me with concern.

"Nothing. I'm doing all the things I never had time to do before because I was working too much."

"I see." He nodded. "The matching outfits are pretty cute. But if you tell anyone I said that, I'll be forced to kill you. Can't have the family thinking I'm going soft."

"Your secret's safe with me. Not sure if you noticed, but I've got overalls in every color now. This is what I'm wearing until I get a new job. I'm an organic-farming, relaxed woman now. I write a few hours a day, and I'll just enjoy this time until I find something. But it's probably going to take some time, so you better get used to the new me."

His eyes widened. "All right. Got it. If you want to come help out at the office, I can always use a hand."

Cage was a veterinarian, and he had his own practice in town. "As tempting as that sounds, I need to find a story and dazzle someone enough to offer me a permanent position."

"Well, if you have time to write in between all your new hobbies, I think you'll land on your feet quickly." He smirked. "How are you doing on money? Do you need a little bit to help carry you over during this time?"

Always the practical one.

"I'm fine. I'm paying one dollar a month in rent because I insisted on renting this place above board, and Maddox and Georgie wrote up a formal lease with the ridiculous rent." I chuckled. "And I had a pretty good savings going because I was hoping to buy a condo in the city in the next year or so, but that won't be happening anytime soon now."

"You'll get in with a much better organization. I think this was actually a blessing because you're not a quitter, so you wouldn't have bailed. But your hand was forced, and you've got experience on your résumé this time. You'll sign with someone soon. Just keep writing."

"Did you just call what happened a blessing? Oh my gosh." I flailed my hands in his face. "Are you still trying to get me to tell you it's okay to fangirl over the man who ruined my life? Do not try to glaze over what he did by calling it a blessing. It's offensive. Ugh, you are all the same." My brothers and Maddox had all found roundabout ways of seeing if I still hated the man because, of course, he happened to be everyone's favorite quarterback in this part of the country.

"First off, I don't *fangirl*, and I take offense to the accusation. The dude has been my favorite QB for years, but of course, I'll agree to hate him right alongside you. Not because I think it's a mature or rational request, but because you're a bit terrifying when you're angry." He smirked.

I rolled my eyes. "Whatever. I never claimed to be mature or rational."

"I couldn't agree more," he said dryly, but I saw the corners of his lips turn up the slightest bit.

"Daddy, what pets did you sees today?" Gracie asked, running toward us with her book bag.

"It was a slow day. But I saw three dogs, one horse, and a pig. The highlight was Mrs. Runither coming in and demanding to be seen." He took another long pull from his glass before setting it on my counter.

"She has animals?" I asked. Mrs. Runither owned Cottonwood Café and was the most sexually inappropriate woman I'd ever met. She harassed her customers about their sex lives, yet it was hard to stay away as her macaroni and cheese was the best in town.

"No." He raised a brow at me. "She wanted me to look at a mole… *on her chest*."

My head tipped back in laughter.

These were the moments that I was grateful to be back home.

"What's did you do, Daddy?" Gracie asked as he pulled her up into his arms. "Did you help the lady?"

"I sent her to a dermatologist." His voice was firm, and I was still laughing. "Thanks for picking her up today."

"Thank you, Auntie. I loves you."

"I loves you more." I kissed each of her rosy cheeks and the tip of her nose as she giggled.

"You want to come over for dinner?" Cage asked as he walked toward the door. I knew my siblings were all worried about me, but I was doing just fine.

Great, actually.

"Thanks, but I'm okay. I'm going to work for a little bit and then go see Mom and Dad."

"All right. We'll see you later." He held a hand up, and I closed the door.

I spent the next hour scanning the internet for sports publications and went through a bunch of submission ideas before walking the few blocks to my parents' house. The sun was just going down, and it was a perfect night for a walk. My phone buzzed, and I knew before I looked that it was the sibling group chat, which was always ongoing.

GEORGIA

Hey, we just got home from work. I was swamped today. What's everyone doing?

FINN

Just finished filming for the day. I think Jessica Carson is actually into me. She just asked me to come to her trailer and hang out. She kept grinding up against me long after they called the scene today.

CAGE

Don't shit where you eat, brother. It has
disaster written all over it.

GEORGIA

What if you live in a tiny house? Wouldn't you
have to shit where you eat?

HUGH

Yeah, I'm guessing Finny boy wants to live in
a tiny house and get busy with his costar.

Stay away from Hotty-McSnotty! I got very
narcissistic vibes from her in the two
interviews I watched with her.

HUGH

I don't think he's thinking of a long future
here, Brinks.

Take it from someone who has experienced
job stress. Not worth it. Walk away.

FINN

She's not my boss. We work together. Sure,
she can be a bit much sometimes. She's got
some serious diva tendencies, but she's hot.

CAGE

You're just bored because Reese has been
gone for so long. You're looking for a
companion, not a hookup. Walk away.

Finn and Reese had been best friends for as long as I could
remember. She'd gone through a bad breakup with her long-
time boyfriend, who was now her ex-fiancé, and she'd been in
Europe for the last several months, working for a design firm
there. The two had always been inseparable, and we all

noticed the difference in him since she'd been gone. He was a lot needier than he'd ever been, but I wouldn't tell him that.

> **HUGH**
> I love when you go deep, Old Wise One.

> **CAGE**
> It's OLE Wise One. Don't call me old, you dick sausage.

> <eggplant emoji> <hotdog emoji>

> **GEORGIA**
> Maybe Finn would bring out a softer side of Jessica. Love can do that to people. Look at Bossman.

> **CAGE**
> <puking emoji>

> **GEORGIA**
> <heart eyes emoji>

> Also, since we're all being a little emotional here about love and happily ever after, I am here to remind you that we still hate the football player from hell. Cage tried to pull his sly, undercover crap and see if he could start getting his "Bieber Fever" on for that rat bastard, and the answer is a big, fat, resounding no.

> **CAGE**
> What the hell is "Bieber Fever"?

> **GEORGIA**
> She's calling you a fangirl. <laughing emoji>

HUGH

I confess. I asked Cage to find out if we were still hating on Hendrix. I tried to change the channel when they were giving updates on where they think he is going to play next year, but old habits die hard, Brinks. I still hate him out of respect for you. I just want to know where he's going to play next season.

FINN

I hate him, too. But did you hear he's leaning toward New York?

CAGE

I also heard Los Angeles is in the running. That's when I ran to turn off the TV because the sound of his name makes me sick.
<eyeroll emoji>

> You're all a bunch of traitors. We do not cheer for the enemy.

GEORGIA

Well, I hate him for sure. But I did catch Maddox watching SportsCenter, and he was glued to the TV when they mentioned him.

> Not a loyal one in the bunch aside from you, Georgie.

CAGE

Don't be dramatic. It's a big ask.

> <middle finger emoji>

FINN

So, wait. Do I go for it with Hotty-McSnotty? Can we circle back to me?

> Walk away. Don't make me say "I told you so." You know I hate to be a know-it-all.

CAGE

> Who is this, and what did you do with Brinks?

I chuckled as several texts came through. Everyone said he should not mix business with pleasure, aside from Georgia, who only wanted to see the best in everyone.

I'd never been that way.

When people showed me who they were, I typically believed them.

And I knew exactly who Lincoln Hendrix was.

two

. . .

Lincoln

MY MOM WAS ASKING MORE questions than I was in
the mood to answer at the moment. I'd stumbled into this
little café as soon as I'd pulled into town, needing to stretch
my legs and get a bite to eat. I'd ordered an iced coffee and a
sandwich and found a table in the back of the quaint
restaurant.

I'd kept my sunglasses and a baseball cap on out of habit,
but no one was in here, so I set them aside. This was exactly
what I needed.

Some quiet.

Some peace.

I couldn't ask for more.

"So, how long do you think you'll stay?" she asked as I
held the phone to my ear.

"I don't know. I haven't even been to the house yet. Drew
said I can stay as long as I want. Apparently, he and Deb are
busy with work and the kids' activities, so they won't be
coming for several months."

"You could come home," Mom said, though she'd offered
it multiple times already.

"I know. And thank you. But I wanted to get out of the

city. I need a break while I figure out my shit. I don't want people grilling me every time I walk out my door. And I want you to have some peace while you continue to get healthier every day." My mom had a house outside of San Francisco, while I lived in a high-rise in the city. But everyone knew me there, and that was what I was trying to avoid at the moment.

I couldn't think.

I couldn't breathe.

"You do what's best for you, Linc. You know I'll support you, no matter what you decide."

There were a few things that I was certain of right now. But my mom's support had always been the most solid thing in my life.

"I know, and I appreciate it. There's a lot to consider, and it's weighing on me."

"Well, I'm here anytime you want to talk."

"You got it. I'll call you in a day or two after I get settled."

"Love you, Linc."

"Love you." I ended the call and took a bite of my sandwich as I glanced around the place. This town was like something out of a movie. It sat on the coast, with a cove in the center of town. My agent, Drew, had been telling me to get a place here for years. He and his family used to spend their summers out here, but now their kids were getting older, and they weren't able to get away as often as they used to.

I'd always been too busy to get away.

Too obligated.

Too intense about training.

But right now, I had options, and I wasn't going to rush into any decisions.

Even if reporters had basically staked out my place in the city, following me to restaurants and hounding friends and family to get the inside scoop about where I was going to play next season.

It annoyed the shit out of me.

14

And the truth was, I didn't know where I was going. I was at the peak of my career. Coach Anders and I didn't see eye to eye, and I'd tried to get behind his plan for the team ever since he'd been hired two seasons ago. But over the last two years, he'd traded half the guys I'd started with. Dudes that had protected me.

Players that I'd had chemistry with.

My brothers that should have been there when we'd won the Super Bowl this year.

So, yeah, we'd done something right, but there'd been a lot of luck involved. Our opponents had had an off day due to a ton of injuries, and the stars had aligned for us.

But I'd taken a beating.

Our guys were young and inexperienced. And I was all about the team and helping one another, but not at the expense of getting my head bashed in over and over.

I reached for my iced coffee and looked up to see that a woman had just come in. She was wearing a pair of overalls and leaning over the counter, laughing.

Long, dark waves ran down her back, and she wiggled her cute ass as she spoke.

My dick jumped to attention.

Damn. It had been a while since I'd been laid.

I didn't trust many people right now, as everyone wanted to know what I was going to do. And there were people willing to pay someone to weasel their way in and find out. So, I was keeping to myself.

I continued watching her until she stood all the way up, and I wondered how the fuck someone managed to make a pair of baggy denim overalls look sexy as hell.

She turned slowly—almost like she felt me staring at her.

When my gaze locked with dark brown eyes, the familiarity had me dropping my sandwich.

I'd seen this woman before.

You've got to be fucking kidding me.

This was the woman who'd followed me into the bathroom a few weeks back. I'd been trying to have a private conversation with my mother.

An important fucking conversation.

Just one damn minute to myself.

It didn't seem like a lot to ask for.

These people had no regard for privacy.

No human decency.

Her jaw fell open, and she glared at me. But I didn't give her the chance to speak. I was on my feet and moving toward her.

"Do I need a restraining order? Did you follow me here?" I hissed, using my height to my advantage as I was a good foot taller than her.

She stormed toward me. "You arrogant, pretentious, narcissistic—"

"Is there an ending to your rant?" I crossed my arms over my chest.

She had some sort of pink scarf thing tied at the top of her head.

Her tan face was free of makeup, and the woman was flawless.

Stunning.

Yet here she was, once again, invading my space.

I'd had her removed from the press conference after she'd crossed the line, and she'd stayed away ever since then. I'd hoped she'd gotten the message.

"For your information, I live here," she said, flailing her arms.

"Is that your story?"

She just stared at me and started backing away as if she couldn't stand the sight of me.

The feeling's mutual, sweetheart.

She may be hot as hell, but she was just another blood-sucking reporter out to make a buck at my expense.

"What's it like to live in a world where you don't see beyond yourself?" she asked, raising a brow as she held a cup filled with pink liquid in one hand.

"Are you seriously trying to interview me now? I promise you, if anyone finds out I'm here, I'll file a restraining order against you so fast, your pretty little head will spin."

Did I need to compliment her when I was threatening her?

"Do you seriously think I'm here for work? That I'm here for you?" she said, shaking her head.

There were grass stains on the knees of her denim overalls and what looked like a bit of dirt on her nose. Was this all a plan to make it appear that she was here on vacation?

"Nice try, sweetheart. Once a bloodsucker, always a bloodsucker. Get back in your car and go home."

Something crossed over her features, and for a minute, it looked like her eyes were watering. But she quickly hardened, narrowing her gaze at me. The teenager behind the counter, who'd made my sandwich and drink and giggled endlessly just minutes ago, was watching us intently. If I wasn't mistaken, it looked like she was shooting daggers at me, as well.

What kind of establishment allowed a man to get stalked and then shamed him for it?

"You are so out of line, and you don't even know it. I hope karma kicks you in the ass. And for the record, I'm not going anywhere. I grew up here, you arrogant prick. So, if you don't want to see me, I suggest you hightail it out of town. Because in Cottonwood Cove, the Reynolds' are a bigger deal than you are, hotshot." She smirked and whipped around, long, brown hair falling down her back.

"Nice try. Go back to the city. There's no story here." I couldn't peel my eyes off her ass as she stormed to the door.

She held her hand high in the air and flipped me the bird as she pushed outside.

What the fuck was this?

I'd only been in Cottonwood Cove for thirty minutes.

How'd she even know that I was here?

I settled back in my chair as the young blonde behind the counter stormed over with a pitcher in her hand and reached for my glass. I hadn't asked for a refill, but she didn't seem to care whether I wanted one or not.

She just glared at me as if I were some kind of criminal.

"Do you allow your customers to get harassed by reporters here? Maybe I picked the wrong town to escape to." I reached for my glass after she set it down.

"I don't know who you are, but I've known Brinkley Reynolds my whole life. She used to babysit me when I was little. And she is a reporter, but she isn't working at the moment because she lost her job. She just moved back home a few weeks ago. I think you misread that one big time, Mister."

Brinkley Reynolds. Yes. Now I remembered the name.

Mister? What was I, a hundred years old? I was twenty-fucking-nine. No one called me mister.

I leaned back in my chair as I processed her words.

"Do you know why she lost her job?" I cleared my throat and braced for her answer.

"Some big, famous football player called her out publicly, and her boss let her go. We're not supposed to talk about it, but here in Cottonwood Cove, we all have one another's backs. Word gets around, you know? I don't know who this guy is, because I don't much care for sports with balls."

What the fuck did that even mean? She'd ruled out half the sports known to man.

She couldn't be more than sixteen years old, and she glared at me once more before marching away.

Had I actually gotten this woman fired? It hadn't been my first time griping about a journalist crossing the line. But I sure as shit didn't know she'd lose her job for it.

I picked up my phone and texted Drew.

> Hey. Remember that reporter I had escorted out of the press conference a few weeks back?

DREW

Not really. I was dealing with my own shit that day, with everyone hounding me about you. What about her?

> I think she got fired.

DREW

Well, she shouldn't have followed you into the shitter.

I scrubbed a hand down the back of my neck, letting out a long breath I hadn't even realized I'd been holding. My mother had been a single mom, and she'd worked her ass off while trying to raise me at the same time. That had been a driving force in my signing with the NFL and being able to help her out and take that pressure off her shoulders. And I sure as shit was not a guy who wanted to cost anyone their livelihood.

> I'm not a complete dick. I wouldn't want to be the reason anyone lost their job.

DREW

How do you know she got fired?

> I just ran into her. Here. She fucking lives here.

DREW

She does? What's her name?

> Brinkley Reynolds.

DREW

Holy fuck. She's a Cottonwood Cove Reynolds?

What the fuck does that mean?

DREW

Everyone knows the Reynolds. Their kids are all rock stars, and they're practically royalty there. Her brother opened a big restaurant that people from the city drive to because the food's so damn good. And the family owns another bar and a restaurant, I think. One of the brothers is an up-and-coming actor. Someone's a doctor. One does something in the book world, and now that you mention it, I think one of them is a journalist.

Great. You sent me to a town with the woman I kicked out of the press conference and proceeded to get her fired? And her family is practically fucking royalty here?

DREW

<head exploding emoji> <shrugging hands emoji>

DREW

Relax, brother. Keep a low profile. It'll be fine. Do you want me to try to call her boss and get her her job back?

Do you know who she even worked for?

DREW

No. But I can find out. You're Lincoln fucking Hendrix. You got her fired. I'm sure we can use your name to get her rehired. I like seeing this human side of you. The one where you feel bad when you're an asshole.

Fuck off. I'm not a total dick, am I?

DREW

Do you want the truth? You do pay me to tell you that you're amazing.

> Then why do you constantly tell me I'm an asshole?

DREW

Kidding, brother. You've got the biggest heart around. You just hide it really well. I'll see what I can find out.

> Thanks. I'm heading to the house now if the teenager at the coffee shop doesn't put a hit out on me for accusing Brinkley Reynolds of stalking me.

DREW

Wow. You really are a dick.

> <Middle finger emoji>

I made my way out of the café and to Drew's house, my cap and sunglasses in place. I was trying to hide my identity for more than one reason at the moment.

three

. . .

Brinkley

"WHAT DID HE SAY?" Georgia asked when I returned to the table. We were having a family dinner at my brother's restaurant, and I'd stepped outside to take a call from my ex-boss. He'd fired me when Lincoln had called me out for crossing a line and invading his privacy. He didn't even allow me to tell my side of the story. It was all because Lincoln Hendrix was paid millions of dollars and was a public figure. He'd had a temper tantrum, and it had cost me my job.

"He offered me my job back." I shook my head and took my seat between my mother and Lila, my brother Hugh's fiancée.

"Well, that's great news." My father held his glass up, and everyone reached for theirs as if we were going to toast in celebration.

"Glasses down," I hissed, looking at each of them one at a time. "He only offered me the job back because that pretentious"—I glanced over at my niece and thought about my words before I said something that would have Cage ripping my head off—"*guy*, you know... the football player, made a call."

"Lincoln Hendrix?" Maddox asked, his eyes wide. He and Lila were already part of the family.

"Do not even get me started about that rat bas—" Damn it. Why did Gracie have to be so little when I wanted to unleash all the ugliness I could muster about this guy? "*Rat basset hound.* Yes. Do not get all starry-eyed about that man. He cost me my job."

"But he obviously made a call to get it back for you," Hugh said, using his thumb to swipe some barbecue sauce off Lila's cheek. I would swoon if I wasn't fuming at the moment.

"The audacity. Like some guy has the power to make a call and get me fired. And then make another call and get me rehired? The nerve. The absolute cajones on this guy."

"What's cajones, Auntie?" Gracie asked, and I couldn't help but laugh when I looked up to see her mouth covered in sauce as she smiled up at me.

"Cajones are testicles," Finn said as he barked out a laugh.

"Finn!" My mother shook her head and chuckled.

"I removed a set of cajones today on a bulldog, actually," Cage said, and the table erupted in more laughter.

"It means... the man has a lot of nerve doing what he's doing." I winked at Gracie.

"Why not just take the job back?" my father asked. "Maybe he realized he made a mistake."

"Please." I rolled my eyes. "The man accused me of stalking him when I stopped in Cup of Cove for a lemonade the other day. He's probably doing this so he can get me fired again. He probably gets off on all that power."

"It seems like a lot of work for a professional athlete, right?" Georgia asked as she looked at me like I had three heads. "I mean, do you really think he wakes up every day and tries to get you hired and fired over and over again? I'm with Dad on this one, Brinks. I think he realized he made a mistake, and he wants to fix it."

Laura Pavlov

"I think he wakes up every day and wonders what will suit him best," I snarled.

I hated this man.

"Well, I admit that I wake up every day wondering what will suit me best. I don't think that's such a bad thing." Finn shrugged, and I rolled my eyes as everyone covered their mouths to keep from laughing.

This was all fun and jokes for everyone, but this man had gotten me fired. It was embarrassing. Sure, I wasn't a well-known journalist, as I had only been at it for a few years, so it hadn't made the news that I'd been let go. But that didn't mean it wasn't horrifying. I'd had to come home with my tail between my legs and give up my apartment in the city.

But aside from that, *Athlete Central* was not an option. My ex-boss, Harvey Talbert, had been horrible to work for. He gave all the good stories to the men in the office, and he'd made offensive remarks about my *sexy legs* and recommended I unbutton a few buttons on my blouse more than once. Plus, the man had a boner for Lincoln Hendrix. I wasn't going back there.

"Whatever. I can't work for that man again. It was time for a change. So, I told Harvey to take his offer"—I glanced over at Gracie, who was watching me like everything I said mattered—"and shove it where the sun don't shine."

"Auntie said to *shove it where the sun don't shine*!" Gracie fist-pumped the ceiling, and I laughed so hard tears sprung from my eyes. I wasn't much of a crier, but the laughter felt damn good. It had been a rough couple of weeks.

"Great. Yet another saying Mrs. Appleton will have to speak to me about. Thanks for that," Cage grumped, and more laughter erupted around the table.

I was still on edge just knowing that my nemesis was here in Cottonwood Cove. Hopefully, he'd gotten the hint, and he'd gotten the hell out of town after our run-in a few days ago.

"Well, we support whatever you want to do," my mom said, putting an arm around my shoulder. "I like the idea of you being home while you figure it all out."

"You don't think you can make freelancing work?" my father asked.

"I think someday, down the road, it will be an option, but not yet. I do think it's time to make the leap to a bigger organization. One that isn't allowed to mistreat their employees. I just need to find a really good story and sell it so I can get my name out there."

"There's that hotshot hockey player that everyone's talking about. Why don't you talk to Hawk?" Cage asked. Our cousin, Everly, was married to one of the best hockey players of all time. He was no longer playing, but he coached and was very involved with the team, not to mention the fact that he knew every player out there.

"That's an idea. I never want to bother him with this stuff, but I could use some help to get my foot in the door."

"I still think that article you wrote about Hawk when he retired was your best work," my sister said.

"Thanks, Georgie. I was proud of that one. That's what I need. Something big to get their attention and see what I'm capable of."

"You can do it, Auntie Brinks," Gracie said, clapping her hands together again. "And it's on our dreams board."

"Thank you, my little angel." I blew her a kiss.

We spent the next hour getting filled in on Lila and Hugh's upcoming wedding, which would be taking place at Georgia and Maddox's home. We were all going to be bridesmaids along with Lila's best friends, Del, Rina, and Sloane. Gracie was going to be the flower girl, and we'd all gushed over Gracie's dress that Lila showed us on her phone. The time was ticking as it was only a little over two months away.

Georgia and Maddox let us know that they had also made their decision, and their wedding was going to be small. They wanted just family and close friends, and they were having their ceremony and reception in Paris.

Ah… the life of a billionaire.

Finn told us about a scene he did yesterday where he was going too fast and almost got bucked off a horse. He said Jessica came running out to help him, and he waggled his brows as he shared the story with us. His new show was going to premiere in a few months, and we were all excited for his breakout role. We were thrilled that we were going to get to view one episode early at my parents' house. He'd been acting for several years, but he was the lead in this new Netflix series, *Big Sky Ranch*, and everyone was talking about it. It was still surreal, thinking about my brother being a movie star.

Cage went on a rant about a few clients that were super high maintenance and had called him at home after hours for ridiculous reasons. Life as a small-town veterinarian was endlessly entertaining, at least for the siblings of the doctor.

My parents just listened happily, thrilled with all the exciting things coming up. I felt a bit like the weak link at the moment. I'd lost my job. I was living in my sister's rental house, trying to pretend to be an organic farmer-slash-free-lance reporter. I needed to go home and find a story. Start creating my future. It wasn't going to just happen. I needed to make it happen. I sent a quick text to my cousin's husband, Hawk, as we all finished up dinner.

> Hey, Hawk. I don't know if Ever told you, but I'm between jobs. I'm looking for a good story. Something big. Do you think you could get me a meeting with Breen Lockhart? Or do you know anyone else that I could interview?

I watched as the three little dots moved around the screen

and chuckled when a picture came through of Everly, Hawk, and their two adorable kiddos' faces all pressed together.

> **HAWK**
>
> Hi, Brinks! We're all sending our love. Unfortunately, the hottest topic in sports right now is Lincoln Hendrix and where he's going to play, but I'm guessing you don't want to talk to him right now.

My cousins all knew that I hated the guy after that whole press conference fiasco. The public wasn't aware of all the gory details, but my family, and most of the people in Cottonwood Cove, all seemed to know about my current situation.

Word always traveled fast in small towns.

But as gossipy as they were—they were equally protective of the people who lived here.

> Yeah. That's a hard no. Unless he wanted to give me his story, which isn't likely considering the man hates me as much as I hate him.

> **HAWK**
>
> I'm still surprised by that because, as I told you, I've known him for years, and he's normally a really good guy, Brinks. But the media attention does get overwhelming, so it sounds like he lost his patience.

> Oh, I'm sorry. I was just looking for my tiny violin. Poor Lincoln Hendrix... He's the hottest thing in the NFL, he makes more money in a week than most will make in their lifetime, and he was number three on The Sexiest Man Alive list this year. I feel so bad for him. <eyeroll emoji>

Laura Pavlov

HAWK

I get it. He did you wrong. Hell hath no fury like a Thomas or a Reynolds girl scorned. <Laughing face emoji> I can get you a meeting with Breen, but you need to watch your back. He's not my favorite. He's cocky, and he's a playboy, so be prepared. But he'll do it. He loves the attention.

Thank you so much. Love you guys. Hope to see you soon. Give big kisses to the babies!

Another photo came through of him and Everly with puckered lips.

HAWK

We love you. I'll be in touch.

We all made our way toward the front of the restaurant and said our goodbyes. Hugh and Lila were informed that there was some sort of crisis in the kitchen.

"Hey, can you stick around and help with a few to-go orders while we handle this?" Hugh asked me after everyone else was out the door and I was still saying goodbye to Lila.

"Of course. I've got it."

I spent the next twenty minutes chatting with Brandy, the hostess, and running back to the kitchen to grab the orders for a few customers. Reynolds' was always packed because they had the best food in town.

I walked back to the kitchen to see Hugh and Lila listening as two of the cooks argued their points after apparently having a big blowup with one another.

There was one final order sitting under the heat lamp, and I checked the receipt.

Captain Jack Sparrow.

I highly doubted Johnny Depp was in Cottonwood Cove, and I couldn't wait to see who the smartass was who'd placed this order.

I took the bag to the front, as the restaurant had all but cleared out. Closing time was around the corner and everyone was making their way out the door.

A few people stopped me on their way out. This was what I loved about my hometown. Everyone knew everyone, and it really was just like one big, happy family.

J.R., who had been the town Santa Claus for as long as I could remember, picked me up and spun me around as I clung to the to-go order in my hand that dangled behind his back.

"Good to see you, sunshine." He set me on my feet, and I pushed up on my tiptoes and kissed his cheek.

"You, too," I said, before turning and hugging his wife, Sandy.

I waved my goodbyes and turned just as the door opened.

And the air left my lungs for the second time this week when I came face-to-face with my nemesis.

Enemy number one.

It didn't help that he was painfully good-looking. And I wasn't easily impressed by men. But this particular man was the whole package. He had the looks, the confidence, and the swagger to balance it all out.

And I despised him… obviously.

He was tall, with muscles straining against his white tee and broad shoulders.

Shoulders of the hottest quarterback in the league.

Green eyes. Blond hair. Chiseled jaw with a little bit of scruff.

The bastard.

He reached for the bill of his baseball cap and turned it around slowly as he met my gaze.

No one was up at the hostess stand, as Brandy was most likely helping the busboy, Lionel, who also happened to be her boyfriend, clear off the tables.

He glanced down at the apron that I was wearing, and his

brows cinched together. I'd only put it on to protect the white blouse and skirt that I wore beneath it.

"You work here now?" he said, his voice low, and I didn't miss the pity in his tone.

Nothing pissed me off more than being pitied.

Well, being escorted out of a press conference and being fired probably trumped being pitied, but I still didn't like it.

I rolled my eyes. "That's none of your business. What do you want?"

"I'm picking up a to-go order." He squared his shoulders, and his face hardened.

It took everything in me not to laugh.

"You must be *Captain Jack Sparrow*?" I mocked.

"Just trying to keep a low profile," he said, glancing around to see that the place was practically empty. "Hey, for the record, I didn't know you'd lost your job over what happened at that press conference. I'm hoping you got a call today?"

Anger coursed through my veins. Who the hell did this guy think he was?

"I don't need you sticking your nose into my business. I'm not taking that job back because I never should have been fired. I was doing exactly what I was supposed to do."

"Just take the goddamn job," he said, his jaw clenching like he was aggravated.

"Oh, I'm sorry if getting me fired has inconvenienced you. I'm going to write as a freelancer until I get hired by a magazine that respects its reporters. So, unless you want me to interview *you*, I'm going to treat you exactly the way that you treated me." I slammed the bag of food against his chest and turned around and shouted to Lionel to come help me.

"You're ridiculous," he said with an annoyingly sexy smirk on his face.

He had no idea just how ridiculous I could be.

four

. . .

Lincoln

SHE'D JUST SLAMMED me in the chest with a bag of ribs and called over some teenage kid, who was a scrawny little thing. The dude couldn't weigh more than a hundred pounds soaking wet.

"Uh, yes, Miss Brinkley, did you need something?" the small dude said, turning his gaze to me before his eyes bulged. "You're, oh my gosh, you're Lincoln Hendrix." He proceeded to bend over to grab his knees as he started hyper-ventilating and wheezing.

"Lionel!" Brinkley snapped, shooting him a look that basi-cally said she'd harm him if he didn't do what she said. "Escort this man out of here, please."

"Really?" I said with a chuckle. "I'm standing next to the door, and I'm on my way out. You're going to make this poor kid have a panic attack just to prove a point?"

"Damn straight. Don't let the door hit you in the ass, *Captain.*"

I barked out a laugh now because she was absolutely out of her mind.

And hot as hell.

"Don't worry about it, Lionel. I was just leaving. Thanks for the food, sweetheart."

Once again, she held her hand up and flipped me the bird. Her pretty, pink lips pursed together, and she raised a brow, waiting for me to leave.

Lionel sheepishly moved toward me and pushed the door open before whispering, "Is there any way that I could get your autograph?"

"Lionel!" she shouted from a few feet away again. "No fraternizing with the enemy."

I quickly took the pen and the pad he was holding in his trembling hand and signed it for him. "You better get back in there. She's a bit terrifying."

He chuckled. "Thanks. She doesn't work here, though. She's just helping out her brother. Come back real soon."

I'd just been escorted out, and he was already inviting me back?

I almost laughed as I held up my hand and waved as I walked down the street.

I'd enjoyed my first few days here.

Life was slower.

I'd had time to think.

Drew and Deb's house was right on the water, and it had its own dock with a boat and all sorts of water toys. I'd be training hard here in the off-season, and the fact that Drew had a state-of-the-art home gym made it very convenient. I'd been out for runs every morning, and I'd even gone for a swim this morning.

This was exactly what I needed to clear my head.

Figure out my shit.

I had a bunch of offers and needed to decide if I'd be moving and playing for a new team next year. My gut told me it was time to go, but I'd always been a loyal guy, and it was hard for me to walk away from my team, even if my coach was a complete asshole. Sure, he was kissing my ass now that we'd shocked the shit out of everyone and made it to the Super Bowl and then somehow pulled off a win. But he wasn't a team player. He didn't build that relationship with our guys. He'd cut too many of my brothers with no warning. He'd made comments to me that he'd cut a bunch of the new guys if they didn't step up. They were young, and they needed time. We needed time as a team to rebuild and find our chemistry. But he was not willing to put in the time or the work for us to do that. I couldn't keep starting over with new guys every time he went on a cutting spree.

And Coach Balboa was coaching out in New York now, and he wanted me to come out there and rebuild that team with him. I'd started my professional career with the man, and he was more like a father to me at this point. When he'd been let go from the team, I'd struggled to stay where I was, but he'd been the one to advise me to do so. He'd brought over two of my best friends, Brett Jacobs and Lenny Waters. Brett was one of the best receivers in the league, and Coach Anders had cut him because he'd had a tough season two years ago when we'd suddenly found ourselves playing for a new coach. But he'd been playing phenomenally this last season, and he was pushing for me to move out there and get our game going again. Lenny was a running back who'd sustained a tough Achilles injury and been cut from our team. Coach Balboa had brought him on, as well, and he was rehabbing that injury and would be playing this coming season for the New York Thunderbirds.

When I got home, I sat outside and looked at the ocean as the waves crashed against the dock.

It was quiet.

Peaceful.

My phone buzzed with a text from Drew.

DREW

She turned down the job. <shrugging emoji>

33

Yeah. I just ran into her when I was picking up food. She told me she wasn't taking the job and to stay out of her business unless I wanted to let her interview me.

DREW

So, give her your story. You're going to have to give it to someone. It'll clear your conscience.

My conscience is fine. I got her the job back, didn't I?

DREW

You did. Did she say why she wasn't taking the job?

Who the fuck knows. Something about finding a story and landing herself a new job. At least, that's what she said before having me escorted out of the restaurant by a teenager who was less than half my size.

DREW

Damn. I like this girl. She doesn't take your shit.

Whatever. She's being stubborn. If she wants the job, it's hers to take. I've done my part. I need to focus on my training and my future. End of story.

DREW

Agreed. I'm just wondering... is she hot?

Who?

DREW

Brinkley Reynolds. Deb said she's gorgeous. I'm wondering if she's just being kind or if it's true.

She's hot. Not that I was looking.

She was fucking hot. Probably the best-looking woman I'd ever laid eyes on. But I wasn't going to admit that. Because she was also being childish and petty about the job and insisting I leave the restaurant.

DREW

Of course, you weren't. It's been a while since you've dated anyone seriously. It's got to get old just banging supermodels and fangirls. Is that why you're being a moody asshole lately?

What are you? My dating therapist? We aren't girlfriends. Fuck off. I'm fine. And if you've forgotten, the last woman I dated sold a bullshit story about my family for a couple of thousand bucks and fucked that douchebag hockey player while we were together. I'm not in a hurry to go there again. It's best to keep things casual while I'm trying to figure out my life.

DREW

Dude, you dated an unknown actress who was a bad breaker-upper. Once you ended things, it was bound to go sour. Perhaps you should try dating a non-famous person who isn't thirsty for their ten minutes of fame.

You set me up with her.

DREW

Don't shoot the messenger. She was a friend of Deb's Pilates instructor. How the hell were we supposed to know she was a stage-five clinger?

I rolled my eyes and leaned back on the couch. I enjoyed sex as much as the next guy, but I hadn't had great experiences with relationships. So, I preferred to keep things casual

Laura Pavlov

most of the time. My life was complicated enough at the moment anyway.

> I'm done talking about my dating life, or lack thereof. I do just fine with the ladies. Don't you worry about it. Talk to you tomorrow.

DREW

> Deb just said that her manicurist is single and that her short stint in prison was just because her ex-boyfriend made her sit in the car when he robbed a gas station. I can't make this shit up, brother.

I laughed and dropped my phone on the couch as I stared out at the water.

For whatever reason, those dark brown eyes flooded my thoughts. The way her chest rose and fell when she hissed at me. The way her long waves fell around her shoulders. And don't even get me started about her plump, pink lips.

Hell, I probably did need to get laid. I had a few hookups I could reach out to, but that would mean inviting them here.

Since everything went down with Jaqueline, I was cautious about that. I preferred to go to hotels and keep things surface-level.

I enjoyed being in control of every situation in my life, and sex was no different.

My mind wandered back to the woman who'd just kicked me out of the restaurant.

I didn't give a shit if Brinkley Reynolds took the job or not.

I'd done my part.

I could rest guilt-free now. She'd turned it down, and that was her choice.

———

I'd gone for a run every day this week, and I loved how quiet it was in the mornings here. I wasn't swamped by reporters, and nobody bothered me in Cottonwood Cove. I'd been to a few restaurants since I'd arrived here, the grocery store and the coffee shop, and people waved and said hello. A few asked for my autograph. But they were respectful. They weren't asking where I was going to play or what my plans were. It reminded me of the early days of my career when attention from the fans felt like an honor and not an obligation. I missed those days. Maybe I'd become too jaded. Built up too many walls to protect myself.

I was heading down the main road just as the sun was starting to come up, and a woman was running toward me. She was pumping her arms, running a similar pace to mine, from what I could tell. Her long strides hit the pavement as she hauled ass in my direction. She wore a black sports bra, black leggings, and a white baseball cap. As we closed the distance, running toward one another from opposite directions, I realized who it was.

Brinkley Reynolds.

Her dark gaze locked with mine as she moved past me, and for reasons I can't explain, I turned around.

Ran after her.

When I pulled up beside her, she startled for a second and tore the earbuds out of her ears.

"Do *I* need to get a restraining order now?" she huffed as she continued striding at a good pace.

"I didn't know you'd be out here, so that would be a bit ridiculous, yeah?"

"What do you want?"

I continued running alongside her and glanced at her profile. Her skin was golden, her exposed abs were feminine yet defined, and her long ponytail swayed from side to side.

I silently warned my dick not to respond to the fact that I couldn't stop looking at the way her tits bounced just the slightest bit with her movements. They weren't big, but they were perky, and my mouth watered at the thought of seeing them beneath the black fabric.

Of wrapping my mouth around them and tugging her long ponytail as I kissed my way up the column of her neck.

Jesus, dude. Pull your shit together.

"I want to know why you aren't taking that job."

We continued running in silence for another two blocks before she came to an abrupt stop in front of a house.

"Why do you care?" she said over her labored breaths as she leaned over her knees and calmed her breathing.

"You're being stubborn. Take the fucking job." I rubbed a hand down the back of my neck as my labored breaths slowed.

"Ah… you feel guilty?"

"I don't feel guilty," I lied. "It's your actions that led to the events that followed. You did follow me into the john. I was pissed. But I'm not the devil. I wouldn't want to take your livelihood from you. I wanted you escorted out of that press conference. End of story." I shrugged.

"As if that wasn't humiliating enough." She glared at me, wiping the sweat from her forehead. The sun had just come out, and it was shining down on her. Pops of amber and gold danced in her dark gaze.

"Do you have any fucking idea what it's like to be hounded by the media? To not have a second to breathe without someone shouting questions at you? To be loved one minute when you play well and hated in the brief moments that you fuck up?" I said, surprising myself with how much I'd just shared.

"Cry me a river. You're the best quarterback in the league. People want to know where you're going to play. They want to know your story, which, by the way, you're the most closed-off athlete that I know. You make millions of dollars doing what you love. You just won a goddamn Super Bowl.

You don't get to play the sympathy card. There are bigger issues in the world than you being hounded by reporters. You're a public figure; you signed up for this."

She had some fucking nerve.

"And you signed up to be a bloodsucking hound who has no respect for the privacy of others. So, I guess we reap what we sow, yeah?" I hissed.

She held a hand up just above her eyes as if she were looking past me, into the distance. "Oh, hey… is that your pirate ship out there, Captain? Why don't you get on it and ship the hell out of town? I can't stand the sight of you."

"The feeling's mutual, sweetheart. Didn't mean to derail your run and make you stop, but obviously, you can't help yourself when you're around me."

"You really are a narcissistic bastard, aren't you?" She raised a brow. "I live here, genius. You do not affect me in any way, shape, or form. You're the one who chased after me. But I'm not going to give you what you want, so you can stop bothering me."

"And what is it that you think I want?" I shook my head in disbelief.

"You want me to take that job so that you don't have to live with the fact that you got me fired."

"You got yourself fired. You crossed a line barging into that bathroom."

"What were you so nervous about anyway? Did you think I'd see your tiny peen and report to the world that the big, bad quarterback isn't packing?" she asked with a wicked smirk.

I laughed. It was impossible not to. I'd been called a lot of things over the years by the media.

Moody. Arrogant. Closed off.

But being accused of having a tiny dick was not one of them.

I intentionally raised my large hand in front of my face and ran it along my scruff.

"Ah… so that's why you followed me into the bathroom. You appear to be obsessed with my cock, and I assure you… no one has ever called it small." I watched as her eyes zeroed in on my hand. "Big hands. Big feet. You know how the saying goes."

"You want to speak on the record?" She raised a brow.

"You want to ask me about the size of my dick and write about it?"

"You sure are full of yourself. For the record, I take my job seriously. So, unless you want to sit down and let me interview you for real, this conversation is over."

"Don't threaten me with a good time. See you around, sweetheart."

"Bite me, jackass." She whipped around and marched toward her house, and I wanted to walk away. Told myself to move. But my eyes were glued to her perfect ass.

When she got to her front door and opened it, she turned around. "Take a picture. It'll last longer."

And then she slammed the door hard.

I covered my mouth to keep from laughing.

She was the most aggravating woman I'd ever met, yet I enjoyed bickering with her more than I enjoyed talking to anyone else.

And I couldn't wait to do it again.

five

. . .

Brinkley

HAWK HAD SET me up to meet with Breen Lockhart, a player who'd been traded to the San Francisco Lions this season. He'd been setting all sorts of league records, including most goals scored in a single season. Hawk had continued to tell me to be cautious, and Everly had gotten on the phone and repeatedly told me to watch my back with him. I didn't need a warning in that department. I was always cautious when it came to men, especially professional athletes.

I had a rule: *All professional athletes were off-limits.*

Mixing work and pleasure was a bad idea. I was already fighting to make a name for myself in a male-dominated field. The last thing I needed was to be accused of sleeping my way to the top.

Breen and I had been on this Zoom call for half an hour, and he'd refused to answer any questions. The man was determined to meet in person.

"Sorry, I prefer face-to-face interviews, especially if you're going to write a big story about me. So we should spend some time together."

"A Zoom call is face-to-face. I told you that I don't live in the city anymore, and when we set up this meeting, you didn't have a problem doing it over Zoom," I reminded him because, so far, this had been a total dead end.

"Well, I don't have a game next weekend, and I've been meaning to get out of town. I think a trip to Cottonwood Cove sounds like a great idea."

I narrowed my gaze. "You're coming here for me to interview you?"

"Yes. You can show me around town, we can get to know one another, and you can ask as many questions as you want. I'm an open book."

"If we meet in person, then you'll be an open book? Because you appear to be a closed book so far, as you haven't answered one question yet."

"All in good time, Brinkley Reynolds." He smiled, and I was fairly certain his charm worked on most women.

Personally, I didn't like it. It was a bit cheesy. He'd spent the entire time circling around my questions. Hell, I'd take that bastard Lincoln Hendrix's closed-off personality over this guy. Because at least with Lincoln, you knew where you stood.

Mind you, he was a complete jackass, but at least he was a straight shooter.

I could work with that.

"Fine. Send me the dates, and I'll reserve the time to meet with you."

"Are you single?" he asked, which was not only completely unprofessional but nervy. He hadn't answered one of my questions, now he thought he was asking the questions?

"I don't date athletes." Even though I was annoyed that he'd asked, I'd prepared for this after what Hawk and Everly had told me. I'd have nothing more than friendship to offer this guy. But building relationships with the people I interviewed was also important in my industry.

"And why is that?" he teased. He was used to getting his way.

"I find that most professional athletes are pretty full of themselves. You travel often and could easily stray, and you, Breen Lockhart, have a reputation for breaking hearts."

"Ahhh... you did your research. Well, we can be friends, right? And friends can spend the day together, talking about their lives? That's what you want, isn't it?"

I rolled my eyes. "I would like to interview you and tell your story."

I needed a damn job, and I wasn't even sure this story would get me in the door. But I was fairly certain that I could sell it to one of the NHL magazines, and at least that would garner me some income while I worked on building my portfolio.

"Okay. I'll send you the dates. See you soon, Brinkley Reynolds."

I ended the call and got to work researching him more than I already had. His story was a decent one. His father and his grandfather had both played for the NHL, and he'd put on his first pair of skates as soon as he started walking. People would eat it up.

They loved a good legacy story.

So, all I had to do was get him to open up and share things that no one knew about him. Dig deeper. Find out the motivation. Did he truly love the sport, or had it become a job?

Lastly, I'd find out what had changed in his life since he'd hit this new level of success.

After I'd read everything that I could find about him, I made an early dinner and sat down to scan the internet.

The first thing to come up was a photo of Lincoln Hendrix, which of course, was trending at the moment. Everyone was biting at the bit to know where he was going to play. Several well-known commentators were making guesses about where he'd go, and no one thought he'd be staying in

San Francisco. It was rumored that he and his coach did not see eye to eye on things.

I didn't blame him for being unhappy with Coach Anders because the guy hadn't done anything to protect Lincoln. He'd taken a real beating this past season. And even though they'd won the Super Bowl, it was known that he'd been the reason they'd pulled it off.

I'd always wondered about his background. He was one of the rare athletes that had managed to keep his personal life pretty private. Aside from a few chatty ex-girlfriends, there wasn't a lot out there about him. His mother attended most of his games, and as far as I knew, he didn't have any siblings. I'd never heard anything about his father, either.

I hated that I wanted to know more. Hated that I'd been thinking about him these last few days since I'd seen him on my run. Hated that every time I'd gone on a run since, I'd looked for him.

I read a few articles about all the predictions that people were making and wondered who would be the lucky one to break the news. Knowing Lincoln, he'd just go out and announce it without any warning.

Everyone in town was talking about how he was here and training hard for the new season. It was funny, here in Cottonwood Cove, no one would ever sell a photo or call a news station to say what he was up to. It was that quintessential small-town mentality. A respect thing. Everyone was a bit protective of the people here. Even if they were here for a short time.

But it didn't stop them from being excited to see him around town.

I closed my laptop and finished dinner before changing my clothes and getting ready to head to my parents' house.

Finn had gotten an early copy of the pilot episode, and we were going to watch it together tonight.

Aside from all the excitement about the famous quarterback being here, Finn's new series, *Big Sky Ranch*, was the talk of the town. I was thrilled for him. He'd always had small roles in things, but this was the first time that he was the lead in a series. He'd been working hard for years, and I was excited for him because this felt like it was going to be his big break.

I walked the few blocks to my parents' house, the home I'd grown up in. The water sat off in the distance, and it was a perfect spring evening. Not too hot just yet, but not cold either.

Large, overgrown trees curved over the street leading to my parents' house, and I made my way up the cobblestone path to the front door.

When I stepped inside, Gracie rushed over and jumped into my arms. I carried her through the house to the large family room. Everyone was there, and Finn was messing around with the remote, but he looked nervous, which was rare for him.

We made our rounds hugging everyone and settled onto the oversized sectional couch. I sat between Georgia and Lila, and my mom had platters of food out on the coffee table. Chicken fingers and tater tots and pizza rolls.

Also known as Reynolds' party food.

It was like the Super Bowl but even better because it was my brother we were going to be cheering on.

"Finn seems nervous," I whispered in Georgia's ear, and Lila leaned forward and nodded.

"I think he is. I hope we love it because he's going to be watching us closely," my baby sister said.

"What if it's awful?" Cage asked, and everyone turned in his direction.

Hugh barked out a laugh as Gracie sat on his lap. "Smooth, dude."

"What? I'm just asking. I'm not good at faking it. So, what do we say?"

"I guess you tell me the truth, ass—" Finn turned around and glared at him before his eyes moved to our niece. "Uh, ask me if you have any questions."

"That was my only question." Cage shrugged, and my mother chuckled when she settled beside him. "Okay, time for you to go to Grammie and Pops room to watch your movie." Cage carried my niece down the hall to my parents' bedroom.

"It's going to be amazing, Finn. We're so proud of you," I said, as I popped a pizza roll into my mouth.

We all agreed, and my father used the remote to put the Roman shades down and darken the room. My parents loved watching movies, so they'd made this room the coziest space in the house, with all the movie theatre vibes.

Once Cage returned, we started the show.

And the next two hours were a bit jaw-dropping.

Finnegan Charles Reynolds was going to be the biggest news in Hollywood in a couple of months.

I had a lump in my throat as I watched him, forgetting that he was the same guy who'd turned my doorknob around in high school and locked me in my bedroom from the outside because he thought it was hilarious.

He'd always been a prankster.

Funny and easy.

But after watching him in this role… Finn was officially an actor.

The credits rolled, and we all sat in silence as he flipped on the lights.

Georgia had tears streaming down her face, and I knew it was more than the car accident that had just happened in the pilot episode. It was pride for our brother, who was about to see his entire life change.

Maddox had his arm around Georgia and shook his head at Finn. "Get ready for what's coming, brother. That was fucking amazing."

"Yeah?" Finn asked, his gaze moving from each of us.

"Finn," I croaked. "I'm so proud of you."

"This is your moment, Finny boy." Hugh pushed to his feet and pulled him in for a hug.

My mother wrapped her arms around him next, and my father just sat there, shaking his head and telling him how impressed he was and going on and on about how breathtaking the scenery was, as well.

Everyone took turns congratulating him. Lila went on about his chemistry with Jessica Carson, his costar. Georgia and I hugged him, making a Finny sandwich. And then it was Cage's turn.

He wrapped an arm around Finn and shook him a little. "You're a goddamn movie star, brother. Don't forget us little people over here once the world knows who you are."

Lila and I were gushing about the horses and how impressed we were with my brother's riding skills. My mom went to go get Gracie out of her bedroom, but she'd fallen asleep watching *The Lion King*, so she'd returned empty-handed.

We sat around talking and laughing and eating all the food as we gushed about how talented our brother was.

I couldn't wait for the rest of the world to find out.

———

"So, you proved to be honest about your claim of being an open book," I said, as I settled across the table at Reynolds' with Breen Lockhart. We'd spent the last few hours walking down to the cove, to my favorite place on the water, where we sat on the sandy beach and chatted for a bit. I'd taken him to all my favorite spots downtown earlier today, and now we'd just arrived at Reynolds' for dinner.

"I told you so. And thanks for showing me around town. I like it here. Aside from that bookstore," he said. I'd laughed at how antsy he'd gotten at my favorite bookstore downtown.

He shivered dramatically, clearly making a point. "I hate books. I hated school. Hockey's the only thing I ever really shined at. And it's quite clear that I really shine. But don't include the stuff about my struggles in school in the article."

"I would never include anything you didn't want in there. But I think it's nice for young kids who look up to you to know that everyone struggles with different things. Even the biggest hockey player in the NHL has struggles."

"I guess so. I tend to focus on all the areas where I thrive, though. The bookstore definitely wasn't my favorite part of the day," he teased. "Everything else was damn good."

"Well, you were a trooper. And you made Mrs. Short's day by stopping in, so thank you. She's owned Once Upon a Time since I was a kid."

"How about your day? Did I make it a good one?" he asked.

Breen was my age, but he appeared younger than me in many ways, mostly with his cocky attitude and the way he bragged about himself any chance he got. He'd been flirting his ass off, and I knew he was a player. But he wasn't awful, and I'd be friends with him as long as he understood that it would never be more than that.

"It was a good day. I think I have plenty of information to get this article written. I'll send it to you before I submit it to make sure it's good to go." I smiled as Danielle brought us each a glass of wine.

"So, this is what it's like to have a female friend?" he asked.

"I guess so, Breen." I'd made it clear the first time he'd been completely inappropriate when we were having lunch and asked me if he could spend the night with me.

"Ahhh... I'm not used to women not wanting more. But I

can live with it. You're beautiful and cool as hell. So, I guess you can be my first."

I chuckled. "You make it sound so dirty."

"Any time you want to make it dirty, you just say the word. I'd lose my playboy ways for a girl like you."

"I'm sure you say that to all the girls."

"He does," a deep voice growled, and I looked up to see an annoyed-looking Lincoln Hendrix standing in front of our table.

What the hell was he doing here?

And why was my heart racing at just the sight of him?

It had been over a week since I'd seen him, and I'd actually been disappointed that I hadn't run into him.

Why did he look so angry?

And why was I so happy that he was here?

six

. . .

Lincoln

BREEN FUCKING Lockhart was not a guy I cared for. And for whatever reason, seeing him with Brinkley Reynolds had my blood boiling.

Was this her fucking boyfriend?

"Lincoln Hendrix? What a pleasant surprise," the dickhead said as he smirked at me.

We were two professional athletes who lived in San Francisco, so we'd met several times. He'd also fucked my ex-girlfriend while we were together and made sure to tell me when we'd run into one another shortly after our breakup a year ago. I'd been happy to be out of the relationship, and there were no broken hearts there, but a dude who was proud to tell you that he'd hooked up with your girl while you were together was not a good guy in my book.

I was far from perfect, but I'd never fuck with someone's relationship, nor would I ever be unfaithful while I was in one.

I'd cut ties long before I'd disrespect a woman.

"Nothing pleasant about it." I raised a brow.

The fucker just chuckled.

"What are you doing here?" Brinkley asked, but she didn't sound as venomous as the last time we'd seen one another.

I hadn't run into her since, and it had irritated the fuck out of me. I'd even tried running at different times in the morning this week to see if she was out there, but I'd had no luck. And I'd come to Reynolds' every night for the last three days to pick up my to-go order, hoping to see her, but she hadn't been here.

And now she was here with this asshole?

"I'm picking up dinner and saw you sitting over here with this one," I said, flicking a thumb at Breen.

"This one? Don't pretend you don't know my name or that I'm not the hottest thing on the ice right now." The fucker smirked.

"Yeah. According to you. You've been relevant for a whole fucking fifteen minutes. And with your head being this big, I'd give it fifteen more minutes before it all blows up."

I'd been around for a while now, and I'd seen athletes like Breen, who finally had their first kickass season after several unimpressive years playing. He'd burned through money, trying to look like a baller his first few years, and now he was actually playing well for the first time in his career, and he couldn't stop talking about it. Success could go to a guy's head quickly, and no one lasted very long once they fell off their pedestals.

Because you couldn't always be on top.

You had to swallow the losses and stay humble through the wins.

Work hard every fucking day, and remember that there was always someone younger, faster, and stronger coming up next.

"Ah… are you still pissed about me fucking your girl back in the day?"

"Sure. I'm really pissed about that," I said, not hiding the sarcasm.

"Okay, let's take a time out. Breen, enjoy your wine. I'm going to get his order, and I'll be back." Brinkley pushed to her feet.

She was wearing dark jeans, a silky white tank top, and a pair of sexy heels.

Why did that piss me off?

She looked fucking good.

Did she make the effort for him?

Her hand wrapped around my bicep, and she urged me through the dining room and down a hallway, which I assumed led to the kitchen. Once we were out of view of everyone, she whipped around.

"What the hell was that?" She threw her hands in the air.

"What are you doing with that dude? He's bad fucking news."

"Well, that's rich, coming from you. He hasn't gotten me fired or been escorted out of any establishments yet." She raised a brow.

"Good Christ, woman. Just trust me on this one."

"I don't know why you care. But for your information, he's a client. I'm writing a story on him," she said as she backed up against the wall in the dark hallway. I stood so close that I could feel her warm breath on my cheek as she spoke. Lavender and honey flooded my senses. And fuck me if my dick didn't jump at her nearness.

"Just watch your back." I ran a hand through my hair. "I don't know why you'd waste your time on a guy like that."

"It's not rocket science. I need to find a job, so I need a story."

I couldn't pull my gaze from her plump, pink lips.

"You were offered your job back. Why not just fucking take it?"

She sighed and shook her head. "Not that you're off the hook for getting me fired, but it was a terrible job, and I'm not going back. It's time to move up. But in order to do that, I need athletes to interview so I have something to offer."

"You don't need dickhead clients."

Why was I moving closer to her? My chest brushed against hers.

"Well then, I guess that rules you out as a potential client?" she said, and her lips turned up in the corners as if she were proud of herself.

"Are you asking me to be your client, sweetheart?" My voice was gruff.

Her gaze searched mine. "You want to tell me your story, Lincoln Hendrix?"

"You want to know my story?"

"Not particularly," she said, rolling her eyes. "But the world wants to hear it, so I wouldn't mind telling it."

"You sure you can handle it?" My tongue swiped out to wet my bottom lip because my mouth was dry from standing this close to her.

"Don't flatter yourself. I can easily handle it."

"If you tell it, you'll need to shadow me while I'm here. Get the whole story. You won't have time for clowns like Breen fucking Lockhart while you're working with me."

What the fuck was I doing?

"Who has the big head now?" she asked as she raised a brow.

And damn, did I want to dip down and taste her sweet mouth.

Press her against this wall and bury myself inside her.

Dip my fingers into those jeans and see how wet she was for me.

Had I ever wanted anyone more?

"I told you. There's nothing small about me."

Her heated gaze locked with mine.

"Coming through!" someone shouted, and we both startled. I stepped to the side, just as a woman came through the doorway leading to the kitchen, carrying a large tray loaded with plates.

She looked at me before glancing over at Brinkley and smiling. "Hey, Brinks. What's going on out here?"

"Hi, Danielle. I was just coming to get his to-go order."

The other woman chuckled and walked off, and Brinkley squared her shoulders.

"Is this for real, or are you messing with me because you don't like my client?"

"If you agree to do it, you do it right. I'll tell you everything over the next few weeks, and I'll let you know what is on and off the record." I held up my hand as she started to ask about where I'd be playing next season. "I haven't decided where I'm going to play yet, and that's the truth. But I'll agree to let you be the first to share it."

"Why are you suddenly doing this?" She narrowed her gaze and crossed her arms over her chest.

"I don't have a fucking clue. Maybe it's the small town rubbing off on me. My agent keeps nagging me to do some interviews, so this will keep him quiet and make everyone happy. And I can do it all right here in Cottonwood Cove."

"Lucky you. And an amazing reporter just happens to live here." She tapped her finger against her lips. "Oh, that's right. You know that. You're the reason she had to tuck her tail between her legs and move back home."

Her tail wasn't the only thing I wanted to put between her legs.

Jesus. What the fuck was going on with me?

I was not that guy.

I didn't fuck around with women who hated me, nor did I mix business with pleasure.

Ever.

She annoyed me. She was stubborn and argumentative.

So what if I'd gotten off to thoughts of her in the shower a few times?

I wouldn't act on it.

"If you can't move forward, this won't work. Maybe it was meant to be. Now you're here, and you can have full access to my life. Who's the lucky one now?"

"I'll do what I have to do to build my business. Count me in." She rolled her eyes. "Stay here. I'll get your food."

I pulled myself together while I waited.

I'd never wanted to open my life to the world. To open myself up that way.

I'd prided myself on keeping my life private.

Separate from football.

She came back immediately and handed me the bag. "So, how does this work?"

"Are you available tomorrow morning to start?"

"I am. I can work on Breen's story outside of our work hours."

I handed her my phone. "Put in your number. I'll text you where to meet me for our run tomorrow morning."

"Oh, I'm running with you now?"

"Do you want to see what I do? The work I put in? All of it?"

"I do."

"I'll text you the time. How are you getting home?"

"What?" she hissed.

"Watch your back with that guy."

"Careful, Captain. You almost seem like you care," she said, backing away with a cocky grin on her face.

"In your dreams, sweetheart."

I made my way to the front of the restaurant before bumping into Lionel, who always seemed to find me every time I came to pick up my food.

"Mr. Hendrix. Um, hi. Er, hello, sir. I thought I saw you come in."

I tried not to laugh. He was always tripping over his

words. "Relax, Lionel. You can call me Lincoln. Brinkley's brother owns this place, right?"

"Hugh? Yeah. He's my boss."

"Is he around, by any chance?" I asked. I didn't know why I was so concerned about her. She wasn't my problem. Hell, I hardly knew the woman.

Well, she was technically working for me now.

The least I could do was make sure she was okay.

"Yep. He's in the kitchen. Do you want me to go get him?" He looked thrilled that I was asking him for something, which was somewhat humorous.

"That would be great. It'll just take a minute."

What the fuck was I doing? Lionel hurried off just as a teenage girl that was always standing behind the hostess stand approached me.

"You're the football player, right? Henry Lincoln?"

"Lincoln Hendrix."

"I'm Brandy, Lionel's girlfriend," she said with a wide grin on her face. "He's a super fan, I guess. He can't stop talking about you. So, I wanted to see if maybe you could help me out with a surprise for his birthday? It's our senior year, so I want to make it extra special."

Welcome to small-town living. Normally, I'd avoid inter-actions like this, but here in Cottonwood Cove, it was just the norm.

"What type of surprise?"

"Well, Lionel is the kicker for our high school football team."

I wasn't expecting that. I hadn't guessed the kid was an athlete, but that was the thing. You never knew what someone had inside them. Hell, I was a scrawny kid once, too.

"I didn't know that. Good for him."

"I thought maybe you and I could plan a surprise out on

the high school football field. He just played his last season and was hoping to play in college, but he hasn't been recruited yet. I know he misses it already. So, I was going to do a picnic out on the football field and bring cupcakes, and I thought maybe you could come out and surprise him. Throw the ball to him a few times. Watch him kick a few touchdowns."

"Field goals?" I corrected her because she clearly didn't have a clue what she was talking about.

"Po-tay-toe. Po-tah-toe. I'm not a sporty girl. But I do love Lionel. And I think it would probably be the best gift I could give him." She shrugged. "Well, we've already done the deed, and I think that's going to be tough to beat." She waggled her brows.

Was I in some kind of small-town twilight zone? Why the fuck was she telling me this?

But go, Lionel. Good for him.

"Yeah. Tell me the day and time to be there, and I'll show up."

Why was I agreeing to do this?

"Next Tuesday. Seven p.m. Cottonwood Cove High School football field." She quickly wrote the information on a piece of paper and folded it up before squealing the highest pitch known to man. I was certain windows were shattering everywhere within a ten-mile radius and dogs were running for cover.

I slipped the paper into my back pocket and nodded.

"You won't regret this, Jimi Hendrix."

For fuck's sake.

"Yeah. You got it."

I turned around just as a tall man with long, dark hair walked toward me.

He wasn't smiling, and I wondered if he knew that I was the guy who'd gotten his sister fired.

I didn't have siblings. I didn't know what people shared with one another when it came to that kind of stuff.

But as he closed the gap and his gaze narrowed, I was fairly certain he knew.

"I'm Hugh Reynolds. How can I help you?" He crossed his arms over his chest. The man stood eye level to me, and we were similar in size, which wasn't the norm, considering I was a big dude.

"Hey. I'm Lincoln Hendrix. I just wanted to give you a heads-up about the guy with your sister over there." I'd never been this guy. I didn't get involved in other people's business because I didn't like people to get in mine. But I couldn't help this burning need to make sure that she was okay.

Maybe it was guilt over what had happened between us weeks ago.

I didn't know.

But I'd always been a man who trusted my gut.

"I know who you are. I'm a big fan, actually. Well, that is until you got my sister fired and she condemned us all to a life of hating you." He raised a brow and smirked. "And now you're concerned about her?"

Obviously, they were close.

I ran a hand down my face. "I didn't know I got her fired. I was pissed that she followed me into that bathroom. It was a dick thing to do. I tried to get her her job back, but she wouldn't take it."

He chuckled, his lips turning up in the corners. "That's Brinks for you. She beats to her own drum. It was time for her to move on. Her old boss was a real dickhead. And we're glad to have her back home for now anyway."

"She's going to start shadowing me tomorrow, and she'll be the first one to break the news about where I'm going to play next season," I said, and I didn't know why I was saying so much to this guy.

"Really? She hadn't shared that with me."

"I just spoke to her, and we agreed on it. She still hates me, but I think her work is more important to her than her dislike for me."

"I see. And you're concerned about Breen Lockhart?" he asked, and there was humor in his tone now.

"He's a dick."

"Wow. Tell me how you really feel." He smirked.

"Listen, you don't know me. I got your sister fired. She hates me." I shrugged as I glanced across the restaurant to see Brinkley laughing at the table where she sat across from Breen. "I understand that you have no reason to listen to me. I just don't trust the guy, and I want to make sure she gets home safely."

"I got you, man. I appreciate it. I will make sure she gets home safely."

"Great. Thanks."

"Yeah, of course. And I see you ordering from here every night, *Captain*." He barked out a laugh. "But you do know that you're welcome to come eat here, right? Brinkley can't ban you from the restaurant."

"Sure. Next time I'll grab a table."

"All right, have a good night. Looking forward to seeing where you play next season."

"You and me both. Your sister will be the first to know." I held up a hand and waved before heading to the door.

"See you later, Abraham Lincoln," the hostess called after me, and I shook my head before exiting the restaurant.

I didn't mind that she didn't have a fucking clue who I was. I actually kind of liked it.

I liked this town.

And the fact that I was just another guy here.

When I got home, there was a message from Drew, telling me that he was getting pressure about when I'd have my decision. If I knew where I wanted to play, I'd tell him. I just wasn't there yet.

> Working on it, brother. I'm going to let Brinkley Reynolds shadow me for the next few weeks and tell my story. She'll break the news about where I'm playing, as well. But I will have boundaries about what I'm willing to share. The whole fucking world doesn't need to know every detail of my life.

DREW

You are a fucking softy, aren't you?

> <middle finger emoji>

I sat down and pulled out my dinner and put on ESPN. There were four guys discussing my future as if we were personal friends. I listened as they weighed out my options, and I shook my head with disbelief as one of the dudes said that he was pretty certain that I was staying in San Francisco. He said that he had a valuable source.

Who the fuck was his source? Because I'd love to talk to them, as well.

I didn't know where I was going, so there was no source that had that answer.

And as soon as I had it, I was going to give it to Brinkley Reynolds.

This would be my way of making amends.

I'd been the reason that she'd lost her job, whether I wanted to admit it or not. And now, she'd get to break this story, and it would be a good way for her to get her foot in the door at another magazine.

It was the right thing to do.

Even if it would pain me to have someone hanging around, asking me questions every day.

I was getting ready for bed and picked up my phone to text her.

> Hey. Let's meet at 7:00 a.m. down by the cove. Are you up for a four-miler?

The three little dots moved around the screen, and I found myself staring impatiently, waiting for her answer.

B.R.

Captain, is this you?

> Are you meeting someone else for a run tomorrow morning?

B.R.

Obviously not. But you could learn some manners about texting someone for the first time. So, let's go over how this will work. How long are you going to let me shadow you?

> Are you home yet?

I didn't know why I asked. Why I cared. But I needed to know before I answered her question.

B.R.

Yes, I'm home. Thanks for going to my brother and asking him to follow me, by the way.

> You're welcome. I can't tell you my story if you aren't around to hear it.

B.R.

So, now Breen Lockhart is a murderer?

> Who knows what that dickhead is capable of.

B.R.

Well, so far... great conversation. Flirty banter. And he bought me dinner. What a bastard.

He's probably fucking your server behind the restaurant because you didn't go home with him.

B.R.

You're such an asshole.

I've been called worse.

B.R.

So, what's the plan? I run a few miles with you, and you'll tell me where you're going to play next season?

In your dreams.

B.R.

Let me guess. You're going to waste my time? Shocker.

I don't know where I'm going to play yet. That's the honest truth. Take it or leave it. You can ask me other questions until I figure it out. I thought you wanted the whole story.

B.R.

What am I allowed to ask?

Whatever you want.

B.R.

Really? You're going to tell me whatever I want to know?

No. I said you could ask me whatever you want. I'll answer what I want to answer. Tomorrow. 7:00 a.m.

B.R.

I hate you.

Right back at you, sweetheart.

Why was I excited to let her interview me? I hated this shit.

But I was counting down the hours until tomorrow morning.

seven

· · ·

Brinkley

MY PHONE VIBRATED as I made my way toward the cove, and I glanced down to see the group chat already going.

HUGH

The football player that we are all supposed to hate has apparently hired Brinks to tell his story, and she's yet to mention it.

CAGE

Absolute bullshit. You demand we hate a guy that we've idolized for years, and now you're working for him and fail to mention that?

Don't get your panties in a twist. He hired me last night. The sun has barely come up. I haven't had a chance to fill you in yet.

GEORGIA

Go Brinks. Do you still hate him?

Of course, I still hate him. He's the devil. But I need this story, and he's willing to tell it.

HUGH

He was also worried about her being with
Breen Lockhart and came out of his way to
ask me to make sure she got home safely.

> Did someone give you a bottle of truth serum
> this morning, Loose Lips Reynolds?

GEORGIA

Swoon. <heart eyes emoji>

HUGH

Just speaking the truth, Brinks.

FINN

Damn. Hard to hate a dude who was looking
out for you.

> It's all part of his game. He and Breen have a
> beef over a personal issue.

CAGE

Release us from this ridiculous demand to
hate the man. I haven't been right since I
agreed to this stupid pact.

> Did you not make us all swear that we'd
> never talk to Jimmy Peters again after he
> stole your fifth-grade book report?

CAGE

I was ten years old. You can befriend the
dude now if you want. Mind you, he's
missing two teeth and reeks of whiskey every
time I see him at Roddy's Motor Shop. But
have at it. He's all yours.

HUGH

He smelled like pickles to me when I was
there last week.

FINN

Interesting. I thought he smelled like deviled eggs.

GEORGIA

I'm kind of hungry now.

> I'm here. First meeting with your favorite QB. You can worship the man if you want, you big traitors.

GEORGIA

Maddox will be so happy. Can you take a selfie with him for me?

> <eyeroll emoji>

CAGE

Send me the selfie.

FINN

I want it, too.

HUGH

Well, if everyone else is getting it, just send it my way.

> <middle finger emoji>

I tucked my phone into my fanny pack and continued walking. I'd always been a morning person, so I didn't mind meeting him this early for a run. I'd played collegiate volleyball. I could hold my own when it came to cardio. And I couldn't wait to see if he was a man of his word or if this was just some sort of twisted game for him.

He'd acted irrationally last night when he saw me with Breen.

Breen was a playboy, and of course, he'd taken his shot.

But he'd missed.

Because I could take care of myself, and I didn't need

warnings from some arrogant NFL player who'd been an ass to me more times than he hadn't.

Now he was suddenly concerned about me?

I made my way through the trees and down toward the cove. It was a gorgeous morning. A perfect day for a run. The sun was shining, and I could hear the water lapping against the shore as I made my way to our meeting point.

It had been a nice break being back home. I hadn't realized how much I'd missed the simple things, like a quiet morning or a peaceful run outside versus a busy gym in the city.

I'd been working in my garden and had even started cooking and exploring new recipes.

Life was slower here.

Calmer.

Easier.

I looked up to see Lincoln standing with his arms folded over his chest, glaring at me.

"You're late." He raised a brow.

I glanced down at my watch and laughed. "It's 7:02. Seriously? You're calling me late?"

"I was here at seven."

I rolled my eyes. "Well, I'm here now. Are you going to tell me what's off-limits and what I'm at liberty to ask you while we run?"

"No. The run is just to get some exercise. We can make small talk. Nothing I say on the run is on the record. Got it?"

I groaned. "Why make me come on the run if I'm not interviewing you?"

"Don't you need a pen and paper or a laptop to do a proper interview?"

I was going to record him, but I did prefer to have my iPad with me.

"Fine. Run first. Questions after."

We walked toward the road, and he turned to look at me. He was tall and too good-looking for his own good.

It made me dislike him even more because I hated that I found him so attractive.

"It's four miles to my place. We can stop there, and you can ask three questions today. So, take your time to choose them wisely while we're on the run."

"Three questions? That's ridiculous," I said as we started running. He moved to the outside of the road, forcing me to the inside, which seemed like a chivalrous gesture for a jackass.

"We've got weeks. No sense rushing it."

Our pace was pretty quick, but nothing I couldn't keep up with. "Did you drive down to the cove? I didn't see a car."

"No. I ran there this morning. I wanted to get a long run in."

I wouldn't lie. I was impressed. But it wasn't too surprising, seeing as the man was considered a machine in the world of football.

"So, am I allowed to make basic small talk while we run? Or does that count as one of my three questions?" I was fairly fluent in sarcasm, and I made sure he knew I was annoyed.

He chuckled. "Small talk is fine. But it goes both ways. You ask something, off the record. I get to ask something. That's how small talk works."

"Says the guy who barely speaks to the press. Now you're the expert on small talk?"

"Offending me will not earn you any points. Stop fighting it and just start with the damn small talk." He glanced over at me with one brow raised before turning his attention back to the road.

"Oh, this is just so twisted," I said as my breathing grew a bit labored. I had a hunch he was pushing the pace in hopes of keeping me quiet. But then, why bring me out here at all? I could have just met him after his run for the interview. "How are you liking Cottonwood Cove?"

"I actually like it. I can finally breathe."

Honest.

Humble.

Unexpected.

"Good answer."

We ran in silence for a few minutes before we turned the corner near Main Street, and he spoke. "Did you grow up here?"

"Yep. I've lived here my whole life, aside from my time away at school. I played collegiate volleyball for four years and then moved to San Francisco to be close to home after I graduated."

"That explains the running skills," he said. "Do you want to move back to the city?"

"Um, you just had your question. It's my turn. Aren't you the small talk expert?"

He laughed. "Touché. Go ahead."

"Are you really going to Cottonwood High School next week to help Brandy surprise Lionel?" I asked because Brandy had cornered my brother and me last night when we were leaving Reynolds' and told us about her surprise.

"Yes. I like Lionel. He's a good kid."

"Yeah. He really is. He's had it rough."

"How so?" he asked.

"His dad ran off with some woman when he was, like, five years old. It's always just been him and his mom. He works at the restaurant to help her pay the bills. He was hoping to get a football scholarship, but nothing's panned out yet, so he's probably going to go to community college here in town."

Lincoln was quiet. Like he was processing my words.

"I know he's a kicker. Is he any good?"

"I've never seen him play, but my brother, Hugh, and his fiancée, Lila, went to all his games this season, and they said he was really good. But it's a small town. He wasn't on anyone's radar, and his mom didn't really know how to go about helping him put himself out there. Lila had him reach out to a few college coaches, but he hasn't heard anything yet."

"It's a tough road. First, you're fighting for a college scholarship, then you're trying to get drafted."

"Says the guy who probably had endless scholarship offers and got drafted before he graduated from college."

"Wrong. I started playing at a small college in the Midwest. It was the only one that wanted me and offered me money. And then I transferred into a bigger program."

I knew he'd graduated from the University of Alabama, but I hadn't realized he'd transferred in. So much about him was unknown.

"I didn't know that."

"It's not something I talk about. I also didn't go in the first round of the draft. Hell, I barely went in the second round. No one expected much from me, but that only made me work harder. That's public knowledge, so I'm guessing you know that."

"I did. Is the college stuff on the record for me to share?" I asked as we turned the corner, moving onto the strand, the path that ran along the water, and he picked up the pace.

"No. It's all small talk, sweetheart. If you want it on the record, you'll have to ask it again as one of your three questions." He chuckled as he glanced over. "I'm the house at the end of the path. Let's go."

I pumped my arms as hard as I could as we sprinted along the water, and I gasped for air.

I couldn't feel my legs, and when we came to a stop, I dry heaved when I bent over to catch my breath. It was a little mortifying when a loud burp escaped, and a large hand came down on my back.

I barely felt it, but it was there. He patted me a few times. "Too much?"

I pushed to stand and wiped my mouth with the back of my hand. "Never."

"Come on. Let's get you hydrated." I followed him as he walked around the side yard and led me to the back door.

Wow. The house was right on the water.

"Is this your house?" I asked as I stepped inside and took in the dark wood beams on the ceiling, which matched the floors. We'd come in through the back door and entered through the kitchen and family room.

"No. This is my agent's house."

"It's beautiful," I said, feeling like I was going to hurl again. I hadn't pushed myself this hard in a long time.

He studied me and then walked to the refrigerator and pulled out a blue Gatorade. "Drink."

"So bossy," I said as my throat constricted, and I dry heaved again.

"Keep your insults in for a few minutes until that hits your system."

I didn't argue this time. I drank, and he pulled out a chair in the kitchen, unscrewed the lid from his bottle, and started chugging it.

After a few sips, I felt remarkably better.

"Thanks for the Gatorade."

"Better?"

"Yes."

He nodded and pushed to his feet. "Are you hungry?"

"No, thank you. I think I'd puke if I ate something right now."

He grabbed two bananas and returned to his seat. "Save this for when you're feeling better."

I nodded. He was bossy. But I didn't mind it at the moment.

"Thanks, Captain." I smiled because I couldn't help myself.

He rolled his eyes. "You like that one, don't you?"

"I mean. Captain Jack Sparrow? How can I resist? He's the best. What made you pick that name?"

He chuckled. "Off the record?"

Something in my chest squeezed at the way he looked at me. Like he'd been burned too many times to trust anyone.

I'd always had a gift for reading people and was fairly certain I was reading him well right now.

"Yeah. I won't print anything you aren't comfortable with."

"My mom threw me a pirate party every year until I was ten years old and I thought I was too cool for a themed party. I loved pirates as a kid, and she loved that I was into it. So, anytime I use an alias, it's Jack Sparrow. But seeing as Brandy, who I didn't know then, answered the phone when I'd called in that first time..." He paused and laughed, and I was surprised by how much I liked the sound of his laugh. "I said it was an order for Jack Sparrow, and she replied, *Captain Jack Sparrow?*" He mimicked her voice so dramatically that it made me laugh harder.

"So, what was I going to say? No? But Lionel must have told her I played football because now she's called me every name under the sun—none of them being my actual name."

"That's pretty hilarious. You don't have to use an alias here. No one is going to sell you out. The press hasn't arrived, have they? If they knew you were here, they'd be all over you, right?"

"Yeah. I've kept a pretty low profile. But those who have seen me haven't done anything about it. I worried your boyfriend, that douchebag Lockhart, would do something, but that would be pretty low, even for him. There's an understanding amongst athletes, even if we don't like one another."

"My boyfriend? He's a client. What is your deal with that guy? He hooked up with your ex? Did she break your heart?" I asked because I'd tried googling it, but nothing had come up about him and Breen. Just that he'd dated Jaqueline Barrett and then she'd gone to every news channel, sharing everything she knew about him afterward.

He clearly didn't open up in relationships either, because she didn't have much to say that wasn't already public knowledge.

"Hell no. And this is still off the record because I don't want to give her any more attention than she's already gotten by selling some story about my mom being a single mom and raising me on her own, which people already know. But she tried to act like she had intimate details, which she didn't. I'd ended it with her because we hardly saw one another. She liked to come to my games and wear my jersey, but we had nothing in common. Just some good fucking sex, I guess. I realized I didn't miss her when we weren't together, and I broke things off. End of story. And that's when Lockhart ran into me at a sports banquet and told me he'd been banging her while we were together. I think he actually thought we were going to bond over it. But it was disrespectful to her, and even though I don't care for her, I don't like people that shit on women." He shrugged.

Not what I expected him to say.

I'd assumed it had hurt his ego, and he was mad for himself.

"You're sort of a rude gentleman," I said, before I could stop the words from leaving my mouth.

He raised a brow, and his lips turned up in the corners the slightest bit. "Whatever. He was proudly talking about it, and it pissed me off. Did he try anything with you?"

"You're serious?"

"Do I strike you as a joker?"

"No. But I don't know why you care so much." I shrugged.

"What? I thought this was small talk." He took another pull from his drink and smirked.

"He asked to take me home, and I turned him down. I was very clear that I was only interested in friendship. My

73

cousin's husband, Hawk Madden, had already warned me long before you stormed the castle." I rolled my eyes.

"Hawk's married to your cousin?"

"Yep."

"Now that's a stand-up dude. I've met him several times, and he's a great guy."

"He said the same about you, which is shocking." I chuckled.

We sat in the quiet for a few minutes, and he devoured his banana. I peeled mine back because I was feeling better. I put the tip in my mouth, and as I was taking a bite, his heated gaze locked with mine.

Holy banana balls.

Had eating a banana ever felt this sexy before? But I couldn't help myself; I slowly slipped it into my mouth, pausing before I took a bite.

Enjoying every moment of torturing him.

My tongue swiped out along my bottom lip, and I didn't miss the way his hands fisted on the table as he watched me.

Getting under Lincoln Hendrix's skin was my new favorite thing.

eight

. . .

Lincoln

WE'D BEEN in the gym at Drew's house for over two hours, and she'd watched me work out and typed a few things into her notes app on her phone. I was fine with her sharing the details of my workout. It wasn't completely traditional.

I was old-school in a lot of ways. Growing up with no money, I'd trained hard in the alley behind our dumpy little house. I used to work side jobs for neighbors, mowing their lawns, washing their cars, and digging holes in their backyards for plants and trees. All those skills had made me stronger when I was a teenager.

So, I still jumped rope every single day, just as I had as a young kid.

Sure, now I did it inside a fancy gym. But I didn't need it. I could train anywhere, under any conditions.

I did my upper-body workout, which I did four days a week in the off-season. I ran, I swam, I biked, I lifted, I jumped, and I pushed myself every single day as hard as I could.

Music was bellowing from the speakers, but she didn't seem to mind. She appeared to be interested in my routine. I hoped letting her in on this side of my life wasn't going to bite me in the ass.

But so far, having someone to run part of my workout with wasn't a bad thing. And seeing the way her eyes scanned across my biceps as I continued my reps long after my arms were burning, pushed me on. There was respect there, and I felt it.

After another hour, I dropped on the mat on my back and groaned.

Another day in the books.

She walked over to my phone on the bench and turned the music down before coming over to sit on the mat a few feet from me.

"How often do you push this hard?" she asked.

"Six days a week in the off-season. It's my time to build and strengthen before the season starts. I always give myself one day to recover."

"It's impressive."

I sat forward so we were facing one another. "I'm sure you've pushed yourself, being a collegiate athlete."

"Yeah. We definitely did. It was a lot of work. I miss it sometimes. But I still run a couple of days a week and swim when I'm home."

Thoughts of Brinkley in a bathing suit flooded my mind.

"You can join me on my swims. I've been cross-training a few days a week."

"Sure. Seeing as now you've made me your training partner, when does the actual interview start?"

I smirked. "I knew you were going to ask that."

"Don't get a big head. I'm a reporter. It was sort of inevitable that I'd ask."

"All right. Three questions today. Make them count."

"I can ask anything?"

"Like I said, I'll answer what I'm comfortable with. If you

ask a question that I don't want to answer, I'll just tell you to move on to the next one."

"Fine." She rolled her eyes. "I'm going to record this, so anything that's not on the record, just be sure to say that so I can make a note later when I type up our conversation."

"Fair enough." My jaw ticked, and I prepared for the worst.

"Why do you look so uncomfortable?"

"I don't like talking about myself outside of football."

I'd never been one to put myself in vulnerable situations, and for whatever reason, I didn't feel like I was in complete control over this interview.

"Then we'll start with football." Her lips turned up in the corners the slightest bit, and her gaze locked with mine. She held up the phone to show me that she was hitting the record button. She said the date and the time, and her demeanor changed in that moment. Her shoulders squared, and she let out a long breath. She took her job seriously, that much was clear.

"Did you know that you wanted to play football when you were young?"

She'd thrown me an easy pass, and I appreciated it.

"From the first moment I held a football in my hands, something changed in me."

"How so?"

"I don't know. I was maybe five or six years old when my grandfather gave me a football. I just remember coming alive. Waking up every day and wanting to play."

I remembered that day with my grandfather like it was yesterday.

"Like it was a part of you?"

"Sure. I'd say that's a fair statement. It was all fun and games back then. I played flag football for years, and then things started changing in high school. It was no longer just a hobby or something I looked forward to doing. It was what I wanted to pursue."

She nodded.

"So, Lincoln, tell us about the next level of play. About getting recruited to college."

I held up two fingers to remind her that this counted as question number two.

She glared in response, and I forced back a smile. I liked irritating her.

"I got one offer to play at a small college in Iowa, where I'd grown up. My high school coach knew Jack Hardin, who coached at Iowa State College, and he took a chance on me. He's also the man who helped me transfer to Alabama from there. I still wasn't their best guy, so I didn't get a ton of playing time when I first arrived. But I was training with top-notch coaches and athletes. Learning. Taking it all in. Working my ass off every day to try to get better."

She paused and studied me for a long minute, as if she was contemplating her next question. I already knew I wasn't going to like it by the look on her face.

"We've all seen your mother out there at every game. Can you tell us about your father and if he played a role in your football journey?"

I could feel my face hardening. My hands fisted, and I made a conscious effort to relax before I spoke. "Next question."

We sat in silence for a minute. "Tell me about the draft."

"Not a lot to tell. I was happy to get drafted by San Francisco. I was their second-string QB when I first came on, and Pete McGuire ended up injured, which put me out on the field before anyone thought I was really ready."

"And you proved everyone wrong, didn't you?"

"Not sure about that, but I'd say the season went well that year. We didn't make it to the Super Bowl, but we finished second in our division."

"That's where you started playing with Brett Jacobs and Lenny Waters, right?"

"Yep. They're my brothers, and I miss playing with them." I knew exactly where she was going to take this.

"That leads us to the question everyone wants to know. There are rumors that you will join them out in New York. I know you haven't made your decision, but is that the team you are considering?"

"That was three, sweetheart. That's enough for today."

She groaned and turned off her phone. "This isn't usually how this works."

"Tell me how it works." I pushed to my feet and held out a hand and pulled her up.

There was a charge when we touched that I couldn't explain.

I quickly dropped her hand.

"Well, as soon as the conversation starts to flow, you're calling it done. That's usually when things start getting good."

"I guess you'll have to be creative, then."

"You're enjoying making this difficult, aren't you?"

"Listen, I'm giving *you* my story. More than I've ever given anyone else. You can shop it around. Use this to leverage your dream job. But we go at my pace. We've got time."

"Fine." She followed me back out to the kitchen, and I guzzled another Gatorade, offering her one, but she held up the one I'd given her earlier to show me she was still working on it.

"So, were those questions okay? You seemed irritated when I asked about your father."

She didn't know when to stop, but she'd learn quickly that I wouldn't suddenly change my mind. She was good, but no one was that good. There were things that were off-limits, and she'd have to respect that.

"I told you that if I didn't want to talk about something, I would tell you to move on."

She narrowed her gaze. "So, is talking about your father off-limits?"

"If I say next, you can assume it's off-limits."

"You're so condescending sometimes."

"You asked. I answered. Deal with it." I was in a foul mood from the mention of my father, but I wasn't about to say that.

Everyone was always curious. As if everything I'd accomplished couldn't have happened without a strong man leading me there.

Well, I was living proof that a strong-ass woman could lead you wherever you wanted to go.

My mother had done that.

She'd believed in me since the first day I'd told her that I was going to be a football player when I grew up. She supported me and showed up for me.

That was what people should be asking about.

"How does this work? We meet once a day? You torture me in a workout and then I get to ask three questions?"

"Correct."

"Okay. What time tomorrow?" she asked, reaching up to tighten the elastic on her ponytail. Her face was free of makeup, and her skin shimmered in the sunlight pouring through the kitchen windows. Her shirt rose the slightest bit, a sliver of her toned stomach peeked out, and my dick hardened again. I was going to have to figure something out about that situation because my body had a physical reaction to this woman, which was not common for me.

But Brinkley Reynolds' presence had me a little off my game.

"Tomorrow, we're going to run and swim. So, meet me here, and bring your swimsuit. We'll do a run and then swim a mile, and then you can ask me three more questions."

"You're just planning to exhaust me so I can't ask much, aren't you?"

"Nah. You'll be fine."

"Damn right."

"Good to know. Let's go. I'll give you a ride home. Plan to be here at 7:00 a.m. tomorrow. Get your questions ready. You didn't find anything out today that you didn't already know." I smirked.

"We didn't know your grandfather bought you your first football," she said as she glared at me. "I'm pacing myself, Captain. You've limited my normal form of questioning, so forgive me if it takes me a minute to get on board with your weird freaking interview process."

I chuckled as I grabbed my keys, and we walked outside before she slipped into the passenger seat. She was quiet in the car, and I figured she was tired. When I pulled up in front of her house, I put the car in park. "Get some rest, sweetheart. Tomorrow's going to be a big day."

"I'll probably go do another workout today. That was nothing for me." She shrugged as I stepped out of the car and came around to her side, but she was already getting out. "You don't need to open my door. I'm quite capable."

I shrugged. "It's a habit. My mother is a stickler for that shit."

"Like I said… you're some sort of rude gentleman."

"I guess I am. I'll see you tomorrow."

"You will." She held her hand up, and this time, she didn't flip me off. She waved. And I stood there like some sort of creeper, watching her move up the walkway to her door.

I quickly pulled my eyes from staring at her ass and got back in my car.

I drove back home and headed straight for the shower.

My head fell against the marble wall, and I gripped my dick.

I needed some relief.

I closed my eyes as I slid my hand up and down my engorged shaft. Hot water pelted my back, and thoughts of Brinkley Reynolds writhing beneath me flooded my thoughts.

My lips gliding down her silky skin.

Over the column of her narrow neck.

Licking and sucking.

My hands covering those perfect tits before I lift her up, her legs wrapping around my waist.

I imagined driving into her over and over and her head falling back as she rode my cock.

And I went right over the edge.

We may not be able to stand one another for long, but there was no doubt we'd fuck like rock stars.

So, I'd allow myself this fantasy in my head.

As long as I didn't act on it in real life.

———

"Did you give her my phone number?" I hissed at Brinkley after we'd gotten back to my kitchen after our run.

We'd worked out together every day for the last week.

We'd run. We'd swum. We'd eaten a few meals back at my house together because we'd been starving after our workouts.

I didn't mind hanging out with her, even if she found reasons to argue with me over the smallest things.

I'd rejected a ton of her questions this week, and she was still angry about it.

She was fucking funny and witty, and I was still pissed at how fucking good she looked in a bikini.

"I didn't give Brandy your phone number, you big baby. You order dinner from Reynolds' all the time, and you give your phone number when you call in." She laughed.

"Oh, I'm a big baby? She's texted me five hundred fucking times about this surprise. I said I'd show up. Now she's got me on a time schedule, and she wants me to stay for a while after. I thought I was tossing a ball, watching the dude kick one or two field goals, and getting the fuck out of there."

She smiled and shook her head. "He idolizes you. You'll be making his birthday really special."

My phone dinged, and I handed it to her. "This is what I'm dealing with."

She took it from me and looked down to read the texts. "Um, wow. She has texted you a lot. She wants you to make a poster for him?"

I groaned. "How the fuck did I get myself into this? I don't even go to birthday parties for my close friends that often. Now I'm practically hosting this fucking birthday party."

"Okay, you're being a little dramatic. It's not that big of a deal. I'll help you."

"Really?"

"Yeah. I'll make the poster if you give me four questions today."

I studied the little diva. "You're fucking kidding me, right?"

"Nope. That's the deal. Or we can just do the usual three, and you're on your own."

"Fine. Four questions. You make the poster, and you have to go with me tonight. I don't want to be a third wheel in some high school lovefest."

"How do you know I don't have plans tonight?"

"Do you? If so, I guess if you want the extra question, you'll cancel your plans." I wanted to know if she had plans. I assumed she didn't have a boyfriend because she'd never mentioned one. But I suddenly needed to know. "Unless your boyfriend will have a problem with that."

She raised a brow and chuckled. "Very sly. It's a good thing you're a football player and not a reporter. That was not smooth. If you want to ask me something, you can just ask. Unlike you, I don't have a ton of rules."

"Well, you're pretty good at avoiding the question because I believe I already asked it, and you still haven't answered. Do you have plans tonight, and will your boyfriend mind if you cancel them?" I crossed my arms over my chest, anxious for her to answer the damn question.

"I don't have a boyfriend, and I don't have plans."

Relief flooded, which made no sense at all. I wasn't trying to date the woman interviewing me, even if I was getting off to thoughts of her in the shower every day. That was because I was a horny dude, nothing more. We were spending a lot of time together, and she was attractive.

End of story.

"Why the hell did you make this so difficult, then?"

"Because I could." She shrugged. "You certainly haven't made my life easy."

"Why? Because you've vomited twice in the last week from a tough workout?"

"I did not vomit. I burped." She cleared her throat and tipped up her chin. "But you haven't made my questioning very easy. So, I'm going to negotiate with you. And I won't go easy on you either."

"Let's hear it."

"I get five questions." She held up her hand when I started to interrupt. "One of those questions is off the record. I get to ask you something that you have passed on this week. I won't write about it, but I want to know."

"Why?" I grouched.

"Because I'm spending weeks with you, and I'm curious. You can ask me anything. It's all off the record."

"No."

"No?" she said. "Fine. You're on your own tonight, then." She flashed a wicked smile.

"You really are a pain in the ass, sweetheart."

"No argument there."

"There's always an argument with you."

"So, what's it going to be? Just the usual three questions?" She smirked.

"Fine. Five. One is off the record." I glared at her.

"Deal."

"Why do I feel like I'm making a deal with the devil?"

She chuckled, and I couldn't help but laugh.

Because I knew she was going to ask me something I didn't want to answer.

But for whatever fucked-up reason, I was willing to play along because I wanted her to come with me tonight.

And that made no sense.

nine

. . .

Brinkley

HE FINISHED UP HIS WORKOUT, and I fought the urge
to stare at him as he walked my way. He'd taken off his shirt
today, and considering we'd swam together multiple times,
I'd seen his chest before. I'd stared. I'd drooled. I'd forced
myself to look away. But today, I was propped up on one of
the benches, and I didn't want to look away.

Let's chalk it up to research.

His arms were pure muscle, his chest chiseled and cut. But
it was his abs that had my attention. The man had at least an
eight-pack. I'd been dying to count them the other day, but I
didn't allow myself that pleasure. Today, I was going to a
high school surprise birthday party with him. The least he
could do was let me peruse his perfect body.

He had a towel over his face, wiping away the sweat, and
my gaze lingered on his tanned torso, moving down to a bit
of dark hair that led to his happy trail. I licked my lips as I
wondered what lay beneath those gym shorts. He'd made
several references to the size of his hands and his feet, and if
the myth was true, he was most definitely packing the
goods.

I was in the moment just as a bulge strained against his

shorts. Hell, the thing grew right before my eyes. I quickly snapped my gaze up to find him watching me.

"Like what you see, sweetheart?" His voice was all tease, but it was gruffer than usual.

"I—no. I was just—" I tripped over my words. I paused to clear my throat and pull myself together. Was it hot in here? "I was thinking about the questions I was going to ask."

"I see," he said, running a hand over the scruff on his face. "Well, let's get to it."

I tried to shake off the fact that his giant schlong had just reacted to my attention. I followed him out to the kitchen, and he pulled out a fruit platter and two bottles of water. He had hired a woman to come here and stock his fridge and clean for him this last week, and I was definitely reaping the benefits of all the food in his house.

We sat at the kitchen table, and I pulled out my iPad that I'd brought with me these last few days so I could record and take notes at the same time. It helped me from staring at the guy the whole time, at least.

"So, I'm going to ask you the one that's off the record first, just so you don't try to weasel out of it by the end."

"Fine. If it ends up outside of this room, I'll cancel the interview indefinitely."

"I'm a professional. You don't need to threaten me. Have I told anyone anything thus far?"

"I don't know. I guess I'll have to see what Brandy knows tonight," he said, but his smile was playful.

The man was impossible to read.

"Okay. I was weighing my choices, but I'm going to go with this one because it's always bothered me."

"I can't wait to hear it," he grumped.

"Why did you have such an over-the-top reaction when I walked into the bathroom that day?" I could still remember it so vividly. The way he'd looked at me like I'd done something terrible to him. He was so angry, and I didn't understand why it was such a big deal. I didn't catch the guy with his pants down. And he'd made it clear that it wouldn't matter if I did.

He pushed to his feet and walked to the counter to tear off two paper towels for us. We already had napkins, which sat beside our plates that were loaded up with fruit, but he was clearly thinking over his answer. He dropped a paper towel down in front of me and then sat back down. His green gaze locked with mine, and he just sat there for the longest moment before he finally spoke.

"A year ago, my mother started chemo. She'd been diagnosed with stage-three breast cancer. And the day you walked into the bathroom was the day we got the results that it hadn't spread, and the chemo had worked. I just needed a fucking minute to process it. I'd thought of every awful thing that she might say when she called, and when it was good news, I was relieved and emotional, and I don't know... I guess I overreacted."

My heart sank. I'd thought of a million reasons why he'd freaked out that day, and none had ever been anything close to this.

A lump formed in my throat, and I tried to find my words, but it took me longer than it normally did.

I wasn't that girl. I didn't get weepy during commercials and fall apart over relationships.

I was usually pretty rock solid. Strong. Determined.

But something about what he'd shared had me off kilter.

"I'm sorry," I whispered, shaking my head a few times in hopes of pushing away the building tears that threatened. "My dad had cancer a few years ago. He's okay now, but it was really scary. It's the reason I moved back to San Francisco after I graduated. So, I understand all those feelings. And I should have respected your privacy."

"Well, don't be nice now. That's not how this works," he

hissed, and then we both laughed at how ridiculous he was being.

"How *does* this work, Captain?" I asked.

"Turn the recorder back on and ask your next question."

I nodded and pulled myself together. I enjoyed this part of our day together because I got to ask what I wanted to ask. But working out with him showed me a different side of him. The man was committed more than anyone that I'd ever met or shadowed or written about.

He woke up every single day and put in the work.

He ate well. He didn't drink a whole lot, and he had shared that during the season, he didn't drink at all. He was the epitome of a superior athlete.

"Tell me how you build chemistry with your teammates," I asked. I'd always wondered why some people just worked together and others didn't. I'd seen some of the best QBs play with top-notch receivers, and they couldn't put a play together. I'd never understood it.

"It's kind of like life, you know?" he asked, tilting his head to the side as he thought about it. His dark blond hair was cut perfectly on the sides and a little longer on top. His eyes were unique in color, and I'd caught myself staring a few times when he wasn't paying attention. A gold rim surrounded his sage green gaze, and pops of caramel showed in the sunlight. "Sometimes you click with people, and some-times you don't. There's no rhyme or reason most of the time. I've been lucky that I've clicked with a lot of amazing players who show up every day and work hard. So, we work at it, right? We keep trying until we get there. Not everyone wants to put in the work. Not everyone needs to, I guess."

I nodded. "I get that. Have you always put in the work?"

It was a wasted question, but I wanted to hear what he'd say. Had this man always been this driven? This determined to be the best?

"Always." He cleared his throat, and my gaze zoned in at

the way his Adam's apple bobbed there. "Things never came easy to me, but I was always willing to give it everything I had to get better. That shit pays off when you keep at it."

"There are a lot of kids out there that probably like hearing that. So, you weren't a superstar as a kid?"

"I didn't say that." He smirked. "But I worked at being a superstar. How about that?"

I nodded, feeling my cheeks heat again at the way he watched me.

"We've been so focused on your professional life, I thought we could take a minute to talk about your personal life. Are you dating anyone? Inquiring minds want to know." I bit down on my bottom lip as I waited for him to answer. I'd been dying to ask. The press made him out to be a bit of a playboy. I wondered if the rumors were true.

"Yeah? Anyone specific want to know?"

I paused the recording. "No one specific. Just answer the damn question."

He chuckled when I hit record on my phone again, and I shot him a warning look. "I date casually. That suits me at the moment. I travel a lot, and I don't have time for complications."

Buzzkill.

One more question.

"Okay. Last question for today. If you weren't a football player, what would you be doing?"

His eyes widened, and he tossed his hands up in a shrug, letting me know he didn't like the question. "I don't know. This is all I've ever wanted to do, and I'm doing it. So, I can't imagine my life off the field just yet."

"You don't have any hobbies?"

He reached for my phone and turned it off. "You already got your last question. And it was a lame one. No one gives a shit what I'd do off the field. Don't waste your questions on dumb shit."

The freaking nerve of this guy.

"Oh, you're telling me how to do my job now?"

"If I think I can do it better, I will," he said, pushing to his feet and walking to the refrigerator to grab a water.

"I've had enough of you today." I reached for my keys and dropped my iPad into my tote bag. "I'm going home."

He leaned against the refrigerator and studied me. "You're not getting out of going tonight."

"I'm quite aware. I made a deal, and I'll follow through. But you're annoying me at the moment, so I'm going to take a time-out."

"What the fuck is a time-out? Are you always such a child?" He stalked toward me, taking long strides.

I turned around and walked toward the door. I didn't appreciate his moodiness most of the time.

"A time-out means I'm tapping out, genius. I'm fairly certain you know what it means, seeing as you were probably put in time-out often as a kid with that attitude of yours," I hissed as I reached for the door handle.

His long fingers wrapped around my wrist, and he turned me around. "Why are you so pissed?"

"You called me dumb," I snapped. "I don't appreciate it. I'm doing your stupid workouts and going along with your ridiculous game of three questions a day. I don't need to be insulted by an arrogant, pig-headed, stubborn, moody, jockboy."

His eyes widened, and he moved closer as my back rested against the front door. His face was so close to mine I could smell the pine and sandalwood mixed with his musty sweat that someone could bottle and sell for a ridiculous amount of money. My chest was rising and falling fast now.

The man's stank was an aphrodisiac.

"Jockboy?"

"You heard me," I said, but my voice was all breathy and

desperate. What the hell was wrong with me? His nearness had some sort of sick effect on me.

"I didn't call you dumb. I said your question was a waste. Tell me why you asked if I was dating," he asked, his voice gruff. I squeezed my thighs together in response.

"Because I'm a reporter," I said, glaring at him when all I wanted to do was wrap my arms around his neck and pull his mouth to mine. Just one taste. "It's my job, or did you forget?"

"I didn't forget anything, sweetheart."

"Are you done harassing me now?" I whispered. Normally, a man calling me *sweetheart* would grate on my nerves, but coming from him, it was sexy. *Ugh.* "I need to leave before you drag me to crash a high school date tonight because you're too much of a chickenshit to go by yourself."

I needed out of this house. His hands were pressed against the door on each side of my face, caging me in now. And I liked it.

That had all sorts of warning bells going off.

I was not going to fall for the guy I was working with.

The man who'd just admitted he didn't date.

What did that even mean?

He just graced endless women with his giant package. Rocked their world and gave them all the orgasms before kicking their ass to the curb.

It didn't sound horrible at the moment.

With his muscled chest right in front of me.

He smiled. "I'll pick you up in an hour. Be ready."

"Can you back your big ole body up and give a girl some room?"

He nodded, his heated gaze locking with mine before he stepped back and reached behind me to pull open the doorknob. His arm grazed the small of my back, and goose bumps ran down my arms.

"See you later, Captain," I said, trying to keep my voice

even when I was more turned on than I'd ever been in my life.

From what? Fighting with this jackass? That was my weakness?

He didn't respond, and I turned around when I slipped into my car. He was still watching me.

With an evil smile on his face.

He knew he was getting under my skin, and he enjoyed it.

The bastard.

ten

. . .

Lincoln

MY PHONE BUZZED through my Bluetooth, and Siri let me know that it was Brett Jacobs. Brinkley and I were driving to the football field, and she was definitely giving me the cold shoulder. Who knew what she was pissed about now. So, maybe I'd trapped her at my front door, for reasons that made no sense to me.

The woman was consuming me, and I wasn't okay with it.

I didn't get consumed by women.

I got consumed by football.

That was it.

Hell, I hadn't even kissed her yet, and she was invading my every thought. I couldn't take a fucking shower without seeing her face.

Those eyes.

That mouth.

Her mouth was normally closed in my fantasies, unless it was wrapped around my cock.

Because usually when she spoke, she was irritated with me.

But this pull I felt toward her was unexplainable.

I needed to put some distance there, but here I was, taking her to crash a high school date with me.

I'd never messed around with drugs of any sort, but I had a hunch that Brinkley Reynolds was my own personal kind of addiction.

And that did not sit well with me.

"I need to take this. Anything you hear is off the record," I said as I glanced at her.

"Of course, it is. Everything is off the record with you, Captain." She rolled her eyes as I answered the call.

"Hey, dude. I've got that reporter I told you about in the car, so watch what you say."

Brinkley glared at me, and I chuckled.

"Oh, the hot one that you got fired?"

The fucker.

"I didn't say she was hot, you dickhead."

"Hey, Brinkley. He did tell me that you were hot. Long, dark hair, dark eyes, and you can hold your own when you run with him. That's high praise coming from big, bad Lincoln Hendrix." He chuckled, and I shook my head.

"Hi, Brett. We actually met two years ago before you left San Francisco. You were very nice and one of the only guys willing to be interviewed, unlike closed-off Hendrix over here," she purred.

Was she fucking flirting with him?

"Closed-off Hendrix!" He barked out a laugh. "You definitely know how to handle his stubborn ass. And I'm always happy to oblige a beautiful woman."

"Does this shit really work for you?" I grumped. "What's up? We're about to pull up to the football field, and I've got to get out of the car because I've somehow been wrangled into surprising some kid for his birthday."

"Brinkley, don't let his asshole personality fool you. He's got the biggest heart in the NFL."

"Well, he's really good at hiding it," she said, looking over at me when I put the car in park.

"It's all an act. I mean, trust me, he's a total asshole to strangers. And he's kind of an asshole to his friends."

"Is there a point to this fucked-up story?" I asked.

"I'm just giving you a hard time. Coach said you're flying out here next week. I think it's time to pull the trigger."

"Did you not hear me tell you that there was a reporter in the car?"

"Please. It's dinnertime there. Well past working hours. If you didn't like her, she wouldn't be in the car with you right now."

"I'm hanging up. I'll be there next week. It's just a discussion. Drew will be there, too."

"Hey, why don't you bring the beautiful Brinkley? If she's shadowing you, she should be coming with you to check out the program."

"Call you later, dickhead."

I ended the call and turned to face her. Her lips were turned up in the corners the slightest bit like she'd just won something.

"What are you smiling about?"

"So, you think I'm hot, huh?" She laughed. She was wearing a cute-as-hell white sundress that fell off her shoulders with a pair of cowboy boots.

"You'll have to ask tomorrow during your allotted question time," I said, pushing out of the car.

"I don't need to ask something that I already know the answer to!" she shouted as I made my way around the car and opened her door.

"So what? He asked if you were good-looking. What was I going to say?"

"Well, we know what you said, don't we?"

I turned so fast she didn't have time to move. Once again,

I had her backed up against the car with both hands on each side of her pretty face.

"Are you telling me you don't think I'm good-looking? I caught you staring earlier, didn't I?"

She flashed me a wicked smile. "You're all right. Definitely not my type."

"Oh, really. And what's your type? Sexist pigs who play hockey?"

"You have a real obsession with Breen Lockhart, don't you? You almost sound jealous."

I stepped back and dropped my arms. "Not the jealous type, sweetheart. Let's go."

She reached into the back seat for the poster she made and handed it to me. We fell into stride beside one another, and we walked toward the football field.

"So, New York is where you're thinking, huh?"

"It's high on the list," I said, not telling her the whole truth. It was the only one on the list besides the team I'd been playing for. I was fairly certain I was ready to make the decision, and it would probably happen very soon. "How about you go with me to New York next week? Nothing will go to print until after I make my decision. But you'll get to meet a few of the guys and see that I'm not a complete asshole when I'm around the people I'm close to. I'll find out how much I can trust you at that point."

"Have I given you any reason not to trust me? You're so skeptical of people," she snarled beside me.

I came to a stop. She was right. She'd gone along with everything I'd asked of her so far, and I'd been an asshole most of the time. "Aside from arguing with me daily, you've done everything I've asked."

"Is that an apology?" she asked, tucking her dark hair behind her ear.

She was so fucking pretty.

"Do you want an apology?"

97

"I do, actually," she said, putting her hands on her hips.

"Good. Ask for it tomorrow as one of your questions." I started walking and chuckled when I heard her grunt from behind me.

"You're such a stubborn ass."

"Been called worse, sweetheart. Usually by you, if I'm being honest."

"If the shoe fits," she hissed as she jogged to catch up to me as I strode toward the field.

"Oh, the shoe fits, but it has to be specially made because it's so big." I winked as we came to a stop at the chain-link fence.

Lionel was sitting on a blanket with Brandy, who looked up and squealed that deafening sound again.

"You came!" she shouted.

The girl had texted me five thousand times. Did I have a choice?

"Let's go." Brinkley elbowed me in the side and reached for the gate before pushing it open. She marched in front of me, her tanned legs striding in her boots toward Brandy and Lionel. I couldn't take my eyes off her ass.

Her hair moved from side to side across her back.

"Mr. Hendrix. Is that you?" Lionel said, pushing to his feet as he hugged Brinkley quickly.

"I told you, you can call me Lincoln." I extended a hand, and he shook it with a bit more strength than I'd expected, and then I handed him the poster that Brinkley made. She'd gone all out, and there was most likely glitter all over my car now. "Happy Birthday, buddy."

"How is this happening?" he said, letting my hand go as he bent over his knees like he'd done the first time I'd met him as he tried to catch his breath.

"I arranged for Jimi Hendrix to meet us out here," Brandy said, and Brinkley's head fell back in a fit of laughter.

"Baby, his name is Lincoln Hendrix. He's the GOAT of the

NFL." Lionel looked at me and shrugged like he was trying to apologize.

Hell, I didn't mind. I liked feeling like a normal dude.

"Yikes. The GOAT. Is that like the booby prize?" Brandy asked.

Brinkley's gaze locked with mine, and she smiled. The sun was just getting ready to tuck behind the clouds, and those last bits of sunshine made her golden skin shimmer.

Lionel groaned. "He's the best of the best. The GOAT means that he's the greatest of all time."

"Go, Jimmy," Brandy said as she clapped her hands together.

Now it was my turn to laugh. "How about you show me how you kick the ball? I heard you're not too bad yourself."

"From my girlfriend?" Lionel quipped, and his face turned bright red.

"From your stats. I looked you up. You've got an impressive record. How about you show me what you can do?"

The next hour was spent watching this kid kick the hell out of the ball. He made every single field goal he attempted. The field lights had come on once it got dark outside, and he went out for a few passes, and I tossed him the ball.

"I suck as a receiver," he said.

"Hey, I'd suck as a receiver, too. You find your place on the field, and then you work your ass off to be the best at it. You're a kicker, Lionel. And a damn good one."

"You're kidding me right now," he said as I tossed him the ball, and we walked back toward Brinkley and Brandy.

"You really want to play college ball? It's not an easy path, brother."

"I want it more than anything."

"All right. I'm going to make a few calls. Put your number in my phone," I said, handing him my cell as he gaped at me. "I'll see what I can do to help."

I startled when I saw his eyes water in the light from

above us. I knew what it was like to feel as if your dream was impossible to reach. I'd been there once or twice myself.

"I, er, thank you, Lincoln. Even if nothing comes out of it, thank you for tonight. This goes down as the best night of my life."

I extended my arm to him again, but he lunged toward me and hugged me.

I patted his back because I wasn't really sure what to do, but the kid didn't move, so I put my other arm around him and let him just sit there for a minute.

Brinkley was smiling bigger than she ever had before. Normally, it was a wicked smile. Or an evil smile. Or a sarcastic smile.

But this one was a genuine smile.

Not an ounce of hate or irritation there.

He finally pulled back, and he swiped at his face, keeping his head down, and I knew in that moment that I'd do whatever I could to help this kid.

We said our goodbyes, and Brandy was still squealing behind us as Brinkley and I made our way to the car. She hadn't said anything yet, and once we were both inside and buckled up, she turned to me.

"That was really nice, Lincoln," she whispered.

"I can't promise anything, but I can get some eyes on him. He's a decent player. He hasn't been coached much, so there's a lot of potential there."

She nodded. "Yeah. All he needs is a chance, right? Then it's in his hands."

"Yep. Are you hungry?" I asked. Hell, I'd dragged her there. The least I could do was feed her.

"Starving."

"What do you feel like?"

"Hmmm…" She thought about it. "What if we just grab some burgers and shakes? That is, if you can handle one night of greasy food?"

"Trust me. I can handle it just fine."

"All right. Head out to Main Street. We'll grab the food, and I'll take you down to my favorite spot on the cove. You've probably never been there. It's a secret locals' place."

"All right. That sounds good."

And that was exactly what we did.

She took off her boots and walked barefoot through the sand, leading me to a spot that had the perfect view of the water and the sky.

"This is pretty amazing," I said after I popped a few fries into my mouth.

"I love it out here."

"I can see why. It's so quiet." The crickets were chirping, and it almost sounded musical in the background.

"Did you like growing up in a small town? Or do you prefer city life?" she asked before taking a bite of her burger and watching me.

I didn't feel the need to remind her that this was off the record. I knew it was, and I felt comfortable that she knew it, too.

"The town I grew up in was a little larger than Cottonwood Cove, but not a city by any stretch. I liked it back then, and being here has reminded me that I like it more now than I thought I would."

"And you don't have any siblings, right?"

"Nope. It was just me and my mom."

"I always wondered what it would be like to be an only child," she said before laughing and shaking her head. "Don't get me wrong. I love my siblings to death. But when I was young, I used to wonder what it would be like to get all the attention."

Now it was my turn to laugh. "Somehow, I imagine you got plenty of attention, sweetheart."

"Why? Because I'm so hot?" A wide grin spread across her face, and my fucking chest squeezed.

I needed to tread carefully before I got in over my head.

I didn't know where I was playing next year.

My life was up in the air.

I did not need complications.

And Brinkley Reynolds was becoming a huge complication.

"You're hot. It's no secret. Don't read into it."

She shrugged. "I think that's the first compliment you've ever given me."

"Yeah? Well, we don't want your head to get too big." I tried to make light of it.

"Don't worry about me getting the wrong idea. You're not my type either." She raised a brow. "I have a hard and fast rule about not dating professional athletes."

We were both posturing and clearly, we were completely full of shit.

I wanted her.

She wanted me.

But that would be about the dumbest thing I could do right now.

"It's a good thing that it's not an option, then. Let's focus on work and get this story done," I said.

Something crossed her face that I couldn't read, but she quickly straightened.

"That's the plan, Captain."

Damn.

In another world, I'd come up with a whole different plan for Brinkley Reynolds.

eleven

. . .

Brinkley

> Don't mind me. I've just boarded a private
> plane to head to New York on a work trip.
> #sorrynotsorry

GEORGIA

Yes! Maddox is thrilled that you've lifted the
hate ban on Lincoln Hendrix.

CAGE

Seeing as the guy tried to get you your job
back and then offered you the story of a
lifetime—I think it's fair to say the ban is
lifted.

HUGH

And he was worried about you getting home,
and now he's taking you on a trip? Yeah...
time to pull out our Hendrix jerseys, boys.

FINN

Are you going to give us any insider news
about where he's playing?

No. He hasn't actually told me where he's going to play, so he could still screw me over if he wants to. But he encouraged me to reach out to Football Live and Sports Today, which are two of the biggest magazines out there, and let them know I'd be breaking the story. I'm getting all sorts of offers now.

CAGE

Sorry. Mr. Wigglestein knocked up Janey Lowery's corgi, Louise, and the Lowerys did not want to breed "porgis". So, it's a real shit show over here. They think it should have been up to her to make that decision.

Up to Janey or the dog?

GEORGIA

Her body. Her decision.

CAGE

Yep. We've heard it all already. She feels Louise, the two-year-old corgi who eats her own shit, should have had a say before Mr. Wigglestein went and humped her in their backyard. This is my life.

Hey, it's a bitch's world; we're just living in it.

HUGH

<laughing face emoji>

GEORGIA

Damn straight. <fist-pump emoji>

CAGE

So, is New York his top choice? Inquiring minds want to know.

If any of you mention where I'm going, I will shave off your eyebrows and cover your face in Sharpie graffiti while you're sleeping. This is top secret. Nothing will ruin a reporter's career faster than chatty siblings.

FINN

Damn. You are terrifying when you're making threats, Brinks.

HUGH

Because you know she'll follow through.

GEORGIA

Damn straight. I've told Maddox he can't tell a soul anything you tell us. He wants to buy season tickets for all of us wherever Lincoln is going to play.

Don't do anything yet. I will let you know right before I break the story.

CAGE

How generous of you. What are you going to do, tell us a whole two minutes before you tell the whole world? You don't think you can throw us a bone and tell us maybe a week early?

HUGH

Did you really go there? You're a brave man. First, you're fighting for the rights of a knocked-up corgi, and now you're lecturing Brinks?

Sleep with one eye open, Dr. Puplovin'. And keep your mouths zipped.

GEORGIA

LOL! My lips are sealed. <kiss emoji>

CAGE

Take it down a notch. Who am I going to tell?
I don't like anyone enough to discuss this
with them, and frankly, I'm not sure I like any
of you today. And Gracie doesn't care about
football. Mr. Wigglestein doesn't give two
fucks about where Lincoln is going to play;
he just wants to be balls deep in Louise, and
I've been forced to separate them while
they're both here with their owners, who are
having meltdowns.

FINN

Where are you?

CAGE

I'm in my office, taking a breather. It's a
fucking Jerry Springer show out there. And
now, my sister is threatening me when I just
asked a simple question.

THE PILOT CAME out to speak to us, and the flight attendant said she'd be bringing us pastries and mimosas shortly.

Sorry. I'll have to plot your demise later.
We're taking off, and I was just offered a
mimosa. No chatting about where I'm going.
Love you guys.

Several emojis came flying across my screen, but I turned off my phone and looked up to see Lincoln watching me. He sat directly across from me, as the two rows faced one another. We were the only two people on this plane, aside from the two pilots and the flight attendant.

Lincoln had been more distant these last few days, since our long chat out at the cove. We'd gotten to know one another that night, but then he'd been more reserved the following morning.

All the flirty banter had halted.

It was my job to follow his lead. I wanted this story.

No. I needed this story.

So, he was in control when it came to how much he wanted to share.

We'd spent the last few days running, swimming, and in the gym. I'd never seen anyone work out as hard as he did. And I respected the hell out of it.

There were a lot of athletes out there who had a ton of natural talent, but they didn't put in the work.

Then there were the athletes who worked hard and were committed.

And then there was Lincoln Hendrix.

The man was next level.

It was no wonder that he was the GOAT of the NFL.

He deserved the title, and that wasn't always the case in professional sports.

The hardest worker didn't always win, but this man—he'd earned it. I hadn't said those words to him yet because he spent most of our time together aggravating me. But I'd softened a lot since we'd started working together. It didn't really matter that he was hot and cold and serving me up a hearty dose of whiplash day after day. I was getting to see the day-to-day life of the best player in the NFL, so I was grateful.

"Is your family okay with you traveling with me?" he asked.

"I'm a grown-up. Of course, they are. And don't worry, they won't tell a soul that we're going to New York. I've threatened them with their lives," I said, just as the plane started moving.

He chuckled. "You don't need to threaten anyone on my behalf. I'm not worried about people talking. I'm just not talking until I have something to share. But word will get out that I'm in New York because it's inevitable. And everyone already suspects I'm leaning that way."

"And would they be right?"

"Yes. I'm not ready to go on the record with that, but the story that you're writing isn't going to print until after I make the final decision, so you can include this conversation in your article if you want to."

"Why are you being so nice all of a sudden?" I asked. My gaze narrowed as I studied him.

He barked out a laugh. "Am I not usually nice to you? I thought we were past that."

"Well, you've been a little weird since we were out at the cove last week." My hands gripped the armchairs on each side of me as we left the runway and the ground behind us. My stomach dipped as we took off.

"Relax. We have the best pilots out there." His eyes locked with mine. "How have I been weird? We've been working out every day, and I've answered your three questions each time you've asked them, haven't I?"

Our flight attendant approached, handing us each a mimosa, but Lincoln requested a black coffee instead. I ordered a chai tea latte and then stared awkwardly at my lovely champagne flute, unsure if it would be unprofessional to drink it. This was work, after all. She set down two baskets of pastries in front of us and left to go get our hot drinks.

His lips turned up in the corners as he watched me. "Drink it. You're fine. I just have a bunch of meetings and need to be on my game today."

He was always on his game, wasn't he?

I took a sip of the sweet citrus and bubbly. "Okay, then. It's delicious."

"Answer the question," he demanded.

I paused when our hot drinks were set in front of us, and I thanked the flight attendant before she stepped away.

"Well, we were very chatty that night. You know, sharing things like normal friends do. But then the next day, you were all business again."

"We have a working relationship." He uncuffed his sleeves and rolled them up, exposing his muscled forearms. I'd never noticed a man's forearms before, but Lincoln's were —spectacular. Unfortunately, his voice was harsh, and it rubbed me wrong.

It was like a wrestling match with him. I'd go from being totally turned on to completely annoyed with him.

"Well, we also spend a lot of time together, and when you share things, there can be a friendship there. Or didn't your alien leaders teach you that?" I raised a brow.

"You know, I think you forget that I'm the client. I'm doing you the favor." His eyes landed on my mouth, and I quickly brushed my fingers there to make sure there was no powdered sugar lingering after taking an oversized bite of the pastry.

"Are you not going to eat these? They are so good," I said over a mouthful of cake.

"Don't talk with your mouth full." He smirked.

I finished chewing. "Don't be so work-focused all the time. We could be friends who also work together."

"You want to be friends, sweetheart?" he asked as he continued to stare at my mouth.

I pulled out my phone and turned my camera around to see what he was looking at, but it was just my lips. I dropped my phone in the empty seat beside me and raised a brow. "I don't see why not. We work out together. We spend hours a day together. We even eat several meals together. Now we're traveling together. So, friendship is the natural thing to happen, right?"

"That's fine."

"It's not fine," I huffed. "I shouldn't have to beg for it. Everyone wants to be my friend. I'm a good time."

He chuckled. "Has anyone ever told you about the number one rule in sales?"

"What are we talking about now?" I asked before leaning

forward and digging in his basket for the other sugared donut. "I take it you aren't going to eat this because your body is a national treasure or something?"

He smirked. "Go ahead and eat it."

"So, what is this big sales tip you're giving me?"

"You said that you wanted to be friends, and I agreed to your request. Stop arguing. You got what you wanted."

"And that's the number one rule in sales?"

"Yes. Stop talking when you get what you want. People talk themselves out of deals all the time." He shrugged, reaching into the basket and taking out a blueberry muffin.

"Well, don't make me sound desperate. I could take or leave this friendship," I said, my voice all tease.

"Is that right?"

"Yep. But since you're so willing, I'll go with it."

He popped part of the muffin into his mouth and brushed his hands together. "So, let's talk about what you'll be doing while we're in New York."

"I'll be shadowing you, right?"

"Most of the time. You'll meet my agent, Drew. We'll be meeting with Coach Balboa and Jeff Robles alone, but you won't sit in on that meeting. That's not something that can be shared in the article." His eyes were hard, and his shoulders were squared as if he were preparing for an argument.

Was I that difficult?

"Ah… the money talk. I get it. It'll be public knowledge when it goes through, but I understand you want to protect your privacy for now." I shrugged and reached for my tea and took a sip.

"I'll tell you what happens after. But it'll be off the record."

"Wow. Thank you for trusting me." I raised a brow.

"Well, we're friends, right? That's what friends do."

"Do you need a lesson on that? It seems kind of foreign to

you." I used my hand to cover my mouth to keep from laughing.

"I have friends, but I keep my circle small. Just the guys I trust. I don't really have female friends, if I'm being honest."

"That's right. You just sleep with them and then kick 'em to the curb." I meant it as a joke, but it didn't come out sounding like one, nor did he look like he found it even remotely humorous.

He leaned forward, not hiding his irritation.

"Have you seen me with a lot of women in the time that you've known me?" he hissed.

"No. But I don't know what you do when we part ways at night."

"Hmmm… let's see, I've eaten dinner with you the last four nights. I've then met you before the sun comes up the following morning. Do you think I'm calling random women to meet me in Cottonwood Cove when the sun goes down?"

"Well, how would I know what you do? It's not lost on me that your jersey number is sixty-nine."

"You noticed that, huh?" He barked out a laugh. "My mom's birthday is June ninth, so when that number was available when I transferred to Alabama in college, she begged me to take it. She thought it was good luck, and I didn't have the heart to tell her that it means something different to anyone with a dirty fucking mind."

"So, you took one for the team," I said, trying not to laugh.

"Sure. And once I started playing more, I wasn't going to jinx myself and change it. So, long story short, I'm fucking exhausted when we finish for the day. I go to bed, just like you do."

"Don't be so cocky about it." I crossed my arms over my chest. "How do you know I'm not out dancing the night away with my endless male suitors?"

His laugh was loud, and it bellowed around the airplane.

"Because you're young, so the fact that you just called them *male suitors* tells me that it's not happening."

"Well, that's only because my new client is running me into the ground. I'm too tired to date at the moment. But it's not because of lack of interest," I assured him.

"You don't have to tell me that, sweetheart. I have no doubt you've got plenty of guys after you." He sipped his coffee as his eyes scanned my face, like he was memorizing every line and every feature.

And then he leaned back and looked out the window like he was mad about something.

As I said...the man was giving me an endless case of whiplash.

twelve

. . .

Lincoln

WHEN WE ARRIVED in New York, we made our way to the hotel. We dropped our bags off in our rooms and headed downstairs to the bar area to meet with Drew. I allowed Brinkley to sit in on this meeting.

I trusted her.

I'd always been a man who trusted my gut, and I didn't have any concerns about her.

Aside from the fact that I couldn't stop staring at her mouth. At her pillowy, pink lips. The way they were perfectly heart-shaped.

Nor the way her dark eyes always met mine head-on.

I tried to put some distance between us after our night at the cove. I'd allowed things to get too personal. The last thing I needed was to fall for the woman writing a story about me. Hell, if things went wrong, she could cause me a lot of grief.

I'd been down that road before.

Right now, I needed to focus on my career. Where I was going to play. Making sure I was in top shape and ready for the season to start.

A fling with Brinkley Reynolds would be a distraction I didn't have time for. She wasn't the type of woman that would go along with something casual, and I wasn't the type of man who could afford to do anything more than that at the moment.

A football player's career wasn't the same as a traditional career. You didn't play until you were sixty-five years old, after which you'd ride off into the sunset and retire. I'd play hard for the years that my body and mind allowed me to.

And I would not fuck that up.

Staying at the top was a lot of work. There were younger, stronger people coming up every single day. I needed to strike while the iron was hot.

Focus.

I glanced over at Brinkley as we rode down in the elevator, and my eyes traveled over her blouse before I could stop them. Her tits were fucking perfect.

I'd seen them several times in sports bras, tank tops, and in her bikini top.

Hell, I'd memorized them when I'd fucked my hand in the shower to thoughts of this woman.

I cleared my throat and forced myself to look away when the doors opened.

"Drew is your agent, and you guys are close, right?" she whispered as my hand found the small of her back.

"Yes. He's one of my best friends. It's his house I'm staying at in Cottonwood Cove."

"Yes. I knew that." She nodded as if she were taking mental notes.

"There he is. Looking strong, my man," Drew said, pulling me into a hug and slapping me on the back. He was a few inches shorter than me, fit and lean.

"Thanks. Good to see you, brother." I turned my attention to the woman beside me and held out a hand. "This is Brinkley Reynolds, the reporter I told you about."

"Yes," he said, glancing over at me with a smirk. "Nice to meet you. I'm glad he brought you with him."

The dickhead.

"Me, too." She smiled and extended her hand. "Nice to meet you, as well."

"It's slightly out of character, as he normally despises journalists."

"You don't say?" She oozed sarcasm. "I wish I could say that I was surprised to hear that, but seeing as he got me fired for doing my job… I think that's a fair statement."

Drew laughed. "He's just a big grump sometimes when he gets hounded. So, I'll give you a heads-up. We have a little situation that happened in the last few hours. Jaqueline was asked about you in an interview this morning, as her five minutes of fame have clearly dwindled. But with your name being everywhere right now, I think she's looking to get herself back in the spotlight. She has that new TV series coming out, so she's obviously out there trying to get any attention that she can."

My chest tightened. I could tell this wasn't going to be good news.

"What did she say?" I asked.

"Well, she was asked by a reporter if she has any idea where you're going to play and if you still speak to one another."

"We don't." My shoulders stiffened. This was the side of this business that I despised.

"I'm aware, Linc. But she said she's been with you while you've been," he paused and held up his pointer and middle finger to make air quotes, "'*in hiding*'. She acted like she knew the inside scoop and that you two had rekindled your relationship."

"What the fuck? Why would she do that?"

"This is ridiculous," Brinkley hissed as she crossed her arms over her chest and shook her head.

"We won't respond, but I just wanted you to be prepared if you get hounded. You're not in Cottonwood Cove anymore.

The bloodhounds are out and rampant in this city," Drew said before turning to Brinkley and wincing. "No offense meant."

She chuckled. "Listen, there are two types of reporters. I don't get offended because I don't make up stories. I may be pushy about getting the truth out of people, but I'd never report on someone's personal life based on gossip."

I nodded as my eyes locked with hers.

She really was a friend of mine, wasn't she?

She was getting all worked up about this instead of trying to spin a story for her own article.

She didn't ask me if any of it was true. She already knew it wasn't.

"I figured as much. This guy doesn't trust easily, and you're here. So that says a lot."

She shrugged, but her lips turned up in the corners just the tiniest bit. Most people wouldn't notice, but I noticed these things about her. Hell, I noticed a lot more than I wanted to admit.

She didn't need to be here with me on this trip.

The truth was—I didn't want to be away from her for the next few days.

I normally craved alone time, but since I'd started working with her, I couldn't get enough of her.

We made our way outside to the car that Drew had waiting for us. My agent led the way, and I had Brinkley move in front of me, my hand on her lower back once I saw the guys with cameras lined up right outside the door. It meant that someone at the hotel had most likely made a call and tipped them off. It was shocking what people would do for money these days.

Sell a person out without so much as a thought.

"Lincoln, are you in town to meet with Coach Balboa?" one of them shouted, and I put my head down, urging her forward.

"No comment," I said.

"Jaqueline Barrett said you two are back together. Is she helping you decide where you're going to play?"

"No comment," I said again.

"Jaqueline alluded that the two of you might be moving in together." This time, the dude shoved his camera right in my face, nearly hitting me in the forehead.

Before I could do anything, Brinkley turned and stepped in front of me.

"Back the fuck off. He said no comment," Brinkley hissed, her teeth grinding together.

Drew chuckled, and I stared with disbelief as the driver of our SUV opened the back door for us to slip inside.

"And who do we have here?" The man aimed his camera directly at her as I blocked his view and hurried her inside the car.

"Your worst fucking nightmare," I said with a wink. "She's the only one I'm giving my story to. Don't waste your time hounding me anymore. You won't get a goddamn thing out of me."

I slipped into the car and pulled the door closed.

"Look at you, girl," Drew said as he turned around to look at us from the front seat.

Brinkley buckled herself in as Drew told the driver where to go.

"That was rude," she said. "He nearly hit you in the face with the camera."

"You didn't need to do that." I glanced over at her, but I'd be lying if I didn't admit I liked it.

Liked seeing that side of her.

"I guess you're right. There are a lot of bloodsuckers out there." She shook her head, and I chuckled.

My hand grazed hers between the seat, and I didn't pull it away.

And neither did she.

———

My meeting with Coach Balboa and Jeff Robles had gone exactly as planned. They'd offered me what we'd discussed, and I'd told them I was ready to make the move.

It was time.

My time playing in San Francisco had come to an end.

I couldn't play for a man that I didn't respect.

This felt right.

This was the coach who'd given me my first break. A man who believed in me and did whatever he needed to do to protect me.

Protect his players.

And play good football at the same time.

Plus, I'd be playing with my brothers again.

Brinkley had gone to a coffee shop near the stadium, and we'd just picked her up.

She hadn't asked me anything about the meeting. She knew I'd share it with her when I was ready.

I'd asked them to hold off on any announcements, as I'd promised the story to a reporter, and I was a man of my word.

She'd break the story soon.

I would continue training in Cottonwood Cove until preseason started and we were expected to report for training camp.

I was grateful for this quiet time away from it all.

"Good meeting, brother. I'm happy for you," Drew said as we pulled up at the hangar to drop him off. He was flying home because his son had a tennis match in the morning that he didn't want to miss.

Brinkley and I would be staying in New York and meeting up with Brett and Lenny and a few other guys from the team.

I jumped out of the car and clapped him on the shoulder, just as Brinkley stepped out of the car, surprising us both.

"It was great to meet you, Drew." She smiled and

extended her hand. "I'm glad he has you looking out for him."

"I feel the same way, boss lady. That was badass what you did earlier. Keep looking out for my boy, okay?" Drew shook her hand and wrapped his other hand around the outside of hers and nodded. "Can't wait to read your story. It's about time someone did this man justice."

"Don't get all sappy. Get home to your family. Thanks for being here," I said, as he held his hand up and waved and walked toward the plane.

"I like him," she said, bumping me with her shoulder.

"Yeah. He's a good guy." I opened the back door and guided her inside.

"We're meeting with your friends tonight? Are you sure you're okay with me going? I can stay at the hotel and order room service if you want some time alone," she said.

But I didn't. I wanted her there.

"No. It'll be fun. You'll love them. If they hit on you, just tell them to fuck off." I chuckled.

She rolled her eyes and then groaned when we pulled up to the hotel and she noticed the cameramen lined up out front.

"Fuck," I hissed as I called the hotel from my phone.

I let them know that there was an issue, and they said that they'd phoned the police and were trying to get them removed. They told me to head around the back of the hotel, so the car pulled away from the curb and made its way around the block to the door at the back of the building.

Security was there to greet us, and they hurried us inside and onto the staff elevator.

Brinkley was quiet the entire time, and I thanked the two men for the escort once we arrived at our floor and stepped off the elevator.

"You okay?" I asked as we made our way down the hallway to the two suites at the end.

Laura Pavlov

"Yeah. I'm fine." She turned around and leaned against her door. "I didn't know how bad it was, Lincoln. I'm sorry for following you into the bathroom that day."

Her dark eyes looked so empathetic it nearly brought me to my knees.

But now, I had thoughts of dropping to my knees and burying my face between her thighs.

Touching her.

Tasting her.

My cock swelled, straining against my zipper.

What the fuck was happening to me?

I was a man who prided himself on control.

It was time to rein it in.

"Don't worry about it. I know you didn't mean anything by it." I backed away from her and slipped the key into my door. "I'll see you in an hour."

She held her hand up and nodded. "I'll be ready."

And fuck me if I didn't want to pull her into my room.

Have my way with her.

Make her feel good.

But instead, I made my way to the bathroom and turned on the coldest shower possible.

This was step one of reining it in.

But I'd allow myself one more time to fantasize about her before I shut off all those feelings.

I'd just made a huge decision for my career.

I should be thinking about my future with the Thunderbirds, not the sexy reporter next door.

thirteen

. . .

Brinkley

I WAS PROBABLY the luckiest woman on the planet at the moment. We'd been taken to a private room at the hotel restaurant, and I was seated at a table with some of the best players in the NFL.

Lincoln sat beside me, and Brett Jacobs was on the other side of me. Lenny Waters sat directly across from me. Pete Garner, the Thunderbirds kicker who also happened to be the best kicker in the league, sat next to him, and Terry Langley, one of the best linemen in the league, was seated at the head of the table.

We'd laughed and talked, and they'd grilled me about how I had gotten Lincoln to hire me to tell his story. Everyone knew the man was tightlipped and guarded his privacy fiercely.

I'd held my own, telling them about his training, and they razzed him about me racing him on our runs most days. I'd only had a few bites to eat because my stomach had felt a little off since I'd had lunch at the café near the offices while Lincoln was at his meeting.

I hoped I wasn't coming down with anything, but I was doing everything in my power to push it away.

"You didn't eat much. Are you okay?" Lincoln leaned close to my ear and whispered. His lips grazed my skin, and chills ran down my back.

I glanced around to see everyone deep in conversation.

"Yeah. Just feeling a little off." I shrugged like it was no big deal. His gaze was laced with concern as he studied me.

"You look a little pale."

"I'm fine," I said, forcing myself to look back at the guys who had just finished another round of cocktails.

I'd passed on the alcoholic beverages, and I was grateful because I was feeling queasy, and any amount of booze would probably have me hurling right now.

The bill came, and Lincoln quickly signed it, letting the guys know he was calling it a night. Everyone got to their feet, and each one of these large men took turns picking me up off the floor and hugging me goodbye.

Brett spun me around, and I thought I was going to vomit, but I did my best to hide it and chuckled.

We waved our goodbyes and headed toward the elevator.

I was sweating profusely now, and I tucked my lips between my teeth and breathed in slowly through my nose.

Lincoln closed the space between us. "You're definitely sick, sweetheart."

"I think I might have food poisoning. I haven't felt right since I ate that sandwich at the café." I bent over my knees and groaned. My stomach was cramping, and I couldn't stand up straight any longer.

He bent down in front of me. "You're okay. I've got you."

His hand moved to my back, making little circles and soothing me in a way I didn't even know would be comforting.

"I think I'm going to be sick," I said, fighting the tears that were threatening to fall.

This was so embarrassing.

"If you need to be sick, just let it out."

"I can't puke in the elevator or the hallway," I said, feeling panicked.

"I'll get it professionally cleaned. Don't worry about it."

The elevator was taking forever. Of course, we had to be on the top floor. I crouched down when the cramp hit me so severely that I couldn't stand up.

When the doors opened, I looked up, unsure how I was going to move. Lincoln's hands moved beneath my thighs and around my neck, and he scooped me up effortlessly. I buried my face in his neck and breathed him in. Turns out, pine and sandalwood were my favorite anti-nausea medicine. At least for the brief few seconds, until the next bout hit me like a tidal wave.

"Oh, God," I groaned, covering my mouth with my hand. "You need to put me down."

Of course, the stubborn ass didn't listen. He just walked briskly toward the door. I found my key in my purse and handed it to him, and he pushed the door open and carried me to the bathroom.

I pointed at the door. "Thanks for everything. You can go. I'm okay."

I dropped to my knees and unleashed the tsunami from my stomach.

I heaved over and over just as the faucet turned on, and I glanced up to see Lincoln wetting a washcloth.

"I told you to leave!" I shrieked as the tears fell down my face.

I didn't think there was anything left in my body at the moment, so I flushed the toilet and leaned against the wall, burying my face in my hands.

Could there be anything more horrifying than vomiting exorcist-style in front of the hottest guy on the planet?

He bent down, his hand finding my chin and forcing me to look up. He used the warm compress to clean up my face and then moved to sit beside me on the floor as he wrapped an arm around me.

"I'm not leaving."

"Why can't you let me be miserable by myself?" I sniffed.

"Because I want to have something to tease you about when we get home." His tone was dry, but I felt his body quake beside me.

I chuckled and groaned at the same time. "I hate you."

"Hate you, too, sweetheart." He pulled me against his chest, and his fingers stroked the side of my face, moving down to my jaw.

It felt so good. I couldn't push him away if I wanted to.

Well, until round two hit.

And it did.

I spent the next several hours violently heaving into the toilet.

I dozed off somewhere along the way, after nothing but bile was left in my body.

I didn't remember how many times I'd gotten sick. I only remembered the beautiful man who'd stayed in the bathroom with me until late into the night.

He'd ordered ginger ale up to the room and forced me to take a few sips.

I didn't know when it had all stopped or how I'd gotten into this bed.

But when I opened my eyes, there was a tiny glimpse of sunlight coming through the crack of the blackout curtains.

I looked down to see I was wearing the hotel robe, with my bra and panties on underneath. My hair was pulled into some sort of messy bun on my head, and I didn't remember doing that.

I sat forward and glanced around. My stomach felt so much better, and the nausea was gone. My stomach grumbled with hunger pains. My gaze caught on the large shape beside my bed, and I blinked a few times to make out what it was.

Lincoln was lying on the floor with a pillow and a very small bath towel draped over his shoulders.

"Hey," I whispered, and he jumped up as if a fire alarm had just gone off. He was on two feet and reaching for me.

"You okay? Are you sick again?" His voice was groggy, his blond hair going in every direction.

"No. No, I'm fine. I feel great, actually. You didn't need to sleep in here."

He sat down on the edge of the bed and ran a hand through his hair. "It's fine. I slept great."

I laughed. "You're such a liar. You slept with a bath towel on the hard floor."

"Hey, you threatened a cameraman for me yesterday. The least I could do is stay with you while the demons who invaded your body found their way out."

I covered my face and chuckled some more. "You're a good friend, Lincoln Hendrix."

"Just to the ones who count."

"Was that a compliment?" I teased, bumping my shoulder with his.

"If you tell anyone, I'll deny it." He turned to look at me, tucking a loose strand of hair behind my ear. "But yeah, it was meant as a compliment. Are you sure you're okay?"

"I am. I'm actually starving." I pushed to my feet and walked to the bathroom to quickly brush my teeth, as I realized my breath was probably horrific.

"Let's get showered and go grab some food," he said.

"Don't we have to catch a plane soon?"

"I pushed it back a few hours. I wasn't sure how you'd be feeling this morning."

I was startled by his kindness at times.

"Can I order one of everything on the menu?" I wiped my face with a clean washcloth and turned to face him.

"That's a sure way to get sick again. Let's start with a normal breakfast and see if you can keep it down."

I smiled and nodded in agreement. "Fine. Hey, how'd I get in this robe, Captain?"

His eyes widened as he scanned my body. "You were covered in vomit. You started tearing your clothes off in between heaves, so I grabbed the robe and wrapped it around you. I didn't see anything that I haven't seen when we were swimming. Scouts honor."

"I wasn't worried about that. I just hoped I didn't embarrass myself any more than I already had by vomiting profusely in front of you."

"Nope. I just didn't know one tiny woman could have that much green slime in her body," he said.

I chucked the washcloth at him and pointed at the door. "Go get cleaned up. I'm going to take a shower."

He nodded and walked backward toward the door. "A shower sounds good."

His heated gaze locked with mine, and my entire body tingled.

As he pulled the door open, he told me to be ready in thirty minutes.

I let out a long breath and turned on the shower.

My attraction to this man was undeniable. But acting on it would be foolish.

There was a reason that I had a no-dating policy when it came to professional athletes.

I'd always dated men that were safe.

My last boyfriend, Kaeran, was a real snooze fest, and my siblings had had a field day with his name.

But at least there was no risk there of getting hurt. I'd always been cautious with men. I'd never been that girl that got all hung up on a guy.

I preferred it to be the other way around.

To stay in control in that area of my life.

But when I was with Lincoln, I didn't feel like I was in control.

It terrified me and excited me all at the same time.

I let the hot water beat down on my back, and I thought about the fact that I was the lucky one who got to write his story.

But our time together would eventually come to an end, and the thought had my stomach churning all over again.

Because I didn't want this time to end.

———

"My eyes were definitely bigger than my stomach," I said as I leaned back in my chair.

"It's good to take it slow."

My phone vibrated on the table, and I reached for it. My family was probably wondering what happened to me, as I hadn't talked to anyone since yesterday morning.

To my surprise, it was an email from *Sports Today*. I gasped as I read the message from their editor, whom I'd submitted the story to on a total long shot. This particular magazine had never responded to anything I'd submitted.

They were the gold standard of the sports news world.

"Oh my gosh, Lincoln," I whisper-gasped.

"What's wrong?"

"*Sports Today* is the top sports magazine in the industry. I sent them a submission regarding the article I'm writing about you, as well as a few past articles that I've written, so they could see my work. I explained all that we would be covering over the next few months," I said, shaking my head in disbelief.

"What did they say?"

"They said they wanted the story, and they were impressed by my writing samples. They want to discuss this with me as soon as possible as well as possibly doing something full time together in the future."

"Look at you. Way to go after what you want. I think they

are all going to be fighting over you, sweetheart." He winked, and my stomach did these weird little flips.

"So, how will this work? It sounds like you know where you're going to play next year," I whispered as I glanced over my shoulder. "I'm guessing you won't want to wait to announce it. And we haven't really discussed how it would all work after the story breaks."

He leaned back in his chair and ran his hand over the scruff on his jaw. "Well, I can't really be the reason you lose another gig, can I?"

"I mean, I have part of a story to write, but I think there's a lot more to dive into."

"Agreed." He leaned forward and reached for his orange juice. "You can break the news on where I'm playing and tease an upcoming story that you're writing, as well."

I tried to keep my smile from taking over my entire face, but I knew I was failing miserably.

"Okay, I'll just ask you a few more questions on our flight home about why you're choosing the Thunderbirds, and then I'll write up your announcement tonight. You can obviously look it over, and then you just say when you want the story to go public."

"I think it's time. And then we'll resume work as usual."

"Sounds like a plan, Captain." My teeth sank into my bottom lip.

I was thrilled, even if a few more weeks with this beautiful man were going to be deliciously torturous.

fourteen

. . .

Lincoln

"WHY ARE WE DOING THIS?" she hissed, and I didn't miss the irritation in her voice.

I'd pulled out the kayak, and we were making our way around the cove. Brinkley couldn't get into a rhythm with her paddles, and it was funny as hell to watch. She didn't like that she wasn't good at something.

Hell, I understood that.

I was a competitive dude.

"Because it's a good upper body and core workout, and sometimes you need to change it up. Stop being a baby and give yourself a minute to figure it out. And stop deflecting and answer the question that you seem to be avoiding."

"I'm not being a baby!" she shouted and looked over her shoulder to glare at me. "I'm just partnered with a man who refuses to let me lead. You're going too fast, and I'm just wasting energy."

"What can I say? I like to lead, sweetheart." Wasn't that the fucking truth. But I wasn't talking about this fucking kayak. This woman was so deep in my head now that I couldn't think straight.

She'd asked her final questions on the plane last night to

write up the announcement about where I'd be playing this season. She'd agreed that I got to ask a few questions this morning during our workout because she'd been relentless on the plane. Yet here she was, deflecting the question and focusing on the goddamn kayak.

I'd dropped her off at her house after we'd arrived back in Cottonwood Cove after a long travel day.

Normally, I'd be anxious about alone time after spending all that time together.

That was the fucked-up thing. I wasn't longing for time away.

I was actually counting the minutes until I saw her again.

"You're such a pompous ass." Her paddle shot into the surface sideways, intentionally causing water to shoot up and hit me in the face.

That was all it took, and I'd had enough. I dropped my paddles into the boat and leaned my body to the side, easily causing the kayak to capsize as we both tumbled into the water.

I knew it wasn't deep since we'd stayed close to the perimeter as we made our way around the cove.

We went under, and I pushed to my feet and stood, shoving the water away from my face and laughing as I watched her. She sputtered water and ran her hands over her hair, which was tied back in a long ponytail, blinking excessively.

"What the hell did you do that for?" My eyes zeroed in on her white tank top, not missing the way her nipples strained beneath the fabric. She attempted to march toward me, but her movements were slowed by the water, and she stopped a few inches in front of me. The water settled just below her perfect tits, and she was surrounded by the aqua sea.

"You were being a brat. I thought I'd help you cool off."

"I'm a brat?" she gasped and shook her head. "That's rich."

"I answered everything you asked on our flight home. You agreed to answer a few questions that I had this morning, and so far, you've done nothing to cooperate."

"Says the most difficult man on the planet." She raised a brow.

"Thank you, sweetheart. I strive to be the best. That means a lot to me." I loved fucking with her.

"It was an insult." She caught my gaze and followed it, looking down to see her headlights were on high beam. A pink hue settled on her cheeks as she crossed her arms over her chest.

"You said that I was the most difficult. That makes me the best, doesn't it?"

She sighed. "I don't know why you care so much. You're the one who got me fired. Why are you invested in the reason that I didn't choose to go back to my old crappy job?"

"Let's see. You hated me for costing you that fucking job, but then when you got it back, you said no. I want to know why."

"You're awfully nosy for a football player. Maybe you should consider being a bloodsucker," she said, and the corners of her lips lifted as if she were proud of her witty comeback.

The girl never missed a beat.

"Answer. The. Fucking. Question."

Her tongue swiped out to wet her plump bottom lip, and my hands fisted beneath the water as I fought the urge to move in. Cover her mouth with mine.

Taste her and touch her and wrap her legs around my waist.

Rub my cock against all that sweetness.

Jesus. I was fucking losing it.

"Fine. Harvey Talbert, my old boss, is a misogynistic pig most of the time. He told me to do whatever I had to do to get you to talk to me. So, I did, and he fired me for it."

"I already knew that. Try again." There was something more there. Someone desperate for a job doesn't turn down an offer when it comes unless there's a reason.

She sighed and looked away. "He never treated me like a reporter. He'd made me uncomfortable a few times."

"How so?" I asked, feeling something unexplainable build inside me.

Anger.

Rage.

She cleared her throat. "The week before he fired me, I'd gone to him, asking him why my interviews weren't getting top billing when I knew they were better than some of the articles that he was running. He suggested that I have dinner with him at his place. He let me know that spending time with him outside of work was the fastest way to get more exposure in the magazine. I turned him down, obviously, and then he let me go shortly after. Obviously, I was just someone that he wanted to fuck, nothing more."

"Are you fucking kidding me?" I didn't even recognize my own voice. I was so pissed. "Why didn't you tell me that in the beginning?"

"First off, it's none of your business. And secondly, we weren't exactly friends." She looked away again, her eyes scanning the water.

My fingers moved beneath her chin, turning her face toward me, waiting for her gaze to find mine. "Well, we're friends now. I will fucking ruin that man."

She shook her head and shrugged. "Just leave it alone. It's probably the reason he only has men working there. And I haven't told anyone about this, including my family. They'd freak out. So… this is off the record, Captain."

"I'm sorry that happened to you. But I'm glad I got you fired from that piece-of-shit job now."

"Well, you're not completely off the hook. You were still a

total jerk to me when you got me escorted out of the press conference."

"Why didn't you just wait until I came out of the restroom?"

"Please. I'd been trying to ask you questions for months. But anytime you were in public, there were journalists swarming you. Most of them are men, and I hate the fact that I'm shorter than all of them." She rolled her eyes. "I'd jump and wave my hands, but you never saw me."

Something in my chest squeezed.

Something unfamiliar and foreign.

I didn't just lust after this woman—I actually cared about her.

I wanted to kill that fucking ex-boss of hers for the way he'd treated her.

And I was pissed at myself for not being more aware of her efforts to talk to me in the past.

My hand still rested beneath her chin, my gaze searching hers. Flickers of gold and copper bounced around those dark, gorgeous eyes. "I see you now, sweetheart."

"It's about damn time," she whispered and then chuckled.

"Agreed. So how about today, we change things up?"

"How so?" she asked.

"We'll finish the workout back at my place, and then I'm going to shadow *you* today. I want to spend a day in the life of Brinkley Reynolds."

She smiled. "What? Why?"

"Because I've let you into my life, and I want to see what yours is like."

"Well, I shadow you most of the day, so that may not be very exciting for you."

I barked out a laugh. "I want you to do what you'd do if you weren't working with me."

"Really?"

"Yes. We're friends, right? That's what friends do."

She nodded. "Okay. Prepare yourself. My days can be very exciting. I don't know if you can handle it."

I let my hand drop from her face because the urge to kiss her was too fucking strong. I stepped back and reached for the kayak and helped her climb back in. Then I jumped in myself, tipping us over two more times before we finally figured out how to both get in without falling. I'd laughed my ass off as she'd sputtered water every time we'd tipped over.

We were both soaked by the time we made our way back to my place.

I finished my weight workout and took a quick shower. Brinkley left to catch a shower herself, and then I was on my way over to meet her at her house.

Was I nervous?

I spent every day with this woman.

Why was spending a day in her life any different from what we did every other day?

My phone rang just as I pulled in front of her place, letting me know it was Drew.

"What's up, brother?"

"Have you been on the internet today? Seen a newspaper?"

"No. I'm in Cottonwood Cove. Nobody here gives a shit about what's happening out in the real world." I laughed. I knew Brinkley's story about where I was going to play wasn't going to break until the end of the week. She'd made a deal with *Sports Today* that she would break the story in their magazine, and they'd made it clear they'd like to bring her on full time in the future, as they hoped they would get the complete story that she was writing about me.

He chuckled. "Brinkley Reynolds' picture is splashed everywhere, dude. That pap caught a photo of her jumping in front of you and telling him to step the fuck off."

I scrubbed a hand down my face. "That fucker. It'll blow over."

"Not sure. People on the internet seem to be loving it. I mean, she's this hot-as-hell woman jumping in to rescue the big, bad Lincoln Hendrix."

"Are you drunk?" I asked dryly.

"Fuck off. I'm telling you, it's a big fucking deal. People are running with it. It'll work out nicely with her announcement, though. Everyone will know you're working together, not dating. Right now, everyone wants to know who she is. But this has definitely drowned out Jaqueline's interviews."

"Never a dull moment."

"Where are you?"

"I'm picking her up. She's going to show me around town. I'm shadowing her today instead of the other way around."

He laughed. "You like her. Why don't you just admit it?"

"I do not. We're friends. We work together. She also has a no-dating-professional-athletes rule. She's pissed at me more often than she's not. And I'm moving across the country soon. There are a million reasons why I shouldn't go there. Can't happen."

"My, oh my. This is so fun to watch. I've never seen you like this, Linc. I've got to admit—I like seeing you squirm."

"I don't squirm. And you're an asshole. But I do need a favor."

"Name it," he said.

"We are never giving so much as a breadcrumb to *Athlete Central* as long as Harvey Talbert is there. Can you make sure all your clients are aware that the dude is a class-A creep?"

"Abso-fucking-lutely. And since I'd reached out to get Brinkley her job back, he's been trying to keep the communication open for some future interviews. I'll shut it all down."

"Thank you. Let him know that as long as I'm an athlete, he won't so much as get a nod from me. He's a fucking piece of shit."

"Well, I guess we know why she didn't take the job back."

"Yep. Thanks, brother. We'll talk soon."

I ended the call and got out of the car. When I made my way up her walkway to the front door, she pulled it open before I knocked.

"My phone has been ringing off the hook. The gig is up, Captain. Apparently, people know I'm working with you. I'm getting all sorts of job offers." She chuckled and then did some sort of little twirly dance.

"Yeah, Drew just called. It'll set up your announcement nicely. And the good news is, you will have options for where you want to work when this is all said and done."

Thoughts of this coming to an end didn't sit well with me.

I shook it off and focused on today. Now.

Just like I always did.

She invited me in, and I glanced around her place. I'd only ever made it to the front door, and I'd never been invited inside. The place was cute and cozy.

Very Brinkley.

She was wearing a white tank top and a pair of denim overalls, just like the first day that I'd met her.

"Exactly. It's all very exciting. Everything is set with *Sports Today*. They sent over my contract for the announcement, and they keep bringing up a future job opportunity for me. It's madness." She smiled and threw her hands up in the air and shrugged.

"You deserve it."

"I do, don't I?" She laughed. "Okay, so… I've got lots of things set up for us to do today. We're starting in the garden. I'm growing my own food, and I love it. Follow me."

She handed me a pair of red floral gloves and laughed when I tried to shove my hands into them with no luck.

"I told you—big hands, sweetheart." I smirked.

She sucked in a breath. "Yeah, you've mentioned that many times."

We spent the next hour with me following her around. I didn't mind it. In fact, following this woman around while she was down on her knees, with a perfect view of her ass, was my new favorite way to spend my day. There just wasn't much happening in her garden, as apparently, she'd planted seeds, and from what I knew from my mother's experience gardening, she had a long way to go.

We talked about the fact that she was going viral on the internet.

She was completely unfazed and much more excited about the professional opportunities that were now coming her way.

We spent the next hour making vision boards. I made fun of her the entire time, as she had me cut out words and photos from magazines and stick them on this canvas board. But I'd be lying if I didn't admit I was having a damn good time.

It didn't matter what I was doing—just that I was doing it with her.

"All right. That's enough of this for the day. Now it's time for all the good stuff. Buckle up, Captain. Things are about to get very exciting."

I didn't need to buckle up.

I was here for it.

fifteen

• • •

Brinkley

"SO, this is what you do when you aren't with me?" Lincoln asked as I guided him to the gated entrance at Maddox and Georgia's house because he'd insisted on driving. I gave him the code to type in, and the grand iron gates opened, and we made our way up the driveway.

"Yes. And it's Saturday, so my sister and Maddox aren't working. She was waiting for me to finish up work with you so I could come over to discuss wedding plans. But since you're working for me today, we get to come early."

"This is a nice house."

"Yes. Georgia's fiancé, Maddox, bought it when he moved from the city to Cottonwood Cove." I'd filled him in on Maddox owning the publishing company where my sister had met him and still worked with him.

I recognized Wyle, Maddox's brother's car in the driveway. I hadn't known he was going to be there. We made our way to the door and rang the bell. Georgia pulled it open; her blonde hair bounced on her shoulders, and she beamed at us.

"Lincoln Hendrix. I apologize now for anything Maddox says that's inappropriate."

Lincoln just chuckled, appearing completely relaxed. We'd

crossed some sort of line with one another, and there was a comfort there now.

There was an obvious attraction, as well. At least on my end. But I would not act on it.

I was finally getting my break professionally. My email inbox was flooded with job opportunities. *Sports Today* had dropped the news this morning that Lincoln's announcement would be coming in a few days, and they'd listed my name as the journalist who would be sharing the news.

No pressure. Just the entire world waiting to hear where he'd be going.

It seemed ridiculous since the news was out that he'd just been in New York, where he was rumored to be going. But fans wanted an official announcement. They were particular that way.

"What could he possibly do?" I asked as Georgia hugged Lincoln and then turned her attention to me.

"Wyle is here, too," she whispered. "That's Maddox's brother, and he's also a super fan. But they promised they would play it cool."

Lincoln just shook his head and smiled.

We made our way through the grand estate and found Maddox and Wyle in the kitchen, huddled together like they were two schoolgirls waiting for their crush to arrive.

"Are you seriously this excited to see him when you haven't seen me in several days?" I asked, raising a brow at my future brother-in-law. "Hey, Wyle. Nice to see you."

"Hey. I just closed on my house, and I needed some, er, eggs. Yeah. I was out of eggs. So, Georgie told me I could come get some." Wyle cleared his throat as his gaze moved to the football star beside me. "Imagine my luck that my favorite quarterback was coming over at the same time."

Maddox came around the island and extended a hand. "Nice to meet you, Lincoln. I'm a—" He paused to look at me, and I rolled my eyes because this was ridiculous.

"Oh my gosh. Just go ahead and gush all over him. It's fine."

"Well, I'm a big fan. Aside from the temporary time that I had to pretend to hate you for Brinkley. And by the way, Brinks, I am equally excited to see you."

Maddox walked over and wrapped his arms around me and hugged me.

"Sure, you are." I laughed when he pulled back. "I heard you've got your man cave almost done. I can't wait to see it."

Maddox's gaze moved from me to my sister. He looked a little nervous, which was unlike him, but I guess that could be the fact that his favorite quarterback was standing in his house.

"Don't worry, baby. There's nothing to be embarrassed about." Georgia chuckled and leaned against Maddox before he wrapped his arms around her. I was so happy for my sister. She'd found the real deal. This man loved her so fiercely, and I absolutely loved it. Loved them together. "Come on. We'll show you his playroom."

"It's a man cave, Tink. A playroom is for a child." Maddox kissed the top of her head and led us down the hallway.

He'd had this custom library done for my sister, so she'd decided to design a room just for him. When she pushed the door open, my jaw fell open. They'd done a lot to this room since I'd seen it last. There was a wall with four large television screens and a leather couch. They'd put in a bar area with cherry wood and a marble countertop in the corner. There was a pool table in the center of the room and dark-framed sports photographs hung all over the wall.

I immediately noticed Lincoln's framed jersey hanging on the wall and walked toward it.

"Hey, I haven't been friends with him for that long. When did you find time to get his jersey framed?" I said, my voice all tease. I actually liked that Maddox was a super fan because Lincoln deserved all the fanfare. The man worked so hard.

"He already had it, and he'd kept it in the garage until you gave the thumbs-up," Georgia said over her laughter.

"I got it for him for Christmas two years ago." Wyle glanced at the jersey before looking over at Lincoln, who was reading something on the wall.

"What are you reading?" I asked as I walked in his direction.

I was stunned to see several of my articles framed and hanging on the walls.

"I loved this article that you wrote about Hawk," Lincoln said. "I just didn't know you wrote it at the time, nor had I put it together until now. You did the man justice, and he deserves that."

I felt a lump form in my throat and turned to see everyone watching me. Maddox raised a brow when I gave him a questioning look.

"It's a sports room. Of course, we want to have your words on the walls in here. We're proud of you," Maddox said. "Hell, I was willing to hate my favorite player for you until he made things right."

"You did give it a try, and I appreciate it. And thank you for including my work in your man cave. I'm honored."

The next hour was spent with Maddox and Wyle asking Lincoln endless questions and talking about some of their favorite moments of the games they'd been to over the years.

Georgia and I sat on the couch, and she showed me her top three favorite dresses that she'd narrowed it down to. We had plans to go with my mom and Lila to the city together to watch her try them on next week. She showed me the color scheme for the wedding, which would be taking place in Paris, France, at the end of the summer. Hugh and Lila's wedding was coming up in a few weeks and would be taking place here at Georgia and Maddox's home. They'd be bringing in a large tent and tables and even port-a-potties for guests.

I couldn't believe my brother and my sister would both be married in a few months. I'd been so busy with work and my new client that I'd lost track of time, and things were getting real now.

We'd ended up ordering takeout and having dinner all together, and now everyone was acting like they'd known Lincoln their entire lives.

"So, do we have to wait until the end of the week to know where you're playing?" Maddox asked, and I glanced over at Lincoln. I hadn't told a soul because it wasn't my secret to tell. Well, not yet, at least.

Lincoln chuckled. "I think I can trust you. I mean, you didn't want to hate me on her behalf, but you followed through. That's a good man."

"Dude. It will go to the grave with us." Wyle held his hands up dramatically.

I laughed and used my hand to cover my mouth. "It's being announced in a few days. You don't have to go to the grave with it."

"You know what I mean," he said, glancing from me to Lincoln.

"I'm heading to New York," Lincoln said, without an ounce of hesitation.

"I knew it!" Maddox shouted. "I bought the season tickets already because I didn't want to risk them selling out."

"Well, be honest, Bossman. You bought season tickets in three places because you didn't totally know where he was going." My sister chuckled.

"You bought tickets for three teams?" I gasped.

"That's if you don't include the fact that we already have the season tickets in San Francisco," Wyle admitted.

"Well, yeah. I had them in San Francisco. I got some in New York. But there was some talk about Chicago and

Tampa." Maddox shrugged. "But I can sell them. It was worth it."

The room erupted in laughter.

"Damn. You do not mess around. Thanks, buddy. Hey, if you guys ever want to come down onto the field, just let me know."

Maddox and Wyle both gaped at him.

"That's a hard yes," Wyle said.

"Well, their father and brothers wouldn't be pleased if we left them out of it."

"Oh my gosh. Cage would lose his shit if you went down on that field without him. Dad, Hugh, and Finn would just spend a few hours pouting," I said.

"I can get you all a pass. It's not a problem." Lincoln winked at me.

Damn, the man was smooth.

Maddox and Wyle were tripping over their words, and Georgia turned to Lincoln and hugged him. "That's really nice of you. Hey, why don't you come to Sunday dinner tomorrow at our parents' house? It would seriously be the best surprise."

He glanced over at me, and I shrugged.

We were friends now, right? I should have thought to invite him myself.

We hugged everyone goodbye, and of course, the guys all exchanged numbers. They invited Lincoln to guys' night at Hugh's house next week for cards and beers.

My brothers were literally going to lose it because they'd get to see him twice this week.

It was late by the time we left their house.

I hadn't expected to stay that long.

Lincoln opened my door, and I got inside and buckled up as he came around and slipped into the driver's seat.

"That was great," he said, glancing over at me. "Thanks for letting me tag along."

"Sure." I chuckled. "I mean, you're hanging on the man's walls because he's such a fan. You were hardly tagging along."

"Hey. You're hanging on the man's walls, too. Don't sell yourself short." He started the car and glanced over one more time. "Am I taking you home?"

I didn't want the night to end. We'd been out all day, and I wasn't ready to say goodbye.

"Are you hungry?" I asked because it had been a few hours since we'd had dinner.

"Starving. But I think everything's closed. It's late." He pulled down the driveway.

I sent a text to Hugh.

> Hey. Is Reynolds' already closed up? I'm with Lincoln, and we are starving. Your apple pie and ice cream sound really good right now.

HUGH

> I just got off the phone with Maddox. Are you fucking kidding me? We're going to go down onto the field at a game? I'd give you my firstborn right now if I had one.

> I figured you'd like that. <winky face emoji>

HUGH

> The restaurant is closed. You've got a key, and you know the alarm code. Go help yourself. Just lock up and set the alarm when you leave. Love you, Brinks.

"Okay, let's go to Reynolds'. Park in the back."

"It's open?" he asked as he drove the short distance to downtown and pulled in behind the restaurant.

"No. But I've got a key, and Hugh said to help ourselves. Get ready for the best pie you've ever had. They have this amazing baker who runs the bakery next door and provides them with the best desserts." Lincoln opened my door, and we made our way inside. I flipped on the lights as we entered through the kitchen.

"Wow. These are some serious sibling perks." He took the pie from me, and I reached for the ice cream and the whipped cream.

I cut us each a slice of pie and popped them into the microwave to get them warmed up just a little bit. I added a scoop of ice cream and sprayed a bunch of whipped cream on top. I tipped my head back and sprayed it into my mouth because I couldn't help myself.

Old habits die hard, I guess.

When I put the cap on the whipped cream and looked up, Lincoln's green eyes were watching me so closely that it made it difficult to breathe.

Well, that and the fact that I had an abnormal amount of sugary cream in my mouth.

I quickly swallowed as he watched me intently.

He moved closer, and his thumb came down on my upper lip.

"You have a little left here," he said, holding his thumb out to me as he offered a small amount of whipped cream.

I didn't know if aliens had taken over my body, but on instinct, my mouth opened. His thumb slipped inside, and I swirled my tongue around it and sucked. Desire flooded, and my gaze never left his.

He pulled his thumb out, and his mouth crashed into mine. My lips parted, and his tongue slipped inside. The kiss was needy and desperate, the way we both clung to one another. He lifted me off the floor and settled my ass on the metal counter in the kitchen. He stood between my thighs, and I could feel his erection through his jeans as it pressed against my center. My fingers were tangled in his hair, and his large hands were on each side of my face, as if he couldn't get close enough. I was so turned on that I couldn't see straight. I bucked against him, needing that friction. Needing to feel him against me.

He kissed me harder.

Faster.

He lifted me from the counter, and my legs wrapped around his waist as he carried me to the wall beside the refrigerator. He pressed my back against the cool wall, and his hands gripped my ass as he slid me up and down his hard cock as I ground up against his gigantic denim-covered bulge. His mouth invaded mine as he licked and nipped and kissed me like he'd die if he stopped. I'd never felt more wanted.

My hands tugged at his hair as I bucked against him, and my entire body started tingling.

Had I ever wanted anyone more?

"Lincoln," I groaned into his mouth as this growing need took over, and my head fell back.

"Let go, sweetheart," he whispered, as he kissed down my neck and continued rocking me faster against him.

I was dry-humping my client in the middle of my brother's kitchen.

And I didn't even care because nothing had ever felt so good.

Stars exploded behind my eyes as my entire body started to shake, and I went right over the edge.

Once my breathing calmed and I was able to open my eyes, I found him watching me.

The look in his gaze was not what I expected.

He didn't look scared that we'd just crossed a line.

He didn't look bothered that I'd finished and he hadn't.

There was no sign of panic.

He looked at me like I was the most beautiful woman he'd ever seen.

Pass me the whipped cream, please.

Because I only wanted more.

sixteen

. . .

Lincoln

I'D BEEN with my fair share of women before.

I'd had a few failed relationships, a few flings, and plenty of casual nights with women that didn't go beyond that.

But this.

Brinkley Reynolds filling her mouth with whipped cream and then rubbing herself against my dick.

Nothing had ever been sexier.

I was done for.

If I never saw a woman come undone again, I would still die a happy man.

Seeing her fall apart from just my mouth on hers. Her body rubbing against mine.

I hadn't even seen her naked or been inside her yet.

Hadn't touched her or tasted her the way I was desperate to.

It didn't matter.

Her gaze searched mine, and I carried her back to the counter and set her down. My fingers stroked her face as I pushed the dark hair behind her ears.

"You okay?" I asked.

"Umm… I've never been better. I'm guessing you've got a little situation going on, though," she purred.

Had there ever been a sexier woman?

I reached for her hand and rested it over my throbbing cock, straining against my jeans.

"Nothing little about the situation going on here, sweetheart," I said, my voice gruff.

Her hand continued to stroke me up and down, and I squeezed my eyes closed.

"You're right about that. You've got quite the package on board, Captain." She waggled her brows.

"You ready to drop the no-dating-professional-athlete's rule?" I said, nipping at her lips.

Her eyes widened. "You don't even date often; why are you asking that?"

"Because I want to date you."

Her eyebrows narrowed, and she shook her head. "Don't say that, Lincoln. Don't say things you don't mean."

She pushed me back and hopped off the counter, moving to her plate of pie and taking a bite as if this were all a big joke.

"Hey." I locked my gaze with hers. "I don't say things that I don't mean. I'd think you'd know that by now."

"Let's see, you haven't dated in quite a while. You can't stand me most of the time, and we work together. Oh… and you're moving across the country. To you, I'm just some small-town smoke show." She crossed her arms over her chest.

I barked out a laugh. "Well, you are hot, and you did grow up in a small town, so if that makes you a small-town smoke show, so fucking be it. But that's not the reason that I want to date you."

"You just want to date me because you're probably horny and you're stuck here in Cottonwood Cove."

The fucking nerve of this woman.

She took another bite of pie and raised her brow at me like I was the crazy one.

I forked some pie, tipped the utensil back, and flung it at her. A chunk of apple and some sort of crumbly shit landed on her cheek, and she gasped.

Now it was my turn to laugh. I hadn't expected to aim so well, but damn, it served her fucking right.

I was as offended for her as I was for myself. First, her accusing me of not knowing what I want and then her saying that I'm only interested in her because she's the only thing here in Cottonwood Cove.

What the fuck was her deal?

She reached for a napkin and wiped her face, turning her back to me.

"I can't believe you did that," she whispered.

My chest squeezed because she was all over the fucking place, and I didn't know what the hell I was doing when it came to her. I moved closer just as she turned around and aimed the can of whipped cream at me and sprayed me in the face.

"Take that, sucker. You have no idea who you're dealing with, Lincoln Hendrix!" She ran to the other side of the island, holding the can in her hand, her eyes wild and full of fire. She was laughing hysterically, and I couldn't help but do the same.

I swiped the whipped cream away from my eyes and shook my head.

I reached for my plate of pie, carrying it with me as I moved around the island that sat between us. Her chest was rising and falling, and our labored breaths filled the air around us.

I stalked toward her, almost predatory.

The way I wanted this woman wasn't anything I'd ever experienced before.

"Put the whipped cream down," I said, closing the distance between us.

She studied me, setting the can on the counter.

I stood right in front of her, my gaze locked with hers. "Open your mouth."

"Someone's feeling full of himself." Her voice was barely a whisper.

I raised a brow, waiting for her to do as I said. Her mouth fell open, and I scooped up some pie and fed it to her. She groaned as she sealed her lips around the fork before I pulled it out, and she chewed slowly.

"I always know what I want. You think because I haven't had a relationship recently that it means that I'm incapable? That's never been my problem."

"So, what's your problem, Captain?" she asked, her voice sexy as hell.

"I haven't found anyone worth doing it with. There was Jaqueline, but it was doomed from the start," I said, taking a bite of pie for myself before I moved the fork back to her sweet mouth.

"Why was that? Because life on the road makes it impossible? Because you have endless women dropping to their knees for you?"

I studied her. She liked to act tough, but she was fucking scared. "We had nothing in common. There was no conversation. No laughter."

"Just hot sex and lots of it, right?" She pursed her lips and squared her shoulders.

"Sure. It was just sex. We both have our pasts. I have nothing to hide. The sex was fine, but at the end of the day, that got old. As did her annoying desire for attention and the spotlight." I set the plate down on the counter. "That's why I normally keep my relationships casual. I have never craved the company of a woman—until now."

"Really? I'm supposed to believe that you crave me?" She

tried to act unaffected, but her cheeks pinked, and I noticed her breaths were coming fast again.

"Yes. Because I do."

"You'll get bored. So, we can agree to a one-night thing, because I can't deny that I want you, too. But that's all it is. One night, then we go back to working together and pretend it never happened."

"Not happening," I said as my hand moved to the side of her neck, my thumb stroking along her jawline. "It's all or nothing."

Was I really fucking turning down one night with her?

This was a first.

She stepped back and shook her head. "Why are you messing with my head?"

"Am I?"

"Yes. I just agreed to a one-night stand. Offered for us to get whatever this is out of our systems. And you're turning me down?" She crossed her arms over her chest, and her face hardened. She was pissed.

"Correct."

"Why?"

"Because I don't want you in my bed for one night, Brinkley Reynolds. It won't be enough for me." My tongue swiped out to wet my lips, and her eyes moved there.

"I don't date athletes. I don't set myself up to get hurt. You get one night, and that's it. Final offer." Her gaze locked with mine, letting me know she wasn't backing down.

But neither the fuck was I.

"No deal." My dick strained so hard behind my zipper that it was painfully uncomfortable. But I was going to stand my ground.

"Fine. Let's leave things as they are, then." She raised a brow.

"All right. Friends?" I held out my hand. I knew I'd wear her down. This pull was too strong with us. I'd gone my entire life never wanting anything real with anyone before now. I wasn't going to fuck it up by starting out the wrong way. This woman was going to be worth the wait.

"You're a stubborn ass." She slapped my hand away and started putting everything back in the refrigerator. She wiped down the counter, and I cleaned up the floor.

Our drive to her house was quiet, and she stared out the window.

When I pulled in front of her house, she turned to face me. "I will send the announcement over to you tonight to look over. We have a few days to make some tweaks if you don't like the wording. But it's pretty brief and to the point."

"Sounds good. And we're off tomorrow, so no workout."

"Right."

"Am I still invited to Sunday dinner, or are you revoking the invitation?"

"Well, seeing as I'm not the one who invited you, I don't think it would be fair to uninvite you."

She was so fucking cute when she was mad.

And what was she even mad about?

The fact that I liked her?

A lot?

"Great. I'll meet you over here, and we can go together."

"Fine. That sounds like a plan. Good night, *friend*." She pushed her door open, and I jumped out of the car.

"Friends don't walk one another to the door," she hissed, glancing over her shoulder at me.

I reached for her arm just as she was about to put the key into the door. I turned her around to face me.

"I will always walk you to the door. Stop being a stubborn ass." I set one hand on each side of her face, caging her in.

"I'm the stubborn ass?" She shook her head and glared at me.

"Yes. You're pissed because I don't want to just fuck you

for one night when you know you want the same thing that I do. That makes *you* a stubborn ass."

"You're so full of yourself. You can't stand the fact that I don't want to date you, can you?"

"No. I can't," I said dryly. "Because you're lying."

"Oh, really? Why would I lie about that?"

I moved closer, invading her space. My forehead rested against hers. "Because you're scared. Because the future is unknown. Because I don't have a great track record in relationships, and from what you've told me, neither do you."

"You'll tire of me, Lincoln. You're moving to New York. I live here."

"You don't even know where you're going to be living in a few months when you publish your story."

"Your story," she said, raising a brow. "It's better that we don't cross the line. Things will get messy."

"I think things are already messy, sweetheart. But I've never been a guy that was afraid of the long game. So, I'll just have to show you that you're wrong." I stepped back and made my way down her path, walking backward as she watched me.

"I'm rarely wrong," she said, and the corners of her lips turned up the slightest bit.

"We'll see about that."

I waited for her to step inside before getting back in my car and driving the short distance to my house.

When I got home, I checked my phone and saw an email from my college coach, Jack Hardin. I'd reached out about Lionel, and he'd gotten back to me. He said they were actually looking for a backup kicker because their first-string kicker had graduated this past year and they were down to one guy. I'd sent him the film that I'd taken of Lionel kicking a few field goals that day out on the field, and he was interested. He also said he knew of a few small programs on the lookout for a kicker, and he'd pass on the word about Lionel.

They weren't huge football programs, but they would allow him to play, and I was hoping they'd offer him something to help pay for his schooling. I sent him Lionel's contact information and then sent Lionel a text, as well, to let him know that he should be looking out for a call.

It was well past midnight, and I didn't expect a response at this hour, but the kid was full of surprises.

> **LIONEL**
>
> I can't believe this. I don't know how to thank you, Lincoln.

> Just keep training and be open to any calls that come your way. If you want to come train with me and Brinkley next week, we can work on building some muscle, which will make you stronger.

What the fuck was I doing?

I guess I remembered the time I was worried about playing in college, and I didn't have a fucking clue how to go about it. Neither did my mom. I didn't have a father to help guide me, and I knew that Lionel didn't either. So, a part of me felt like I could offer that to him in a way. At least help him out where his own father had failed him.

> **LIONEL**
>
> I would love to. I will do anything you say.

If only Brinkley Reynolds would say those same words to me.

Then the world would be a perfect place.

seventeen

. . .

Brinkley

LINCOLN and I drove to my parents' house after he arrived at my house. He was acting like nothing had gone down last night. Meanwhile, I hadn't slept a wink. I'd tossed and turned with memories of the world's best orgasm flooding my mind all night long.

Jesus.

The fact that the most erotic, sexy, amazing moment of my life had happened at my brother's restaurant in the middle of the kitchen was beyond anything I could comprehend. I'd gone for some pie and left with a whole lot more than that.

Was I sweating now?

We pulled up in front of my parents' house and he came around to help me out of the car.

"Your cheeks are pretty flushed. Want to tell me what you're thinking about?" he said with a cocky smirk.

"What? I'm not flushed. It's hot outside." I couldn't look at him.

"It's seventy-five degrees tonight. Actually, it's pretty cool with the breeze. I think you're thinking about that kiss last night."

"Of course, you do. Because you're arrogant and cocky

and—" I threw my hands in the air because I was flustered. He was right. That kiss was all I could think about.

He wrapped his fingers around my wrist and turned me to face him. "You can't stop thinking about it because neither can I. It was a good fucking kiss. The best I've ever had."

"Stop," I whispered, glancing around to make sure no one was watching us because I was suddenly ridiculously turned on.

"The way you rocked up and down my cock like you fucking owned it... Because you do, Brinkley. This can all be yours if you want it. I'll make you come so many times you won't be able to see straight, sweetheart."

The bastard.

My breaths were labored, and desire pooled between my thighs. This was not good.

I pressed my fingers to my temples. "Okay, this stops now. My parents live here. No more talk about last night. Let's go."

He chuckled, and we started walking again. "You a little frustrated, baby?"

"I'm fine," I hissed as we walked up the cobblestone side-walk toward the front door. I turned around and poked my finger hard into his chest, and I wanted to tear his buttons open and kiss every inch of him. My God. What was happening to me? "Best behavior, Captain."

"Always." The back of his hand grazed mine, and goose bumps ran down my arms and legs.

Once we stepped inside, all hell broke loose. Everyone gawked and fawned over the football star.

"Lincoln, I can't believe you're really here," my mother said. The woman didn't give a damn about football, but she was suddenly very interested in the man.

Maddox and Wyle were there, and of course, they were laughing and talking and telling my brothers that he was coming to guys' night this week.

Cage introduced Gracie to Lincoln, but my brother could barely form a sentence when he tried to speak.

Hugh and Finn were completely comfortable and acting like they'd been best friends with the guy for years.

"I think he's having a good time," Georgia said as we stood several feet away from them, sipping our wine. Lila walked over to join us, as my mom was busy in the kitchen.

"He does. And this can be an overwhelming group." Lila chuckled.

"Yeah. I mean, they're all falling all over him. I don't know why he wouldn't enjoy that. The man has a big ego."

Georgia studied me. "It's okay to say that you like him. He seems like a really good guy."

"I agree. Don't fight it, girl. He's hot. You're hot," Lila said, waggling her brows.

"He's fine. We're friends."

"Oh, I know that face. You like him," Georgia whispered before grabbing mine and Lila's hands and tugging us toward the hallway. "Tell me."

"It's nothing. I'm attracted to him. We accidentally kissed last night. And then he pretended that he wanted to actually date me. Give it a real try. See where it goes. It's ridiculous. I was on board with a one-time fling—no risk of anyone's feelings getting hurt. But he wanted to go and make it complicated."

"You've never even had a one-night stand. Why are you pushing for that?" Georgia asked.

"I mean, maybe he knows one night just won't be enough," Lila whispered.

"I'm not against having a one-nighter. I just haven't found anyone that I wanted to give it a try with and that I was super attracted to. Plus, he's not the dating type. He's a freaking football star. Come on. Am I the only one that sees it? This would never work."

"Football stars date all the time. It's not unheard of." Lila shrugged.

"And he never stops staring at you. Maddox and I both noticed it when you were over yesterday. And you're always together. Why are you so afraid to give it a try?"

"There are a million reasons why it won't work."

"There were a million reasons why your brother and I would never work, and look at us," Lila said.

Georgia chuckled. "Agreed. And the idea of Maddox and I felt impossible at first. Give me one good reason why it can't work," Georgia said, putting her hands on her hips, and Lila stood beside her, waiting, as well.

"I can name several. He's a freaking football star. He's moving across the country. We annoy each other daily."

Georgia studied me for a long moment before she spoke. "You really like him, and you're afraid of getting hurt. That's new for you, isn't it?"

"What are you talking about?"

"Come on, Brinks. You've never dated a man who challenged you. You tend to date really passive guys who you tire of quickly. But there's no risk there, is there?"

"Yeah, I have to agree. That Kaeran guy had the personality of a snail," Lila said, and she and Georgia broke out in a fit of laughter.

"What are you talking about? Obviously, I prefer to date guys that I don't fight with. That's sort of a good thing." I chuckled and looked up when Lincoln said my name.

"That's just the arrogant football player bragging about how you're getting all these job offers because you're so talented. He's such a pig," Georgia said, making no attempt to hide her sarcasm.

"The nerve of him." Lila smirked.

Thankfully, my mother called us all to the table for dinner.

"Okay, enough of this conversation. Let's go eat. I'm starving."

We all sat around the table, and my father looked so starstruck it was difficult not to laugh.

Lincoln sat beside me, with Cage and Gracie on the other side of him. Hugh and Lila were directly across from us, and Georgia and Maddox sat beside them with Wyle on the other side of them. Finn was next to me, and my parents were each at the head of the table.

We passed the platters of chicken and mashed potatoes and corn on the cob around the table as Gracie asked Lincoln several questions about football. It was adorable the way he answered each one as she listened intently.

"I want to thank you for what you're doing for Lionel," Hugh said as he passed the rolls to Lila. "He worked with me this morning, and he was all excited that you texted him last night."

"What is he doing for Lionel?" my father asked.

"He's helping him out with the hope that Lionel can continue his football career in college. Even if he just walks onto a team, it would be good for him to go away and experience college. The dude has been working for a long time, and he deserves a chance to just be a normal college kid, and if he got to play for a team, it would be the icing on the cake," my brother said.

"He's a good kid. I'm happy to help."

I glanced over at him. "Did you speak to the coach?"

"Yeah. He's going to reach out, and he passed his name to a few other programs."

Wow. He'd really followed through. I was impressed.

I hadn't realized he'd made the call.

"So, Lincoln, I don't know a whole lot about you outside of being a football star," my mother said as she scooped some salad onto her plate. "Are you married or dating?"

Leave it to my parents to make things completely awkward.

"Mom," I groaned. "We work together. That's not something you should ask."

Everyone chuckled, and my mom smiled at me.

"Brinks," she mimicked me, and there was more laughter. "You spend every day with this man, you just flew across the country with him, and he's at our home for dinner. This is called small talk, my love."

"Grammie loves small talk," Gracie sang out, and I sighed.

"Actually, Alana, it's funny you should ask. I'm not married, but I am trying to date your daughter. She's just putting up a big fight because she's a bit stubborn, which I'm guessing isn't news to any of you?"

No. He. Didn't.

The table was silent as they all tried to hide their smiles, which was not the norm for a Reynolds' family dinner. My eyes probably doubled in size as I gaped at him.

"She is painfully stubborn. I couldn't agree more," Cage said, breaking the silence. "But if you do win her over, do we get season tickets for life?"

Hugh and Finn laughed, and I rolled my eyes.

"Maddox already got you all season tickets, so don't be pimping me out," I hissed.

"What does pimping mean?" Gracie asked.

Damn it. I couldn't even have a meltdown without feeling like an asshole.

"I'd be happy to answer this one," Wyle said, and the entire table turned and shouted the word: *No.*

More laughter.

"It's an adult word," Cage said, shooting me a look. "One your auntie shouldn't be using. And thank you, Maddox, for the tickets, and Lincoln, whatever perks dating our sister gets us, I'd be down for."

My hands came down on the table hard, and I shook my head. "You are all a bunch of traitors."

"Hey, we love you. We just really love Lincoln," Finn said before chomping down on his corn on the cob.

"You all have been a lot easier to win over than this one." Lincoln flicked his thumb at me before reaching for his glass of wine.

"She's never been easy," Cage said, shaking his head. "The girl has exhausted me most of my life. The other three—piece of cake."

Everyone at the table lost it as Finn threw his hands in the air. "Hey. We have names. We may be easy, but we have feelings, too."

"Um, I was called 'this one'," I said, elbowing Lincoln in the arm. "And you were far from easy yourself, Cage."

"All right. Let's relax," my father said while still trying to pull himself together.

"Easy or strong or difficult or hilarious… we love you all the same."

"Wait. What does that mean?" I asked, because not one single person had yet to say that I wasn't exhausting. "Mom, am I exhausting?"

"Honey. You're perfect just the way you are."

"I think that says it all," Finn said with a wide grin on his face.

"Whatever. You can all side with the football god over here. But I've had more successful relationships than he has."

"I think Mom is best equipped for this one." Georgia winked. "Lincoln, did you know our mom was a therapist?"

"Yes. Brinkley did tell me that. So, let's hear it, Alana. Why won't she date me?"

"I am going to torture you slowly when we leave here," I whisper-hissed in Lincoln's ear, and he turned and waggled his brows.

"I'm looking forward to it, sweetheart," he said, close to my ear.

"So, obviously I don't know Lincoln's dating past, but I

know Brinkley's. Three serious relationships. Not one of them was someone any of us thought you'd wind up with. They were all—hmmm… *mild in personality.*"

"Interesting." Lincoln chuckled. "I'm guessing she had a lot of control over those relationships. Not a lot of risk there."

"Bingo," my mother said.

What the hell was this?

"Are you kidding me right now? Okay, let's hear it. How many long-lasting relationships have you had, Lincoln Hendrix?" I raised a brow.

"Well, I had a high school girlfriend for two years, and we broke up when we went to college."

"Let me guess. You became the big man on campus and kicked little small-town Suzie to the curb?"

"Wrong. I went to a small college and hardly anyone knew my name. My girlfriend's name was not Suzie—her name was Lucy—and she fell in love with her college professor and ended things with me."

"What a little tartlet," Georgia said, and everyone laughed.

"It's fine. The relationship had run its course. I think she married the dude and has a kid or two now. All worked out well."

"Next?" I asked, arms folded over my chest.

"I transferred to Alabama and met Barbie. We dated for almost a year. She wanted to get married and have kids, and I didn't. So, she gave me an ultimatum, and I walked away."

"See? Afraid of commitment." I glanced around the table, looking for people to back me.

"I was twenty years old. Marriage and kids were not on my radar. I was honest. She was honest. No one got hurt."

"I mean, I get that. I hardly think anyone at this table wanted to get married when they were twenty years old," Cage said, obviously siding with Lincoln. "Continue, Linc."

Linc?

My brother didn't use nicknames for anyone but his daughter and his siblings.

Clearly, Lincoln had won the man over.

"I got drafted right out of college, and my focus was football." He glanced at me. "I've had two girlfriends over the last seven years. Neither lasted more than a year. Lynette couldn't handle the fact that I traveled so much. She was jealous, and my lifestyle was too much for her. Jaqueline was an actress who wanted her ten minutes of fame and sold a story about my mother to the tabloids, and she was also unfaithful. So, I've remained single because it's easier. And God knows that Brinkley isn't easy, but for whatever reason, I just don't care. It doesn't scare me." He turned toward me. "You don't scare me, Brinkley Reynolds."

"Wow. She scares everyone. This is a first," Finn said, and Cage agreed.

"Auntie Brinks doesn't scare me either, Links. Hey, Links and Brinks. That's a rhyme, Daddy."

Everyone laughed, but I just stared at the man beside me. "Aren't you always closed off and guarded? What's with all the confessions tonight?"

"I like you, and I like your family. Deal with it. I'm not going anywhere."

"I think he wins this one, honey," my mother said.

"I say we keep him," Wyle said, and everyone cheered.

"I say we keep him, too, Auntie." Gracie came over and climbed on my lap.

I acted annoyed, but they'd all hit a nerve.

Because I wanted to keep him, too.

But wanting someone came with a lot of risks.

And that terrified me.

eighteen

. . .

Lincoln

I'D NEVER BEEN QUITE SO chatty in a group before, but the Reynolds' sure made it easy. I felt comfortable, and I had a really good time.

I'd always wondered what it would be like to have a large family.

One who loved big.

They were the real deal, and it didn't surprise me because I knew Brinkley's family would be amazing. She talked about them often.

She was quiet after we got into the car. I drove toward her house.

"Hey, let's go back to that spot at the cove."

"Yeah? You like it there, huh?"

"I do. I always think best on the shore. Listening to the waves. I used to go out there all the time as a teenager. No one understood my passion or my drive back then. Hell, I don't know if most people understand it now." She chuckled, but there was something in her words that told me she meant it.

"They understand you, and they love you. There's no shame in being strong or passionate or driven."

I pulled the car down near the cove, and we found a blanket in my trunk. We got out and walked down to the sand. The tide was coming in, and the water moved pretty far up the shore.

She spread the blanket out and plopped down a few feet from the water line and pulled off her sandals. "God, I love it here."

"Yeah, it's nice. I can see why it's your favorite place."

She turned to face me. "I can't believe how much you shared tonight with my family. That's very out of character."

"It is. But I like them. And I have grown to trust you, and for whatever reason, that makes me trust them."

"Do you think this is just some sort of conquest now?" She held up her hand to stop me when I was about to argue with her. "I'm just saying. Maybe you just like winning, and you don't like that I'm not giving you what you want."

"Is that really what you think?"

"I don't know what to think. I mean, where can this even go? It's so complicated. I work for you, and you can have anyone you want. Why me?"

I moved closer, pulling her hands in mine. "First off, if I was just trying to win something, I would have taken you up on your offer last night, wouldn't I? Instead, I didn't take your shitty offer. I wanted more. I want more now. I had dinner with your family. That's the kind of shit I normally dread. But I did it because I want you. That's it. It's not that complicated. But I'm not a teenage boy who sneaks around. If I'm with a woman for one night, sure, it's private. But if I'm with someone, the way I want to be with you—I won't hide that. I'd want everyone to know that you're mine."

"It doesn't work the same for me. I finally have offers in a profession that I've worked really hard to break into. I can't let the world know that I'm sleeping with my first client. It's already hard enough as a woman trying to find a place for myself in this field."

I nodded. She made a good point.

A fair point.

"I understand that. And I can work with that. What I can't work with is one night with you. I'm not here for that. I haven't felt like this before, and I want to see where it goes. So, if you feel the same way, we can keep it between us for now. As long as you and I know that it's—"

"That it's what?" she whispered.

"You and me. Together. No one else. I don't share, Brinkley. I want you and only you. And we can keep it quiet until you land a job, and you publish the story that you wrote about me. We can say we got together later when we're ready to share it."

"You think we're going to last that long?" she asked, her eyes watery as the light from the moon shone down on her. "You don't think we'll kill each other first?"

"I guess we'll have to see. But I can tell you this much," I said, placing my hand beneath her chin and turning her face to look at me. "I have very few things that I've been sure about in my life, and this is one of them."

"Tell me what you're sure about," she said, moving closer and climbing onto my lap. She wore a little white dress, and my arms wrapped around her.

"My mother's love. I've never doubted it for one day of my life." My fingers intertwined with hers. "Football was it for me, and I knew it at a young age, and I've never wavered." I cleared my throat. "And the pull that I feel toward you is different from anything I've ever felt before. So, I'm trusting it."

She looked away, staring out at the water. "I think you're going to break my heart, Lincoln Hendrix."

"That's just fear talking, sweetheart. I get it. What's happening here is scary as shit." I chuckled. "But since when do you or I let fear stop us from anything?"

She turned to face me as a tear slipped down her cheek. "I've never felt like this. And it terrifies me."

"I've got you, Brinkley Reynolds."

She nodded, and a few more tears fell, and she swiped at her cheeks. "Okay, then. I'm all in, Captain. You better not crash this boat."

That was all I needed. My fingers tangled in her hair, and I pulled her mouth down to mine.

This time, our kiss was slower. Like we both knew we could take our time because there wasn't an expiration date attached to it. She turned in my arms so she was straddling me. Our mouths never lost contact.

Our tongues tangled, and our hands explored.

The waves crashed against the shore a few feet away, and I could stay here forever, kissing this girl.

Under the moon.

On the shore.

She ground up against me, and my cock swelled in my jeans. I pulled back to look at her. Her lips were swollen from kissing me for the last thirty minutes.

She tugged at her dress, pulling it down and exposing a strapless white lace bra beneath. My fingers traced over her breasts before moving to her back and unlatching the bra. The fabric fell between us, exposing her perfect tits. I'd fantasized about them so many times, yet they were even more perfect than I could have imagined. My fingers teased her nipples, and she groaned. I wrapped my hands around her small waist and lifted her just enough so my mouth could cover her breast. I licked and sucked and flicked her hard peak with my tongue before moving to the other side. I took my time, moving from one to the next as she arched her back and reveled in it.

"Lincoln, I want you so badly," she whispered.

"You don't have a fucking clue, sweetheart." I lifted her up and placed her on her back on the blanket. I tossed the bra to the side and glanced around to make sure no one was around. I hovered above her. "If you knew how many times I've gotten off to thoughts of you and this body."

"Tell me more," she purred as her teeth sank into her juicy bottom lip.

"I'd grip my cock every single day in the shower after our workouts." I leaned forward and kissed her neck, making my way down her body. "I'd stroke myself over and over to thoughts of your smart mouth, your perfect tits, and this pussy that I wanted to claim as mine."

"Oh my God," she whispered.

I pulled her dress down past her waist and thighs before tossing it beside us, leaving her in nothing but a lacy white thong.

"Have you thought of me when you were alone?"

She sucked in a breath and nodded. "A lot."

"How often?"

"Every day. Sometimes twice a day." She smiled up at me.

"Tell me what I was doing to you."

"I will when you take off some of those clothes. I don't like being the only one undressed."

I pushed up on my knees and unbuttoned my shirt, shoving it off my shoulders. Brinkley sat forward and reached for the button on my jeans.

So eager. I wrapped my fingers around her wrists and pulled them away. "Not yet. I want to taste you first. Is that something you've thought about?"

"Mmm-hmmm," she said as I dropped down, pushing her legs apart.

"All this pretty lace I need to work around." I kissed her over the fabric, my fingers tracing along her inner thigh.

"Lincoln," she whispered as her fingers tugged at my hair.

"Do you have any idea how long I've thought about this moment right now? About burying myself between your pretty thighs?"

"How long?" she asked as she writhed beneath me, and I ran my fingers over the lace covering her pussy.

Back and forth slowly.

"Since the night you had me escorted out of Reynolds', I've wanted to drop to my knees right there. Spread you wide. Taste you. Make you cry out my name over and over."

"Please," she moaned.

I slipped the lacy fabric to the side and replaced my fingers with my tongue. Her hips jerked in response, and I lifted her legs and settled them over my shoulders to give me even better access.

"Is this what you want?" I asked as I continued teasing her with my tongue.

Breathing in all that sweetness that I'd been craving for weeks.

"Oh my God. Yes."

I gripped her hips and took my time licking and sucking and tasting her, over and over. I'd bring her to the edge and then pull back.

Her thighs tightened against me, and she bucked harder.

Faster.

And this time, I didn't pull back.

I slipped one finger inside, and she gasped.

"So fucking tight," I said as I slipped in and out of her before sliding in another finger and feeling her tighten around me.

She bucked faster, her breaths filling the space around us.

I sealed my mouth over her clit and sucked before flicking my tongue against her sensitive bundle.

I felt it before it happened. The way her body trembled and shook before she cried out my name. I stayed right there, waiting for her to ride out every last bit of pleasure.

Once her breathing slowed and her body settled, I reluctantly pulled my fingers out and sat up on my knees, slipping them into my mouth as I watched her.

Laura Pavlov

"Wow," she whispered. "That was something, Captain."

I leaned down and pushed her dark hair away from her face. "You're all sass and fire when you speak, but you're pure fucking sugar between your legs, sweetheart. I don't think I'll ever get enough."

"You can have as much as you want," she said with a chuckle. "But now it's your turn."

She pushed up and shoved me back enough for her to get up on her knees, facing me. She reached for my jeans and unbuttoned them before sliding them down my thighs. Next, she reached for the band of my boxer briefs, and I didn't miss the way her breath caught as she slid them down, my cock springing free.

"Holy shit," she whispered. "I don't think there's any way that's going to fit."

Now it was my turn to chuckle. "We'll take our time. There's no rush."

She bit down on her juicy bottom lip. "Okay. You know I don't scare easily. Please tell me you have a condom?"

I pushed to my feet and shoved my clothing all the way off before reaching into the back pocket of my jeans for my wallet. I pulled out a condom and tore off the top, removing the latex from the packet. She reached for it and took it from me. I thought she was going to slide it on, but instead, she surprised me as she gripped my cock. Her tongue came out to lick the tip, and she swirled her tongue around several times.

"Jesus," I hissed. "You're killing me."

She looked up at me, long lashes flanking those gorgeous, dark eyes. The light from the moon shone down on her like a fucking halo.

Her mouth came over my dick, her hand at the base as she slowly moved up and down. My head fell back, eyes closed, and I reveled in the moment.

Nothing had ever felt better.

I pulled back, placing a hand on each side of her face just

enough that she released me with a pop, looking up at me with confusion.

"You feel too good. And I want to be inside you now."

She nodded, her hands trembling as she slipped the latex over my swollen cock.

I covered her hands with mine to help her along and then urged her back.

Her legs fell open, making room for me, and I teased her entrance with my tip, rubbing it up and down along her seam.

"Is this what you want, sweetheart?" I asked.

"Yes."

I moved in slowly, just a little bit at first. My gaze locked with hers. Her eyes were hooded. Lips plump and begging to be kissed. I ran my tongue along her bottom lip before my mouth claimed hers. I pressed forward, using all the restraint I had to take it slow.

Inch by glorious fucking inch.

She was so tight.

So wet.

"Don't stop," she whispered. "I want to feel all of you."

I pulled back to look at her, making sure she was okay, and I pushed forward. I continued to move, her hand on my face now, letting me know she wanted more.

"You're so fucking perfect," I said as I pushed all the way in. I paused for a minute to give her time to adjust to me.

"Nothing has ever felt this good. You were worth the wait," she said, her voice a sexy mix of need and desire.

I watched her. Waited. And her lips turned up the slightest bit in the corners, and she gave me a small nod.

I pulled back, slowly at first, before thrusting back in. She arched up in response, letting me know that she loved it. My mouth covered her perfect tit, and I flicked her hard peak with my tongue.

I swear this woman was fucking made for me.

She tugged at my hair, pulling my mouth up to hers. Our tongues tangled as I thrust in and out of her.

We found our rhythm. Meeting one another thrust for thrust.

I knew she was fucking close because she squeezed my cock with force. Her walls tightened around me, her breaths out of control. I wanted to watch her fall apart this time. I pulled back, taking both of her hands in mine and pinning them above her head. My other hand moved between us, knowing exactly where she needed me to touch her.

And I watched as this beautiful woman's eyes closed, lips swollen from where I'd kissed her, chest rising and falling.

"Lincoln," she cried out. Her body shook, and I moved faster.

Once.

Twice.

And I exploded, going right over the edge with her.

Waves splashed against the sand.

A breeze moved around us.

And I wished I could stay right here with her forever.

On the shore.

nineteen

. . .

Brinkley

MY BREATHING finally slowed after two of the most epic orgasms of my life. Lincoln Hendrix was not only a rock star on the field, but he knew his way around a woman's body. I'd never had an orgasm with a man before, though I'd obviously had plenty by myself.

This was new.

And let me tell you—the man delivered.

If there was a GOAT award for delivering the best orgasms, he would hold that title, as well.

I couldn't believe that I was lying on the beach butt naked, or that I'd literally cried out his name like something you'd see in a porno movie. I'd never been so turned on in my life. I'd never allowed myself to be this vulnerable with a man. Losing control like this.

And I was here for it.

Control was overrated.

He pulled out of me and tugged off the condom, tying the end and setting it beside our clothing. I figured he'd grab his clothes, so I sat forward to reach for mine, but he stopped me.

He came to sit beside me, pulling me onto his lap. He

reached for the corners of the blanket and wrapped it around us.

We sat there, looking out at the water.

"I didn't hurt you, did I?"

My gentle giant? He acted all tough on the outside, but he was a softy beneath.

"Of course not. If you didn't notice, I wasn't crying in pain. That was pure pleasure, Captain."

He tightened his arms around me. "Yeah. I noticed. Just want to make sure you're okay."

I tipped my head back to look at him. "That was amazing."

"Did you expect anything less?"

"Ah… there he is. My cocky football star."

He kissed the tip of my nose and looked back out at the water.

"Your family is pretty amazing. Must have been fun growing up with all those kids in the house."

"Yes. It was the best. But it was also chaotic and crazy. We love hard. We fight hard. But we always have one another's backs, no matter what."

"That's cool. It's like your own built-in football team."

A loud laugh escaped. "Never thought of it like that, but yes, I've got my teammates for life, I guess."

He was quiet for a minute, and there were so many things I wanted to ask him.

"You and your mama are really close, huh?"

"We are. She's the best. She's already looking at homes in New York now. The woman has supported me for my entire life."

"She sounds incredible."

"She is. You're going to love her."

My stomach flipped at the way he spoke about the future. Like it was a no-brainer that I'd meet his mother.

"I look forward to it." I cleared my throat.

"Something you want to ask me, sweetheart?"

"Yeah. It's not for the story; it's just for me."

"Then there is nothing off the table. Ask away."

"Well, I know you don't like to talk about your father. But I just wondered if you talk to him?"

He let out a long breath, and I waited. "My father left shortly after I was born. Just took off and wanted a new life, I guess. They were young, and she got pregnant when she was only nineteen years old. My mom used her name on my birth certificate because she was fully prepared to raise me on her own, which she did. He kept in touch with my mother and would check in a couple of times a year, and then he eventually stopped reaching out. He remarried a few years later and had a new family. Last I heard, he had a son and a daughter. I've never met them and have no idea where they live. Where he lives."

I turned to face him, placing a hand on his cheek. "Wow. He sounds like a selfish asshole."

"Probably a fair description."

"Do you want to meet his other children?"

"I used to wonder about it. I don't even know if they know about me. But at the end of the day, I don't know him or them, nor do I consider them my family. The man left my mom to fend for both of us on her own. He never paid child support because she didn't put his name down on the birth certificate. She said he used to send money now and then to try to help out. My mom worked really hard to make ends meet when I was growing up. That's why I was pretty horrified that I'd gotten you fired. I'd never intentionally take someone's livelihood from them."

"I know that now that I actually know you. Your mom sounds like such a rock star. So, she struggled financially?"

"Oh, yeah. I didn't grow up with a lot, as far as material items, but there was a shit ton of love in that house. We lived on peanut butter sandwiches and macaroni and cheese. But we always had a good time together. We'd play cards and board games, and there was always a lot of love in our home. That's probably why I overreacted when you walked into that bathroom. I'd been on edge ever since she got diagnosed. She's kind of it for me as far as family goes."

My heart ached for a young Lincoln and his mother, who were clearly on their own.

"I know how scary it is," I said, leaning my head against his chest. The sound of his heartbeat soothed me. "I told you that my father was diagnosed with colon cancer when I was in college. It was the reason I came back to San Francisco when I graduated. I'd interned for a big magazine back east that had offered me a position, but I knew I needed to be close to home. It was a scary couple of years."

"He's okay now?"

I nodded. "He is. And hopefully, it stays that way. Every time the poor guy even coughs, we all get nervous."

Lincoln chuckled. "I get that. I did my research when my mom got sick. Wanted to be sure we got her the best care possible. I'm always on her about eating right and getting rest. She pushes herself. Never misses any of my games."

"She loves you."

"She does. And she deserves a break. She's lived her entire life for me. I want her to do things for herself, you know?"

"Yeah. My aunt Beth lost her battle to pancreatic cancer when my cousins were young, and Uncle Jack just focused on them. Making sure they were okay. But now they're grown, and we all worry about him. I think my cousins would be okay with him dating now, well, aside from Dilly." I laughed, and he shot me a puzzled look. "She's just super protective over him, and I don't know that anyone would be good enough for him in her eyes."

"I get that. My mom's dated a few guys, nothing serious. But I didn't find a single one of those dudes to be nearly good enough for her."

I shook my head. "I get it. You're protective over the people you love. It's a good quality to have."

We sat there quietly, listening to the waves for a few minutes.

"Tell me why you love your job. Where do you see it going?" he asked.

"I've always loved sports. I spent my childhood and teen years trying hard to beat my brothers at everything. So, choosing a career in the sports industry was a no-brainer. But I also have a love for knowledge. Information. Learning about people and what makes them tick."

"You are a nosy little one," he teased.

I elbowed him in the stomach, and he tightened his grip on me. "I majored in journalism, and I interned at *Strive Forward* magazine, and my mentor was this super cool woman, Audrey. She would tell me how much power there was in the written word. The ability to communicate with hundreds to thousands to millions of people. The ability to make people fall in love with a sport, a person, or a place. The ability to change people's perception about an individual if they've been presented unfairly. It was a way to use your voice for good. And I found it inspiring, I guess. But I also know there's another side. The side of the bloodsuckers," I said with a chuckle. "But I always wanted to be fair. Tell the truth. And I was drawn to you because no one really knew your story."

"Jesus. I'm not above saying when I'm wrong, and I was very wrong about you. I shouldn't have called anyone a bloodsucker. Years of being stalked and hounded by the press put a bad taste in my mouth. But it wasn't a fair assessment. It's just like anything—there is good and bad everywhere. There are good football players, and then there are people that are out there for the money and the fame. So, I apologize for the way we met, even if I don't regret it."

"And why is that?" I tipped my head back and studied him.

"Because you wouldn't have come home. We wouldn't be sitting here right now, after the best sex of my life—butt-ass naked on the shore."

"Was it the best sex you've ever had?" I asked.

"Fuck yeah. It was for me." He raised a brow.

I smiled. "It was for me, too. I wasn't going to show all my cards so easily, but since you did, I'll admit it, too."

"And you wanted to do it just once. I told you, once would never be enough."

"You were right," I said as he flipped me over onto my back, and I broke out in a fit of hysterical laughter. "This one time, you were right."

"Only this one time?" he asked, leaning down and kissing me hard.

"This time was the only one that really mattered."

He nodded. His gaze was soft as he took me in. "Come on. Let's get out of here before we get caught naked and end up on the cover of every newspaper and magazine in town. They're already talking about you jumping to my defense in the press."

He helped me to my feet, and we both quickly slipped back into our clothes.

"It has to be close to midnight now. We need to get some sleep. We've got to be up early for our run in the morning."

He took my hand and led me to the car. "Yep. And it's not going to be easy getting any sleep with you naked in my bed."

I sucked in a breath. I wondered if we'd each go to our own places once we left the cove.

"That's presumptuous," I teased. "You just think I'll sleep at your house?"

"You want me to chase you, sweetheart?" he said, not hiding his sarcasm. "Because I will. If that's what you need.

But I want you in my bed. I want to wrap myself around you and wake up to you in the morning."

"Well, when you put it that way." I shrugged after I got into the car, and he reached over to buckle my seat belt. Normally, I'd slap someone's hand away for doing that, but at the moment, I'd let this man do just about anything to me.

"Good. Let's go home."

I closed my eyes as we drove toward his house. I couldn't remember a time that I'd been this relaxed.

This happy.

This content.

———

The last few days had been busy between Lincoln's insane workouts and me in talks with *Sports Today,* as I'd be breaking this news with them. I'd been busy making tweaks to the final statement that had been released this morning.

Lincoln Hendrix Will Be Signing with the New York Thunderbirds.

It was now public knowledge that Lincoln was telling me his story, and I was also the same woman who'd jumped to his defense last week when we'd been in the city.

My phone rang, and I watched Lincoln through the sliding glass doors as he pushed a gigantic tire up and down the driveway as an extra core workout that he liked to do. He wore a pair of basketball shorts, no shirt, and a navy baseball cap turned backward on his head.

There should be some sort of rule about sexy men wearing their caps backward. It caused my ovaries to go into overdrive.

Every. Damn. Time.

His chest was tanned and chiseled, and the muscles in his arms strained each time he pushed the oversized tire another couple of feet.

I answered the phone and put it on speaker.

"Hey, Ever," I said, happy to see my cousin's name on the screen.

"Hi, superstar. So, you broke the news about where Lincoln's playing next year, and it's all everyone is talking about here. I'm in the city with Hawk and the kids for a game, and this story is *everywhere*."

"Yeah, I think people have been waiting to see what he was going to do. I know local fans won't be thrilled, but I'm sure a lot of them will follow him to the Thunderbirds."

"I think so, too," she said. "The vibe I've heard is that everyone sort of blames Tony Anders for not protecting him."

"It would be the truth."

"So, are you going to tell me what's going on with you two? First, you defend the man against a paparazzo, and don't even get me started that Lincoln is twice your size, and you still decided to jump in. I think what people love most about that photo going viral is the way that he was looking at you."

"What do you mean?" I asked, trying not to chuckle because it was ridiculous that I'd jumped in front of him, but I'd do it again if I felt like he was being threatened.

"Well, for starters, you're like a fierce mama bear, ready to throw down, and he looks like—" She paused and laughed. "He's looking at you like you set the sun, Brinks. Just complete adoration."

"Says my cousin. Clearly, you're reading into it a bit." I smiled, even though I knew she couldn't see me. These last few days had been filled with endless together time for me and Lincoln. Workouts. Sex. Laughter. Fights. Board games. Late-night dinners. And tonight, we were taking out the boat for the first time.

"Spill it, Cuzzy. Take it from someone who knows that look well."

I sighed. We'd never kept secrets in our family. Our

cousins used to spend their summers here in Cottonwood Cove, and we grew up together. "I like him."

"You don't say?" She oozed sarcasm. "I mean, the man is beautiful. He's a freaking rock star on the field. And from what Georgie told me last week, you two are always together."

"Well, I am working for him, in a way. So, we are together a lot. We'll call that research." I chuckled.

"I'm sure you're very thorough."

We were both laughing now.

"I do my best."

"I'm guessing you're keeping this on the down-low until the story breaks and you secure a job?"

"Absolutely. I don't need to be known as the woman who slept her way to the top."

"It sucks that we have to worry about that. He doesn't have to worry about a thing, and that's how it was with Hawk. I had to be very careful myself, and we kept it hidden for quite a while. But people are going to judge, regardless. You're going to have people that hate you for stealing the heart of the hottest football player out there right now. Jealousy is an ugly beast."

I hated the thought of everyone knowing and getting into our business. "Well, until I have a signed contract for a full-time position, we'll be keeping this to ourselves. And the Thomas sisters, of course."

"Well, you know we take it to the grave. I'm happy for you. I miss you. I'll see you soon. We'll all be in Cottonwood Cove for Hugh and Lila's wedding next month."

"I can't wait. It's coming up so soon. And then Paris for Georgie's. Thank goodness you're all married because it's hard to keep up with these weddings."

She laughed. "Damn straight. Maybe you'll be next, Brinks."

"Okay. I'm hanging up. That's ridiculous."

"We'll see about that. Love you."

"Love you more."

I ended the call and shook my head.

Marriage wasn't even in the realm of my imagination. Don't get me wrong, I was thrilled for Lila and Georgia. But I had too much to accomplish before I even considered that.

Didn't I?

Why did the thought excite me as much as it terrified me?

I looked up to see Lincoln walking toward me from the backyard. His gaze locked with mine, and I had my answer.

It terrified me because a lifetime with Lincoln Hendrix made my stomach flutter.

And that was never supposed to happen.

But here we were.

twenty

. . .

Lincoln

"IS this what you do every day?" Lionel asked after he heaved into a bush for the third time.

Brinkley stood there, rubbing her hand across his back to comfort him as she spoke. "Don't be too hard on yourself. His workouts are not normal."

My gaze locked with hers.

That's right, sweetheart. My favorite workouts were with her in the bedroom at the start and end of every day.

Her cheeks pinked because she knew what I was thinking, but she rolled her eyes and smirked like I was ridiculous. This was our shtick. Me saying how crazy I was about her, and her acting like I was going to tire of her any day now.

But that wasn't going to happen.

It was a big part of the reason that I wanted my mom to come out this weekend. I'd told her I'd met someone, and she was excited to meet Brinkley.

They were the two most important women in my life, and I wanted them to meet.

"I can feel I'm getting stronger, though," Lionel said. He'd worked out with us four days this week, and he'd puked every time. The poor kid would need to double his calories to make up for these workouts and the fact that he couldn't make it through a workout without chucking his breakfast.

"You are getting stronger. So, what did Coach Hardin say when you spoke to him yesterday?" I asked, and we all three dropped down to sit in the grass, looking out at the water.

"He said they're interested. He isn't sure if he has any money left in the budget because it's so late now and the recruiting season is basically over. But he wants me to come out there, so my mom is pricing some tickets."

"Don't worry about that. I've got you. I'll get you there," I said, and Brinkley's eyes snapped up to meet mine. "Do you want to play there?"

"Yes. They have a really good business school, which is what I want to major in."

"Then how about you and I go check it out?"

"What? You're coming with me?"

"Fuck yeah, I am. I'll talk to your mom and make sure she's good with it. You need to have someone there asking the right questions. We're not going to let you go out there and get pushed around, Lionel. You've got decent stats, and you haven't even really been coached yet. The potential is there. I believe it. So, we'll make sure that Coach Hardin, and anyone else who reaches out, knows it."

"I don't know how to thank you."

"How about you double up your calories after your workouts so you don't wither away? Can you do that for me?" The kid's biggest issue at the moment was the fact that he needed to put some weight and some muscle on his bones.

"I could start making you green juices from my garden if things would ever grow. I've been waiting forever," Brinkley said, shaking her head, which made me laugh.

Every damn day we went and checked on that ridiculous garden. It had a long way to go, and whole vegetables and fruits were not going to just start popping up that quickly. It would take time.

I wanted to do something for her, and I knew that she would never ask for help with anything.

So, Georgia had met a few people from the nursery at the house this morning for me, to oversee some updates to the garden that I wanted to surprise Brinkley with.

"Thanks, Miss Brinkley," Lionel said as we started walking toward the house where his car was parked. "I'll try to bulk up some."

There was an awkward pause there, and I knew something was up.

I knew the look on his face.

He wanted this but didn't have the means to do it.

His mother lived on a fixed income, from what Brinkley had told me. She couldn't just double her grocery bill. I should have thought of that before I called him out for it.

I clapped him on the shoulder. "I've got some things that helped me a lot when I was trying to put on some weight back in the day. Let me look into it for you."

He nodded as he stopped in front of his car. "I appreciate it. And I get free dinner at Reynolds' when I work, and I don't think Hugh would mind if I increased my portions a bit."

"Of course, he wouldn't." Brinkley smiled.

"I'll see you both tomorrow if you're still okay with me joining in?" he asked.

"Absolutely." I held up my hand and waved.

After he pulled down the driveway, Brinkley turned to me. "Look at you. You're going with him to see the school?"

"It's not a big deal," I said, avoiding her stare.

"You're a big softy, Captain."

She ran for the back door, and I chased her. I scooped her up and dropped her onto the couch, hovering over her.

"Do I strike you as a softy?" I teased as I thrust my erection against her.

She laughed and tugged me down before my mouth crashed into hers.

Laura Pavlov

When I pulled back, she glanced at her wrist to check the time. "Shit. I've got to grab a fast shower and then pick up Gracie from preschool. My parents weren't able to pick her up today, so I'm going to go get her."

"I'll come with you," I said, scooping her up and carrying her toward the bedroom.

I set her down on the bathroom counter, and her lips turned up in the corners. "Really? We're going to the Tipsy Tea; you sure you want to come with us?"

"I am." I smirked before turning on the shower as we both stripped our clothes off and stepped in.

Obviously, we couldn't keep our hands to ourselves, so showering together was my new favorite thing. I pressed her against the wall and thrust into her, as my lips found hers.

We were like a finely tuned ship. We could go at it for hours, or we could find our release in minutes. Our bodies fit together like they were made for one another.

We quickly dried off, and Brinkley slicked her hair back into a bun at the nape of her neck. She dabbed a little gloss on her lips, did something to her eyelashes, and we were out the door.

I'd insisted on driving, so we'd moved the car seat thingy into my car. Brinkley guided me to the school and talked me through the pickup line. I'd never heard of a drive-through where you got a child at the end of the line, but I also had very little experience with children.

"There she is," Brinkley said as she rolled the window down and waved.

A woman escorted Gracie to the car. She was probably the cutest kid I'd ever seen. She wore a navy plaid jumper, a white blouse beneath, and some navy knee socks. Her hair was pulled up in two buns on top of her head. But she wasn't donning the big smile she'd worn the last time I'd seen her.

"Have a good one. We'll see you tomorrow, Gracie," the woman said.

"Goodbye," Gracie said quietly. "Hi, Auntie Brinks and Links."

Brinkley glanced at me, her brows cinched together as I pulled out of the circular drive and headed toward downtown.

"Hey, how was your day?"

"Fine."

"Fine? It's not like you to be this quiet. Did something happen today?"

She didn't respond. I glanced in my rearview mirror as I pulled in front of the tea place, and Gracie just stared out the window.

"Something is up," Brinkley whispered close to my ear before she unbuckled herself.

We got out of the car and walked into the Tipsy Tea, which was some sort of little girl store, and everything was pink and floral. It smelled like watermelon bubblegum. An elderly woman walked over, and Brinkley introduced me.

"This is Matilda. She owns this gorgeous store. Matilda, this is Lincoln."

"Nice to meet you, Lincoln. Congrats on signing with the Thunderbirds. We'll miss you playing for San Francisco, but my husband and I will be cheering you on all the same this year."

"I appreciate it."

"I'm guessing it's a special day with Auntie Brinks, and you'll get to pick out a lovely prize?" Matilda bent down to greet Gracie before shooting a look at Brinkley.

Apparently, everyone here was fluent in the behavior of this kid, aside from me. Hell, sometimes I don't feel like talking. Doesn't mean anything other than I don't feel like talking.

"Yes, ma'am," Gracie said, and she gave a small smile.

"Great, well, you enjoy yourselves. We got some new

things in this morning, so go wander around and check it out."

She waved and walked toward the cash register.

Brinkley followed Gracie down an aisle with a whole lot of pink shit, and her phone buzzed.

"Oh. It's John Jones from *Football Live* calling," she gasped.

"Go take it outside. I've got this."

"Okay. Thank you. I'll be right back, Gracie. Stay with Links."

Gracie nodded as Brinkley darted out of the store. We came to a stop in front of a pair of pink cowboy boots.

"Do you like those?" I asked as she studied them.

"I do. But that's a fancy present." She picked one up and smiled at it.

"I think we should try those on." I bent down and unbuckled her navy school shoes and looked on the bottom for the size before finding a pair of boots of the same size. She held onto my shoulder with her tiny hands, and I helped her slip into them.

"Preston told me that I'm weird because my dog's name is Bob Picklepants." She shrugged. Was this some sort of little girl confessional? I didn't know what was happening, but I'd go with it.

"Preston sounds like a tool. I like the name Bob Pick-lepants. And there's nothing weird about you, Gracie Reynolds. I say you rock these pink boots at school tomorrow and ignore him."

Her brows cinched as if she were considering saying something but wasn't sure. "He said I'm weird because I don't have a mama, too."

My motherfucking chest tightened so much it was painful. I took her little hand in mine as I remained bent down so I could look into her dark eyes that were so similar to Brinkley's. They were watering just the slightest bit, and I wanted to beat the fuck out of this Preston kid for hurting her.

"Do you know that I didn't have a dad growing up? And I'm certainly not weird, am I? I think it makes us extra cool because we've got one parent that loves us enough for two. Not many people can say that."

Her eyes widened, and her lips turned up in the corners with a genuine smile as she used the back of her hand to wipe away the single tear that had just rolled down her cheek. This little girl was something special.

"You're not weird, Links. We're both extra cool," she said, as if I'd just fixed all her problems.

I wanted to drive right down to that school tomorrow and give Preston a piece of my fucking mind.

Kids, man. They could be brutal.

"I think that pink hat would look awfully cute on you with the boots," I said, because now she was looking down at her feet and smiling.

"I can't get two prizes in one day," she said. "That's not the rules."

"Well, I'm here today. I think we should get a couple of things." I reached for the hat, but before I placed it on her, she tugged at her two little buns sitting on her head.

"We needs to take these out first or the hat won't fit. Can you help me?"

I gently tried to remove the elastic from each one, but I didn't want to yank her hair. She shocked me when she placed a hand on my cheek and smiled. "You won't hurt me, Links. Daddy says I'm the toughest girl around, next to Auntie Brinks."

I chuckled as her hair sprung loose and dark spiral curls fell down around her shoulders. I plopped the hat on her head and pushed to stand all the way up.

I'd never even known that tiny humans could be this adorable.

She hurried to the mirror and gasped.

"I look extra cool, don't I, Links?"

"You sure do."

Matilda came walking over and clapped her hands together. "Well, aren't you the cutest girl in the world. And you'll look perfect at the fair this summer."

"I insist on getting them," I said.

"I can't believe it. Can I wear them out of the store, Miss Matilda?"

"You sure can."

I held her little navy shoes in my hand and glanced around. "Is there anything else that you like?"

Those dark eyes grew wide again, and she covered her mouth with both hands, as if she couldn't believe I'd asked the question, and I swear I'd get this little girl one of everything in this store if she asked for it.

Matilda pointed to the back of the store and said that they'd gotten some new dresses in, so I followed Gracie over there. But she'd passed by the sundresses that were hanging on a rack and gasped when she saw a rack full of white, puffy dresses that looked more like wedding gowns.

"Links," she whispered, and her little voice shook. "Look at that one. It's a real princess dress. Not a pretend one."

Matilda chuckled and pulled down the one Gracie was pointing to.

"This is a flower girl dress. I think you're going to be a flower girl in your uncle Hugh's wedding and your aunt Georgia's weddings. But didn't you already get dresses for those?"

"Yes." Gracie nodded. "They are real pretty but not fancy like this one."

"I think you should try it on. You can wear it to Sunday dinner at your grandparents' house," I said.

Matilda chuckled, and Gracie jumped up and down as the older woman said she'd help her try it on. I waited and walked over to the front of the store to see Brinkley on the phone, pacing in circles out in front of the store as she spoke.

"Links!" Gracie shouted, and I made my way back. She twirled around and did some sort of curtsy, managing to keep her pink cowboy hat on her head. "Look at me. I'm a real, live princess."

Matilda walked out, carrying her school uniform and raising a brow at me as if this was going to be a tough one to turn down.

But that wasn't going to happen.

This girl had gotten her heart hurt today, and if a fancy dress and some boots and a hat made her smile, I'd do it ten times over.

Hell, I'd give her my goddamn kidney if she needed it right now.

This was nothing.

"I don't see how we can walk out of here without it," I teased. "Let's get it."

"Do you want to wear it out of the store with the boots and the hat?" the older woman asked.

"Yes, ma'am!" Gracie jumped up and attempted to give me a high-five, but she missed, which made me laugh. Matilda cut off the tags and made her way around the counter.

I handed over my credit card, and we tossed her school clothes and shoes into a bag.

"Thank you, Links. This is the best day ever." Gracie smiled up at me as I reached for her hand to lead her toward the exit, just as the door opened and Brinkley walked in.

One brow raised, she put her hands on her hips. "What's going on here?"

"Me and Links is extra cool, Auntie."

Damn straight.

Enough said.

twenty-one

. . .

Brinkley

WE MADE our way over to Cottonwood Café because the place was a rite of passage in town. And Lincoln had been avoiding it because he'd heard the rumors about the dirty old bird that worked there.

"So, tell me how we ended up with this beautiful dress and the cute boots and hat?" I asked as Gracie walked between us, with one hand in mine and the other in Lincoln's. When I'd stepped out of the adorable boutique, they'd been friendly, but now they appeared to be besties. And my niece, who had been completely off when we'd picked her up, seemed to be back to her old self.

"Don't you love these boots, Auntie?" Gracie said, kicking her foot up from beneath the frilly white flower girl dress to show the pink cowboy boots. "Links says I look very cool."

She was literally surrounded by an abnormal amount of tulle, and she wore the cutest pink cowboy hat and boots, and my heart was threatening to explode.

I loved this little girl so much.

And the fact that this man had just pampered her the way that he had and turned her spirits around—my heart couldn't take much more.

I was dying to know what had happened. Gracie had been upset when I'd stepped outside to take that call and now these two seemed to be fast friends, so I assumed she'd shared something with him.

"Links is right," I said, over my laughter. "But Daddy is going to be a little annoyed, seeing as he has that whole spending rule."

Lincoln's head snapped in my direction. "What kind of rule?"

"I'm only allowed to get her presents under ten dollars on our outings unless it's her birthday or Christmas."

"When's your birthday?" Lincoln asked her as he scrubbed a hand over the scruff on his jaw.

"It's coming up," she said. "It's right after Uncle Hughey and Auntie Lila's wedding, right, Auntie?"

"Yep. June twenty-third, baby girl. It's my favorite day of the year."

"Perfect. We can call this an early birthday gift," he said as he reached for the door. Then he surprised me by leaning down and whisper-shouting to her. "But don't you worry. I'll get you something good for your birthday, too."

Unbelievable.

"Like I said—you're a softy."

"I preferred it when you called me a rude gentleman." He leaned close to my ear, and his warm breath tickled my neck.

Damn, this man did crazy things to me.

This last week had been a whirlwind. So much for taking it slow. Our passion for one another was as strong as our disagreements were. And we had plenty.

He was bossy as hell, and I didn't like being told what to do.

Tonight, we were staying at my house. He'd gotten his way the last few nights, but I was putting my foot down.

"Well, looky here. It's about time you brought the football player over. I've heard you've been everywhere in town but my place," Mrs. Runither purred as she moved into Lincoln's space.

It took everything I had not to laugh as his shoulders stiffened. He held on to Gracie's hand like she was a security blanket.

"Uh, hello. I've just been busy." Lincoln gave a half nod and took the slightest step backward. But Mrs. Runither didn't miss a beat. She wasn't about to let a fine-ass man distance himself without a fight. She moved along with him, and he startled, glancing over at me.

"There's J.R!" Gracie shouted and asked if she could go say hello, and I told her she could. Lincoln looked very unhappy when she dropped his hand and Mrs. Runither took it in hers and intertwined her fingers with his.

This was a new one for her.

"My, oh my. Look at these hands. I like a man who knows how to handle his balls," she said, and I nearly lost it because Lincoln's discomfort was impossible to miss.

He tugged his hand back and shoved them into the pockets of his jeans.

"Tell me, Lincoln Hendrix. Do you like a tiger in the bedroom? Or do you prefer your women to be submissive?"

"Are you really just going to stand there watching?" he hissed at me, and I covered my mouth with both hands because this was just too good.

It wouldn't even matter if the mac and cheese was horrible at this point.

"Mrs. Runither, I'm not sure how to answer that question, but I can tell you this," he said, looking like his cocky self all of a sudden. "I prefer not to be asked inappropriate questions when I go out to eat."

"Oh, he likes to play cat and mouse? You know I love a man who likes to play." She winked at me. "Come on, y'all. Let's get you a table so we can feed the football star. Nothing better than a well-fed man. Am I right, Brinkley?"

"I prefer to be well-fed myself; I don't really care how much the big guy eats." My voice was all tease.

We stopped to say a quick hello to J.R., then Lincoln scooped up Gracie and carried her to the table with us. I wasn't sure if he was trying to help her, considering she kept tripping over her long dress, or if he was using her as a shield from the old horndog, Runither.

When the elderly woman stepped away and we'd settled into the booth, Lincoln leaned forward so only I could hear him. "I will pay you back for that. Get ready for a tiger in the bedroom."

I whipped my head to make sure Gracie wasn't listening, but she was too busy waving at J.R.

"Promises, promises. You made the woman's day. It wouldn't kill you to flirt with her." I smirked.

"You're barking up the wrong tree, sweetheart. She's not my type."

"What's your types, Links?" Gracie suddenly turned her attention to us.

"I'm looking at it." He stared at me before leaning down and kissing my niece's forehead.

The man was full of surprises.

———

We'd dropped Gracie off at Cage's house, and he didn't even give Lincoln any shit for buying her so many things. Instead, he praised the man and thanked him for spoiling his daughter.

When we pulled up in front of my house, I turned to him. "I think I need some fans of my own."

He chuckled. "What are you talking about?"

"My brother. He's always grumpy and irritated, but when you're around, he's ridiculously cheerful. *Thank you so much for spoiling my girl*," I said in my cheesiest voice, mimicking

Cage.

"Hey, don't be jealous that your brother appreciates me and your niece called me her bestie. Serves you right for feeding me to that piranha, Runither. Do you know what happened when I asked you to walk with me to the bathroom and you refused to go with me? Do you?" he said, all loud and boisterous, which made me laugh.

"She followed me. And she was grabbing at my shoulders and reached up and ran those long, creepy nails through my scalp, claiming there was a feather in my hair. I think she drew blood. She really dug her claws in there." He leaned forward, resting his big head between my breasts.

I couldn't stop laughing. I ran my fingers through his hair and held my phone up with the flashlight to humor him. "Um. There's no blood here, buddy. I think you're going to make it. How'd you get away from her?"

He whipped his head back up to look at me. "I belched in her face and said I was sick. My mother would be disgusted. But seeing as you threw me to the wolves, I had no choice."

"Hey, if football doesn't work out for you, I think you have a future in the dramatic arts, you big baby." I pushed out of the car, and he did the same, coming around to catch my door before I stepped all the way out.

"I'm a big baby? I was violated. Where's the sympathy?" He crowded me as my back rested against the car, and he pushed in closer.

"Do you need some pampering, Lincoln Hendrix?" I teased, my hands fisting in his T-shirt and tugging his mouth down to mine.

"I thought I was your dirty little secret for now. You want to kiss me in the middle of the street, sweetheart?"

Desire pooled between my legs, and I sucked in a breath. His lips grazed mine, and I squeezed my eyes closed. It was dark out, and I doubted anyone was watching.

But the last thing I wanted to do was blow up my career before it even began.

"Let's go inside," I whispered.

His hand moved down between us and slipped beneath my short dress. His finger pushed my lace thong to the side and dipped in just the slightest bit.

"So fucking wet." He pulled his hand away and popped his finger into his mouth and groaned. "I guess you'll have to wait, seeing as you don't want everyone to know that you're mine."

"You're evil," I said, falling forward and resting my head on his chest.

He chuckled and moved so fast that I didn't know what was happening until he tossed me over his shoulder like I weighed nothing. His hand found my ass as it moved beneath my dress again, and he jogged up to the house. He turned around as I laughed hysterically so that I could put the key into the door. Once I pushed it open, he carried me inside and dropped me onto the couch.

"What am I going to do with you, Captain?" I asked, teasing.

"Whatever the fuck you want to do." He leaned down and kissed me hard before tugging me to my feet.

I started to pull him toward my bedroom when he stopped me. "Don't you need to water the damn garden first?"

He was such a baby about the fact that we had to come over here daily to take care of it. It may not be impressive at the moment, but someday, this garden would feed whoever lived here. I'd probably be long gone before that happened, but I wasn't ready to throw in the towel yet. Plus, my herb garden was coming along.

"Ahhh... you do care. How about I water and you weed?"

"There are no weeds because there are no plants. There are

literally sticks and metal shit for the plants that have yet to grow." He barked out a laugh.

"Oh, you're just hilarious," I said, trying to hide the fact that I wasn't being sarcastic. The man was really funny. I flipped on the lights out back and reached for my gloves before pushing open the door. When I stepped outside, my mouth fell open.

There were tomatoes and cucumbers and corn. Two trees that hadn't been there yesterday were full of avocados and lemons. There were bushes with blackberries and raspberries, and heads of lettuce were along the back wall.

"What is this?" I asked, my voice just above a whisper.

"Surprise." He came around from behind and wrapped his arms around me. His chin rested on top of my head because he was ridiculously tall. "Now you can make whatever you want from your garden."

I'd had a few romantic gestures in my day, but this was beyond anything I could have ever imagined. It wasn't about buying a fancy present with Lincoln. Hell, he'd seen my niece hurting today, and he'd let her pick out whatever she wanted to make her smile. And he knew that I was determined to make this garden grow, so he'd found a way to make it happen.

Beneath this broody athlete was such a tender heart, and he continued to surprise me at every turn.

One minute, he was racing me in the water during our swims and dunking my head as he sped past me, and the next, he was planting a garden for me or rocking my world.

"This is—" I turned around to look at him and threw my hands up in the air.

"Is Brinkley Reynolds speechless? All I had to do to keep you from yelling at me is put in a garden?" he teased as he moved closer.

"I'm not speechless. I'm processing." I placed my hands

on his shoulders and jumped up, wrapping my legs around his waist. "You're not too bad for a secret boyfriend."

"Good. Maybe you should keep me." His voice was gruff.

Maybe I should.

twenty-two

. . .

Lincoln

"SO, is this how you two spend your days?" my mom asked as she set the plates down with sandwiches and chips, placing a large bowl of fruit in the center of the table.

My mom and Brinkley had hit it off when they'd met yesterday. The only problem I had now was that Brinkley wouldn't stay the night at the house with me while my mom was here. Nor was she okay with me sneaking over to her place last night because she said my mother would know I had left. She didn't want to make a bad impression.

What about the fucking impression she was making on my dick?

Sure, I'd gone without sex for weeks before I'd met her.

But now that I'd had her, I didn't function well without her in my bed.

And that was a huge fucking problem.

I'd spent most of my life making sure I didn't need to depend on anyone.

My job was to take care of my mom and take care of myself.

But now this woman had complicated things.

And I was in a foul mood due to a bad case of raging blue balls.

Try running six miles with an erection.

It's no fun.

"Yes, he puts in the work every single day. It's impressive." Brinkley smiled at me.

She thought it was hilarious that I was struggling after one day without her body pressed against mine.

There was nothing fucking funny about it.

"Always has. Do you know this boy used to wake up at five o'clock in the morning to mow everyone in the neighborhood's lawns when he was in middle school? He was born with a shrewd work ethic."

"The apple doesn't fall far from the tree." I winked at her. She was leaving out the fact that she'd been up at the same time, heading out to clean houses. She'd worked two jobs a day, six days a week, most of my life. The only time she'd ever taken off was to attend my games. Every single one of them. My mom worked her ass off to provide for me, and I would never take that for granted.

"Lincoln tells me that you're going to be moving to New York with him?"

"I am. Can't miss my boy's games, you know?" Mom said before taking a bite of her sandwich. She looked thin, which always concerned me. I had groceries delivered to her every week. Organic, healthy, whole foods. I'd been doing this since before she found out she had cancer. When you spend years eating shit food because you live on a budget, it's hard to remember that what you put into your body actually matters. It really fucking matters.

But old habits die hard.

My mother would go without food in order to give me more. That shit would never happen again in my lifetime.

She deserved to live out the rest of her days being fucking waited on like a goddamn royal.

So, the fact that I could buy her a beautiful home in whatever city she chose to live in and keep her refrigerator well-stocked—was the least I could do.

"I love that you never miss his games. That's how my parents were with us, too. And it was hard with five kids, but one of them was always there, no matter what. Sometimes they had to split up if two of us had something on the same day." Brinkley chuckled as she reached for her sun tea.

"That must have been so fun, growing up in a house full of kids." Mom shook her head with a big smile on her face. "I always wanted a big family. But now I'll just have to hope this one gives me a bunch of grandkids."

Jesus, Mom.

Take it down a notch.

She knew we were seeing one another, and she asked me last night after I took Brinkley home how serious it was.

We hadn't been together that long, but for whatever reason, it felt serious to me.

If the connection I felt was the meter for how serious I was about her, I'd be walking this girl down the aisle today.

But who the hell knew what was going to happen in two months when I headed to New York for official training camp at the end of July.

It was too soon to talk about that shit.

But not too soon to think about it. We were keeping things quiet for now, but we hadn't talked about what would happen after the story was released. Because I'd be leaving when that happened. And she didn't know where she was going.

"All right. I think that's a bit more than anyone needed to know. We've got plenty of time for that." I took the last bite of my sandwich.

My mom's eyes widened, and she smiled. "Well, that's a first."

"What's a first?" I asked as Brinkley looked between me and my mother.

"Well, whenever I'd joke about grandbabies in the past, you'd always say that football was your one and only love, and unless I wanted little footballs to babysit, I should give it up."

Brinkley's head fell back in laughter. "I can hear him saying that."

"You're overthinking it. I was just saying that we have plenty of time before you start taking care of a bunch of tiny footballs," I teased, trying to make light of the fact that she was right. It was the first time that the thought didn't make me want to crawl out of my skin.

It didn't mean I'd changed my mind. I had no example for a father, and I knew the damage that a man could do to a kid if he wasn't there or didn't step up to the plate.

I hated that I was the only kid on the flag football team who didn't have a father in the stands. There were a million examples of how shitty it had been, knowing that my father had chosen to walk away from me.

That wasn't an easy thing for a kid to process.

But I guess, in a way, seeing Brinkley with her family showed me the other side. How fucking good a family could actually be when everyone stuck around.

I wouldn't analyze it too deeply. My life was about to change drastically, and I didn't know what the future looked like.

"You're ridiculous," Brinkley said, smiling at me with this tender look in her eyes.

"Linc told me that your brother and your sister are both getting married this summer. Are they getting married here in Cottonwood Cove?"

"My brother, Hugh, and Lila are going to get married here. My sister Georgia, and her fiancé, Maddox, have a gorgeous home looking out at the cove. They have the yard for it, so Hugh and Lila are going to have the ceremony and reception there next month." She fiddled with her napkin in her lap. "And Georgia and Maddox are having a small wedding in Paris in September. So, we've got a lot to look forward to over the next few months."

"Wow. Your parents must be thrilled." My mother clapped her hands together like she'd never heard anything this impressive.

Didn't people get married every day?

The woman was an over-celebrator. Always had been. And I wouldn't change a fucking thing.

"Yeah. They are thrilled about it. I think it's hard in our family with the example my parents set in a way, you know?"

"What do you mean?" I asked, curious about this because we had never discussed it. And we discussed a lot. We worked out for hours every day with just conversation or music, so you could get to know someone pretty quickly that way.

"Well, they've been married for thirty-three years, and they're still ridiculously in love. My dad freaks out every year when my mom goes on a girls' trip with her best friend. He wanders around the grocery store aimlessly like he's missing a limb." She laughed and shook her head. "He still tells the story about how he knew she was the one because all the hair on his arms stood on end when they met. So, I think we all have the bar set pretty high. And we don't want to settle for anything less than the real deal."

Interesting.

This, I could relate to.

I never believed in settling.

"That is the sweetest thing I've ever heard. I love that they have that kind of love. And it's an amazing thing for their children to grow up surrounded by it. What do your parents do, Brinkley?"

"My mom is a therapist. So, she's a fabulous listener and not shy on the advice." She smiled. "And my dad owns a bar and a restaurant in town, but when he got diagnosed with cancer a few years back, he stepped away from the business. My brother, Hugh, and his fiancée run everything now. My dad does constant projects around the house, and they're traveling a lot now. And apparently, they'll be heading to New York because the whole family has season tickets to see the Thunderbirds."

More clapping from my mother. Her glass was always endlessly half full. She loved to make a big deal out of the good things, and she had a gift for spinning bad news.

When I'd get upset about other kids going on trips with their fathers or throwing the football with their dads, she'd always say that we were lucky that he walked away if he wasn't going to be what we needed.

Surround yourself with good people, Lincoln.

She said those words to me every day growing up. I'd kept my circle small. I'd used those words to guide me when I made the decision to leave San Francisco and the team I'd been playing for since I started my professional career.

Simple words with a whole lot of meaning behind them.

And right now, I was surrounded by the two best women that I knew.

"Well, then, I hope I'll get to see you at a game this season," my mom said.

"Oh, yes, I hope so. We haven't really talked about that stuff yet," Brinkley said, glancing at me with a smile.

"Are you a reporter now, Mama?" I teased.

"No. I just thought—I, er, you two are spending a lot of time together. I just wondered where you saw it going."

"Annnnd that's our cue. We should get going if we're going to take the boat out." I pushed to my feet.

Brinkley laughed over her words. "Has he not told you about the three-question rule?"

"What's that about?"

"He only allows me to ask three questions a day. I try to

sneak in a fourth question all the time, but he sticks to his rules."

"He's always been a bit of a rule follower." Mom chuckled. "I'm just going to go to my room and get changed. Give me about thirty minutes?"

"Take your time," I said as I watched her go down the hallway into her room and close the door.

"Why are you getting all agitated? Her questions didn't bother me," Brinkley whispered.

I took her hand and tugged her down the hallway to the bedroom and closed the door.

My mouth was on hers the second the door was closed. "I'll tell you why I'm agitated. I fucking missed you. Your smart mouth. Your body." I kissed down her neck.

"Your mom is right down the hall," she hissed, but her fingers were tangled in my hair, tugging me closer.

"What if we're quiet?" I said against her ear and nipped at her lobe. She nodded.

I pulled back and moved her to the dresser, where a large mirror sat on the wall above it. I turned her around, and she watched me in the mirror, her hooded gaze locked with mine.

"I missed you, too," she said, her voice low and laced with desire. She shoved her shorts down her legs and kicked them to the side before jutting her ass back in my direction.

I took in her peach-shaped ass and white thong that was doing very little to cover it. "God. I love your fucking body so much, sweetheart."

"I need you now." Her head fell back against my chest, and I reached into my pocket for a condom and had my shorts and briefs down within seconds. I rolled the latex over my throbbing cock and watched her in the mirror.

I leaned down and tore the lace fabric right off her body, and her eyes widened. I tossed her now-decimated thong on the floor and ran my fingers along her pussy.

"So fucking wet and ready," I whisper-growled against her ear, and her breaths were labored.

I teased her with my tip before pushing in, slowly at first.

Her eyes closed, lips parted.

I shoved the straps of her tank top and bra down her shoulders, exposing her beautiful tits, as I pulled out and thrust back in. I squeezed her breasts, teasing her nipples as we found our rhythm.

Faster.

Harder.

She met me thrust for thrust. Every single fucking time.

Her body was made for mine.

She was made for me.

"Lincoln," she whispered and placed her hand over her mouth to remain quiet. Our breaths were out of control, and my cock swelled inside her, as we were both overcome with desire.

My need for this woman was feral.

Completely out of my control at this point.

My hand moved around her hips, finding her clit and knowing just what she needed.

"Come for me, baby," I demanded.

Her body shook and convulsed as she went right over the edge. She bit down on her hand to keep from screaming.

I pumped into her one more time.

And that was all it took.

I followed her into oblivion.

I came so hard I couldn't see straight.

And I only wanted more.

twenty-three

. . .

Brinkley

"I LOVE YOUR MOM," I said, no hesitation in my voice. Those weren't words I tossed around lightly, but Abi Hendrix was an amazing woman.

"She loves you, too," Lincoln said as we settled onto the couch on the back deck, looking out at the water.

"She's so open. She told me all about her cancer journey when we stayed up chatting last night."

"Is that when you made me drive you home after? My mom is more than aware that we're sleeping together."

I rolled my eyes. "I know. But she was here for a weekend. I don't need to be getting busy with her son while she's in the house."

"Getting busy? Is that what we're doing?" A loud laugh escaped.

The sun had just tucked behind the horizon and the sky was a mix of oranges and yellows and pinks. It looked like a watercolor painting. We loved to sit out here every night and watch the sun go down.

I'd never spent this much time with a man before. We were together all day, every day. My work and personal life had completely meshed together. I'm sure I'd broken a million professional rules, but for whatever reason, I didn't care.

I couldn't pull back now if I wanted to.

And I didn't want to.

"I think we're doing more than that," I said. "I noticed you shut the conversation down quickly when your mom asked about the future."

He turned to face me, studying me for the longest time before he spoke. "I didn't think it was a conversation that my mother should be part of. Are you ready to have it?"

I raised a brow. "Sure. Let's do it."

"All right. Well, where do you see this going?"

Now it was my turn to laugh. "Are you putting this on me?"

"No. I just wanted to give you a chance to go first."

"Who's the rude gentleman now?"

He chuckled. "I'm not afraid to tell you how I feel, Brinkley."

"I'm listening."

"I don't only love your smart mouth and your hot-as-shit body," he said as he moved closer.

"You are off to a really good start, Captain."

"I'm not joking." He placed his fingers beneath my chin and forced me to meet his gaze. "I fucking love you. I'm all in."

I sucked in a breath. I could feel my eyes watering, and I blinked several times.

"What does that mean?" I whispered as a tear rolled down my cheek.

"Exactly what I said. I love you."

I nodded as his thumb swiped across the moisture moving down my face.

"I love you so much it freaks me out," I said, my voice trembling as the words left my mouth. "But I don't know how this works after we leave this bubble, and that terrifies me."

"Life is scary, baby. But I've got you. You don't need to be afraid."

"It's different for you," I said as he pulled me onto his lap.

"How so?"

"You're in love with a regular person. I'm in love with Lincoln Hendrix, the GOAT of the NFL. There's going to be women throwing themselves at you, and I don't even know where I'll be living. I have a few options on the table, but I'm leaning toward going with *Sports Today*, which would mean I would live in San Francisco."

"You're thinking too much, sweetheart. We'll figure it out. Other women won't be throwing themselves at me because I won't be looking. There's only one woman I see. One woman that I want."

"Maybe that's because I'm the only one here in Cottonwood Cove. This bubble is going to pop, and the real world is going to be waiting for you."

"Do you think I'm that guy? I've never cheated at anything in my life. I don't take shortcuts. If this isn't working, I'd have enough respect for you to talk to you about it first. I'd expect the same in return. I keep my circle small because I like it that way. But I'm loyal to the people that I love, and I think you know that deep down. Hell, I think you're drawn to it. We're similar that way."

I nodded. He was right. I was the same way. I kept my circle small, and I was fiercely protective of the people that I loved, as well.

"I agree. But temptation will be there. The press will be hounding you again. Our lives won't be private any longer."

"I didn't say it would be easy, but it'll be worth it. And if you end up in San Francisco, I'll fly out to see you or fly you out to see me as much as we can. I've got access to planes, and we'll make it work. People do it all the time."

I couldn't believe we were having this conversation.

That we'd both been completely honest about how we felt.

It was scary and exhilarating all at the same time.

"So, we're doing this?"

"I'd say we don't have a choice at this point. There's no turning back now. I'm too far gone," he said, and he wrapped his arms tighter around me.

He was right.

We were both too far gone.

———

"You are such a traitor. You've only known him for a few months, and you're cheering for him over your own sister?"

"Correct," Cage said dryly, and everyone laughed.

We'd come to Maddox and Georgia's house because Hugh and Lila had met their wedding planner over here to discuss the final details for their wedding, and we'd stopped by to see everyone. Cage and Gracie were out running errands, so they'd stopped by, as well. Finn was doing the final scenes for *Big Sky Ranch*, and he'd been working a lot lately.

Of course, once we'd shown up, that led to Georgia insisting we play pickleball. Let's just say that Lincoln Hendrix may be amazing with a football, but I did play volleyball for a long time. And with my sister being oddly talented at the sport of pickleball, she'd taught me a thing or two.

He and I had gone at it for the last hour, and he'd managed to edge me out, all with the annoying cheering from my oldest brother.

"I cheers for Auntie Brinks and Links!" Gracie shouted.

"He is the best football player out there, so don't take the loss too hard," Hugh said, placing an arm around my shoulder.

"It's fine." I rolled my eyes and handed my racket to my sister before glaring at Cage. "You best sleep with one eye open."

"Hey, remember that I played you first, and you gloated about beating me. Linc doesn't gloat."

"Please. He gloats so much he does it in his sleep!" I threw my hands in the air.

"Only when I have reason to gloat in my sleep, sweetheart."

Cage and Hugh high-fived him, and I punched him in the shoulder.

"We're leaving. I need to go check on the garden."

My brothers both laughed because they found it hilarious that I was so invested.

"You should see it," Lincoln said as he reached for my hand. "It's taken off."

Maddox and Georgia smirked at one another because they knew he'd been the reason it was currently a garden that could hold its own on any home and garden show. "She's got a green thumb."

Normally, I would call him out for covering for me, but I was annoyed with Cage, so I let this one go.

We said our goodbyes and drove to my house. We spent very little time there because, with Lincoln having a place on the water, along with an amazing home gym, it was the obvious choice most days.

But the garden was my thing. And yes, he'd had a watering system put in, so I didn't need to be out there with the hose every day. But I liked to go choose some items from the garden that we could use for dinner or for breakfast the next day.

There was something very satisfying about growing the food that you ate.

When we pulled in front of my house, we both stared at the tall guy sitting on my front steps.

"Who the fuck is that?" Lincoln grumped.

"I don't know. But let's greet him a bit friendlier than that."

I got out of the car, which earned me an eye roll from my boyfriend, who had hurried around to open my door.

"It's not a goddamn race," he said under his breath as he pinned me to the car. "But I do need to get you alone."

"Did you forget that we have a stranger waiting for us a few feet away?" I said with a laugh.

He pulled back, and I patted my hair into place and walked toward the house. Our unknown visitor was standing up now, and the closer we got, the clearer it was that he was strikingly good-looking. He was tall, close in height to Lincoln, with broad shoulders and wavy brown hair, and he appeared to be in his early twenties, if not younger.

"I didn't expect to see you here, Lincoln." He studied the man beside me, but not the way someone having a true fan moment would. This was different.

"Do I know you?" Lincoln asked. "Who the fuck were you expecting?"

I turned to look at Lincoln. The man was such a hothead when it came to people he didn't know. "Turn it down a notch, Captain."

"Are you Brinkley Reynolds?" the guy asked.

Lincoln stepped in front of me, wrapping his fingers around my wrist to keep me behind him. "Are you a fucking reporter?"

"Do I look like a fucking reporter?" The guy raised a brow with the same bad attitude as my boyfriend.

"I'm going to ask you one last time. Who. The. Fuck. Are. You?"

I stepped out of Lincoln's grip to stand beside him.

The guy crossed his arms over his chest. "I'm Romeo Knight. I'm fairly certain that you're my brother."

Lincoln's shoulders stiffened, and his jaw strained when I glanced up to look at him.

"Your last name is Knight? Who's your father?" That was all Lincoln asked.

"Keith Knight." He continued to stare at Lincoln, and you could cut the tension with a knife.

I stepped forward, desperate to lighten things up. "Hi, Romeo. I'm Brinkley Reynolds. How'd you find my house?"

He went on to explain how he'd recently learned that he had a brother. He'd tried messaging a few times on social media. When my article came out, he'd learned that I was writing a story about Lincoln and interviewing him while he trained. So, he'd researched me and found out where I lived. He assumed he'd have better luck finding a reporter than a football star who lived a very private life.

"Her address is not listed on a public site." Lincoln was really hung up on the fact that Romeo had found my house, and he had yet to acknowledge that this was potentially his brother.

"I stopped at the Cottonwood Café, and the girl behind the counter told me where I could find your house." He had an edge to him, very similar to the disposition of the man beside me. Between the attitude, the striking looks, and the height, that was as far as the similarities ran. Romeo was tan, with dark eyes and darker hair.

"She just gave you her address? What if you were a trained fucking killer?" Lincoln hissed, and Romeo rolled his eyes.

"I am a boxer, but I've yet to kill anyone."

"How am I supposed to know if you're really who you say you are?"

"Our father's birthday is on Christmas. He was born in Clearance, Iowa. He and your mom dated in high school, and she got pregnant after they graduated. The story goes that he ran off shortly after you were born. Your mother didn't put his name on the birth certificate, and you took her last name."

"What are you here for, money? Did my father send you?"

"Fuck you. I don't need your money. I guess you're as big

of an asshole as the media has made you out to be." He stalked down the walkway.

"Lincoln. This is most likely your brother. He isn't the one who left you. He just found out about you," I said as I squeezed his hand.

"Fuck," he said under his breath. "Romeo. Hold up."

Romeo turned around, not making any effort to hide his annoyance. "You beckoned, your highness?"

They had a similar dry sense of humor, no doubt about it.

"Why are you coming around now?" Lincoln asked.

He shoved his hands into his pockets and glanced away before looking back in our direction. "I didn't know about you, dude. At least not beyond being a famous football player. He never told me, but all the skeletons came out of the closet after he passed away a few weeks ago."

My chest ached at his words because he was hurting as much as Lincoln was. Just for different reasons.

"He's dead?"

"He is. Had a heart attack ringside at my last fight. He was my coach." His teeth sank into his bottom lip, and it was impossible to miss the emotions that were clearly still fresh and raw.

"And he sent you a message from the grave?" Lincoln asked, and I glared at him for being so cold about it.

He had his reasons for being angry, but Romeo hadn't done anything wrong.

"No, dickhead. He's not sending me messages from the grave. My grandmother told me at his funeral that you were his biggest regret. And then my mom did some digging because apparently, he'd never told her either. She found a box he'd hidden in their closet with a copy of your birth certificate, a lock of your hair, and a few baby photos. He had a ton of newspaper clippings from all your games over the years. We found a letter that he wrote to you in the box, and I guess I thought I should bring it to you."

Lincoln just stared as if he were processing the information.

"Where do you live? Did you travel far to get here?" Lincoln asked.

"I drove from Magnolia Falls." He looked toward the street, and I followed his gaze to the old motorcycle a few feet in front of where Lincoln had parked.

"That's like an eight-hour drive," I said. "You must be exhausted."

"I got an early start this morning," he said, clearing his throat. "I'm fine."

"Where are you staying?" Lincoln asked.

"I'll find a motel, or I'll head back tonight. I'm not worried about it." Romeo Knight was pretty good at masking his emotions, that much was clear. His cool demeanor was similar to his brother's.

"Does your mom know that you're here?"

He chuckled. "I'm twenty-one years old. I hardly need to tell my mother where I'm going. But Tia knows."

"Who's Tia?" Lincoln pressed.

"My sister. Technically, I guess she's *our* sister. She's eighteen. She's been sending you messages to your social media accounts, as well. I decided to just hop on my bike and come find Brinkley Reynolds and see if she'd tell me where I could find you. Thought you at least deserved the letter he'd written you."

Lincoln ran a hand down his face and glanced over at me.

"Well, you drove all this way. You've got to be starving. You want to come inside?"

Whether he liked it or not.

They were family.

twenty-four

· · ·

Lincoln

WE'D SPENT the last hour talking about football and boxing, and I was fairly certain the dude was telling the truth. He didn't want anything from me, other than to meet me and deliver this fucking letter.

I'd shot a text to my mom, and she'd verified that the information he'd shared about my father was true, and she said last she'd heard from him, he was living in Magnolia Falls with his wife and two kids.

So, I had a fucking brother and sister.

And the dude was kind of a cool cat, and we definitely shared the same distaste when it came to meeting new people.

But Brinkley had asked him no less than four thousand intrusive fucking questions, and he'd answered every single one of them.

I could see that he was a straight shooter, and he didn't appear to be a bullshitter.

He'd shared that his father, a.k.a. my sperm donor, had battled with drugs and alcohol when Romeo and Tia were young, but he'd turned his life around over a decade ago, minus a few falls off the wagon. His mom was a strong woman who'd stuck by the man through all the ups and downs. They'd struggled financially, and his father had stepped up these last few years. He'd worked at a boxing gym for as long as he could remember, and the man had eventually become a partner in the place. Romeo basically grew up at the gym, as they didn't have much money, and fighting became a way he could make some side money. He and his father had bonded over the sport over the years, and he was his coach when Romeo decided to take his career to the next level.

He'd won a big fight a few months ago against a dude who'd been a pro for a long time, and the win had bumped him to a professional boxer status. He hadn't fought again since his last fight when his father had dropped to the ground during the third round, and he didn't know if he'd ever fight again.

"I'm sure it was very traumatic to witness that," Brinkley said as she refilled our glasses of sun tea and set out some more grapes, crackers, and cheese.

"It's fine. Shit happens. Right now, I'm running the gym. Doing what I can to keep the lights on. My dad's partner, Rocco, is in his early eighties, so he's not there all that often."

He and I were devouring the platter of snacks.

"I see we both have healthy appetites," I said, changing the subject because this was a lot to unpack.

"Yeah. My mom complains about how much I eat. But spending all that time in the gym will get your appetite going. I guess I don't need to tell you that."

"Well, how about we grab some food and head back to my place? There's more room there."

Brinkley smiled before reaching for her glass.

"You don't need to feed me, dude."

"Take it easy. It's a meal. And you came a long way." I scrubbed a hand down my face. "I'm not ready to take the letter just yet. So how about you do me a solid and come back to my house and spend the night there so my girl can continue grilling you? We can eat some good food, and I'll think about reading the fucking letter."

He smirked. "I can do that."

"Do you like ribs?" she asked him. "My brother has a restaurant in town, and we can swing by and grab dinner."

"Sure. That sounds good." He reached for his wallet. Clearly, he wanted to make sure I knew he didn't want anything from me.

She held up her hand. "Not necessary. It's on the house. Perks of my brother owning the best restaurant in town."

He cleared his throat, noticeably uncomfortable with the gesture, but he nodded.

I gave Romeo the address, and he agreed to meet us at the house in half an hour. He said he needed to go fill his tank with gas, and a part of me wondered if he'd just take off and never look back.

I pulled up to Reynolds' and insisted on running in to pick up the food, so I could tell Brandy to ring it up. Hugh didn't need to be comping my meals.

Apparently, my new brother and I had a thing or two in common.

Hugh wasn't there tonight, so I knew I could get away with it.

Brinkley was on the phone with her mother when I got in the car, and she ended the call.

"You know, if you want to talk about this, I'm here to listen," she said.

I barked out a laugh. "Did you just ask your therapist mother how to talk to me about this?"

"Well, you know I prefer to just press you for information. My mom said I should offer to open the lines of communication but let you go at your own speed. It's a lot, Captain. But I've got to say, he's got your grumpy, guarded demeanor. It must be genetic."

"Is that supposed to be a compliment?"

"If you like grumpy, guarded people, it is. I happen to be a fan." She smirked. "For real, though, is it hard to hear that your father is gone?"

"I think if I'd had any intent on finding him as an adult, it probably would be. But I made peace with the fact that I didn't have a father years ago. But I'm not going to lie—it's hard to hear that I have two siblings I've never met."

"Maybe this is just how it was supposed to happen. After your father was gone," she said as I pulled into the garage. His bike wasn't out front. "Do you think he'll even show up?"

"I don't know. I mean, he came here to deliver a letter to me, and he seems like the kind of guy who follows through with his plans. Plus, we lightened up these last few hours. I think he'll show up."

"I think he will, too."

"And he's clearly got skills being a professional boxer at such a young age."

"Your father obviously had athletic genes. He has two sons that are professional athletes. One being the GOAT," she said. I pushed out of the car and grabbed the food before walking around to open her door.

"I'm sure seeing your parent drop to the ground in front of you during a fight has got to do some damage, huh?"

"I imagine it would be pretty traumatic."

We both turned as we heard the rumble of an engine coming down the street. He drove up the driveway and turned off his bike before pulling off his helmet and placing it on the seat. He walked toward us with his backpack slung over his shoulder.

"This is your house?" he asked as he followed us inside.

"No. It's my agent's house."

We ate dinner, and the conversation felt more relaxed. Brinkley opened a bottle of wine, pouring us each a glass. It definitely took the edge off. Romeo's phone rang several times, and he glanced down before looking back up at me.

"Listen, this is Tia. She wants to FaceTime and say hello. Are you cool with that? If not, she'll never stop calling."

I dropped the last rib bone onto my plate and reached for my napkin, nodding slowly as Brinkley shot me a look. We communicated well without needing to speak lately. This was a familiar look—one she'd graced me with often.

Be nice, Asshole.

"Yeah. Answer the damn phone." I chuckled.

He held the phone in front of his face. "For fuck's sake, Tia. You're relentless."

"I got your text that you found him. What is he like?"

"Well, seeing as he's sitting here listening, it would be hard to talk shit about him. But his girlfriend is cool as hell." He winked at Brinkley, and I rolled my eyes.

Like I said, the dude was a cool cat.

"So, tell me about him and his girlfriend," Tia whisper-shouted, as if we all couldn't hear her. I barked out a laugh.

"Why don't you see for yourself," Romeo said, flipping his phone so the camera was facing me and Brinkley. "This is Lincoln. He's a bit of a dickhead, but he's growing on me. And this is his better half, Brinkley Reynolds."

"He's dating the reporter?"

"Them dating is still a secret, and they trusted me with that info, so don't make them think I'm a traitor, all right? And you know` they can hear you, right? You're on Face-Time," he said, and there was a lightness about him when he spoke to his sister. He passed me his phone so that Brinkley and I could see her.

"Oh, hey, guys. Sorry about that. I'm just excited. And of course, mum's the word on the *secret romance*. Who would I even tell?" She shrugged. She looked like Romeo, but she had green eyes that appeared to be very similar to mine. My mother's eyes were blue, and she'd always told me I had the same gaze as my father.

"It's so nice to meet you, Tia," Brinkley said, leaning her head on my shoulder.

"I see this brother is not a big talker either. I have to pull teeth to get Romeo to talk most of the time. It must be genetic. Thank God I have Mom's genes." She tucked her dark hair behind her ear.

"It's nice to meet you. It's just a lot to process," I said.

"Oh, really?" She rolled her eyes and chuckled. "I just lost my father and found out I have a brother that I didn't know about—*that's a lot to process*. You scored. Romeo and I are the best. You're a lucky bastard."

Brinkley fell back in her chair in a fit of laughter. "I already like you, Tia."

"I like you, too. When do I get to meet you guys?"

I let out a long breath. I wasn't sure where any of this was going, but I'd be lying if I said I didn't want to get to know them better. I'd been ditched, and they'd been lied to, so no one here was at fault.

"I head back to training camp at the end of July. Would you want to come visit before then? Or do you prefer I come there?"

Brinkley's gaze was so tender when she glanced at me it made my chest squeeze. This was a lot, but I wasn't going to run from it. I was handling it.

Hell, I was practically embracing it.

I'd already invited Romeo to stay the night.

That was an olive branch I never saw coming.

"Well, since you're the big-time football player, and I'm an eighteen-year-old, jobless senior in high school, I'd say it would be better if you come here. My brother used every spare penny he had to make the trip there."

"Fuck, Tia. Shut the hell up. It's hardly every penny I have. You don't know what's in my bank account." Romeo turned the phone and looked pissed off as he glared at the screen.

"I know that you filled Mom's refrigerator with groceries for us before you left. You paid for Dad's funeral. I can't imagine you have much left after that."

"If you want to come here to meet him, I can get you here. Got it?"

Fuck. This dude and his pride.

"Sorry. Let me talk to my other brother. He actually seems like the better of the two evils at the moment." Romeo handed me his phone, running a hand down his face and shaking his head with irritation.

That earned a laugh from both me and Brinkley.

"Listen, Tia. I can come there, or I can fly you here." I held my hand up to the broody bastard who looked like he wanted to punch me in the face. "Dude, I have access to a plane; stop being a stubborn ass."

"You tell him, Lincoln. He's so stubborn sometimes."

"I can hear you," Romeo said dryly.

"When are you coming home, Romeo?"

"Tomorrow," he answered quickly. "They're letting me crash here for the night, and then I'll head home. I've got to get back to work."

"I think the gym can survive without you for a few days. I'm so bummed I'm missing this sleepover tonight. *Hashtag sibling goals*."

"Tia, I think you and I are going to get along really well." Brinkley smiled.

"Me, too. So, we'll figure out a time to get together soon. I can't wait to meet you both. Thanks for looking out for Romeo."

"Annnd I think we're done here. I'll call you tomorrow, okay?" Romeo said as I handed him the phone back.

"Goodnight, brother dearest. I love you."

"Yep. Love you." He ended the call.

"You two are close, huh?" I asked.

"Yeah. She's a pain in my ass, but I love her."

We sat there quietly for a minute. "You want to see the gym here? It's pretty badass."

"Hell, yeah. Now you're speaking my language."

We took him on a quick tour of the house, and after a lengthy argument, with him insisting on sleeping on the couch, he agreed to stay in the guest room, as there were four empty bedrooms in this place.

When we got to the gym, he took it in and didn't hide his surprise. "Damn. This is top-notch. What I wouldn't give to have a home fucking gym like this."

"We'll be getting up early to work out tomorrow. How about you stick around a little longer, and you can join us?" Brinkley asked.

Romeo glanced around, taking a minute to think it over. "I could do that. Remember, I'm younger than you, so you might not be able to keep up, old man."

I smirked. "We'll see about that."

And just like that, I was falling into a rhythm with my new brother.

———

Romeo ended up staying over a second night, and we'd worked out two mornings in a row together. The dude was a badass. There were very few people who could manage to do both my cardio and my strength training workout. But this guy challenged me every step of the way.

He'd grabbed a quick shower and enjoyed the breakfast Brinkley had made for us before insisting he had to get back home to work.

He waited until Brinkley stepped away to use the restroom, and he turned to face me. The envelope was in his hand. "Are you going to stop being a pussy and read the damn letter?"

"Fuck off. I'm not being a pussy," I said, snatching it from his hand and smirking. "It's just… I know he's your dad, but I don't know the guy. So, I'm not sure how I feel about reading a letter from a dude that I never knew, who is no longer here."

"Well, you never knew me before, and now you're a bit of a clingy motherfucker." He laughed. "Listen. The man wasn't perfect, but he was a good guy, Lincoln. He made some mistakes, and they haunted him. I don't know what the fucking letter says, but he wanted you to have it. He sure as fuck didn't leave a letter for me and Tia."

I nodded. "All right. I'll read it, just not right now. And don't ever call me clingy again."

A wide grin spread across his face. He'd been doing that a lot this morning. There was a comfort there now, and we'd gotten past the awkward stage. It was crazy to think we'd only known one another for forty-eight hours, but somehow, it felt like I'd known the guy all my life.

"Dude, you're about to get really well acquainted with clingy. But remember, you gave Tia your number, not me. The girl has no boundaries. She'll be so far in your business, you won't know what hit you."

Tia had texted me three times this morning, and she'd texted Brinkley far more than that. Neither of us minded.

"It'll be fine. I want to talk to you about something."

"Shoot."

"I know money is tight after the funeral, and I just want to give you and Tia a little something to get on your feet." I pulled out the wad of money in my back pocket that I'd planned to give him.

His gaze hardened. "Lincoln, I appreciate it. That's not what I came here for. If you want to help out Tia, I won't get in your way. She deserves a break. She works really hard at school, and she helps out our mom a lot. But I'm good."

"Damn, you're stubborn. I can help. Why won't you let me?"

"I would if I needed it." He clapped me on the shoulder. "And I'll see you in a couple of weeks when you and Brinkley come to Magnolia Falls."

"All right. Call me when you make it home, okay?"

Brinkley came out and wrapped him in a hug. "I'm glad you came, Romeo. You're stuck with us now."

"I'm good with that." He winked. The dude had swagger, no doubt about it. And it made me fucking proud.

We walked him outside, and he extended a hand to me. "Thanks for letting me crash here."

I pulled him in for a hug, keeping my voice low. "You're always welcome wherever I am. You got it?"

"Same for you." He pulled back and then reached for his helmet.

"Remember to shoot me a text when you get home," I reminded him.

"Like I said, you're a little clingy, brother." Romeo barked out a laugh before firing up his engine.

Brother.

My chest squeezed at his words, and I saluted him before flashing him the bird.

I knew in my gut that, moving forward, he and Tia were going to be permanent fixtures in my life.

And I was totally okay with that.

twenty-five

· · ·

Brinkley

WE'D JUST FINISHED a six-mile run, and my legs were rubbery and weak. "I can't keep up with you lately, and you know it's hard for me to admit that."

Lincoln turned to look at me with concern and grabbed me by the thighs and flipped me over his shoulder. "I'll carry you, then."

"It doesn't mean I can't walk; it just means you're getting faster." I smacked his ass as my body relaxed against him.

"I'm training harder than I ever have, and I like having you push me on the runs."

I sighed and pushed up, sliding down his body until my feet hit the ground. "Then I guess I'll just have to keep pushing alongside you."

"Tell me about your two offers," he said.

I'd tried to fill him in on the latest with my job prospects when we'd started our run, but my breathing was so labored right out of the gate that I'd been unable to form a complete sentence.

"So, both *Football Live* and *Sports Today* want to buy the rights to your story. *Sports Today* is obviously big time, and they let me break the news about your plans for next year when we made that announcement. But I like the woman at *Football Live* magazine a lot. And they have a female president over there, which I, of course, love. But then I got a really nice call from Audrey. Do you remember me mentioning her? She was my mentor during my internship at *Strive Forward* magazine. They are hiring, as well, and she said they'd be thrilled to have me."

"So, you have three really good offers. The others aren't in the running?"

"No. I definitely want to go with one of these three. It's just, you know, there's a lot to consider."

The back of his hand grazed mine as we walked, and he glanced over at me. "What is there to consider?"

"All three are talking about full-time positions, which is important for me moving forward. So, it comes down to pay, benefits, and how much control I will actually have over what I write and where it's featured. And then the big kahuna—where I'd be located."

He came to a stop and turned to face me. "Where do you want to be located?"

I laughed because he was so funny about certain things. He'd made it clear he wanted to be together. In fact, he couldn't wait for this story to break so we could go public with our relationship. But he had not pushed me at all to sign in New York, even though we both knew it would make our lives easier.

"I don't really have a say in that, you know? But obviously, I'd like to be close to you. Both *Football Live* and *Sports Today* are based in San Francisco, but that doesn't mean that I couldn't work remotely down the road. You know, once I prove myself. And then *Strive Forward* magazine is located in New York, which would obviously be very convenient, as well."

"I'm not going to lie, I'd fucking love to wake up with you every day like we're doing right now. But I know your career is important to you, and I want to support that. So, wherever you go, we'll make it work. Do I prefer you to be in New York with me? Fuck, yeah. But I can't really demand that, can I?" His gaze locked with mine, and a loud laugh escaped when I realized that he was actually asking for permission to be a caveman.

"Um, no. You can't demand that."

"Fuck. That's what I thought." He shrugged, and we started walking again. "So, you'll go interview with all three of them, and your gut will tell you what to do."

"Do you always listen to your gut?"

"I do. It's never failed me. Not with football, not with you, and it even told me to hear out Romeo when he showed up on your front porch. Your instincts are there for a reason. And if you don't know what to do, you can always ask me, and I'll be happy to tell you what to do."

I laughed. "You are so ridiculous. You're not my boss; you're my lover."

We walked through the backyard and into the house.

"You can be the boss of me anytime you want, sweetheart."

"Yeah? I can tell you whatever I want you to do, and you'll do it?"

"Correct." He handed me a bottle of water and tugged me close.

"How about we read that letter?" It had been sitting on the counter for the last two days since Romeo left, and he kept putting it off.

"What do I get if I read the fucking letter?" He thrust against me, letting me know exactly what he wanted.

"How about we read the letter, and then you can have your way with me in the shower?"

"Fine. You read it. I'll listen." He handed me the letter and moved to the table where we settled across from one another. Lincoln had a thick skin, and he wanted everyone to believe he didn't care because he didn't know his father. But it was something that had always bothered him, so he obviously cared. And I hoped that this could be a form of closure for him.

I opened the sealed envelope and pulled out the lined notebook paper before glancing up at him to make sure he was okay with me moving forward. He gave me a slight nod, and I unfolded the paper.

A photo of what looked like a young Lincoln and Abi was inside the letter, and I handed him the photo. He stared at it for a few moments and then nodded at me to start.

The letter was handwritten in black ink.

I turned the paper around to show him the date.

"He wrote this last fall," I said, and Lincoln nodded.

"Lincoln, Hell, I've tried to write this letter a million times, and I couldn't find the words. But tonight, I watched you play the Cougars and dominate the football game on TV. It's hard for me to wrap my head around it—that I had any part in creating such a magnificent man. I've been keeping tabs on you where I could without getting too close, and I have to shake my head every time I learn more about you. A straight-A student, a superior athlete, and a great son to Abi. I'm not deserving of any ounce of your light, so I'll watch from a distance. But I need you to know that I didn't walk away because I didn't love you and your mom. I walked away because I didn't love myself." I paused to clear my throat and take a sip of water. I glanced up at Lincoln, and his face was hard as he listened. So, I returned my gaze to the paper.

"I'm not here to make excuses. I didn't have a great upbringing, and I wasn't worthy of your mother. I knew it the first time I met her, but I couldn't walk away back then. The pull was too strong. She was all goodness and sunshine and warmth. Something I didn't feel deserving of back then. And when she got pregnant with you, I panicked. I wasn't ready. She embraced it. Worked double shifts and read everything she could about becoming a mother. I turned to the bottle and drugs and anything I could to escape. When you came

into the world, I was there. I watched you take your first breath," I said, and my voice cracked. I could feel the pain in his words. Lincoln's face remained hard, and I continued.

"Your mother told me I hadn't earned the right to give you my name, and she was right. I'd abandoned her long before you entered the world. She'd made it clear that if I wasn't going to step up and be the man you both deserved, she'd do it all on her own. And there was no doubt in my mind that she meant it. So, I stuck around for a few days and then tucked tail and ran." I paused to take a breath because this was heavier than I'd imagined it would be and watched as Lincoln took a long pull from his water bottle. The way his Adam's apple bobbed in his throat and his jaw ticked from clenching his teeth so hard had my heart squeezing.

"You okay?"

"Yep. Finish it up. Let's get this done."

I nodded. *"I know I don't deserve the title of being your father. I've known it every day since the day you were born. But I want you to know that it has nothing to do with you and everything to do with me. I wish I'd been man enough to step up to the plate back then. Man enough to show up on your birthdays and Christmas and attend your football games. It's the very least I could have done. But fear had a choke hold on me, Lincoln. And I didn't want to face what I'd done to you, so I let more and more time go by, terrified to look into your eyes and see the disappointment that I knew would be there.*

"I am writing this now because I've recently learned that I have a lot of health issues. My family doesn't know it, and I'm doing what I can to step up the only way I know how in the time I have left. I have two more children, Romeo and Tia. It's important to me that you know I don't love them any more than I love you.

There has not been one day in your life that has gone by that I haven't thought of you. I've carried this picture of you in my wallet every day. Every single day, I apologize to you in my prayers. Yeah, I've fucked up a lot in my life, but I still pray every night. And you're the first thought and the first one I pray for before I go to sleep. I may not have been able to make things right in my lifetime, but I'd be really happy if my three children could find their way to one another. They don't know about you, and I won't tell them because you are the one who deserves the right to make that decision. So, I'm going to leave this letter for my wife and hope it finds its way to you. And then the ball will be in your court." I paused again and let out a long breath.

"Sometimes, Lincoln, we aren't strong enough to find the courage to make things right, but it's never too late to say I'm sorry. And I'm truly sorry for failing you as a father, as a man, and as a friend. I'm honored to watch you play on TV and to know that a little piece of me lives on in you. My amazing son, I hope you'll find it in your heart to forgive me and get to know your siblings. They're really good people, just like their mama and their older brother who they don't know about.

With love, Keith Knight."

I set down the paper and looked up. Lincoln's eyes were wet with emotion, and his hands were fisted on the table. I reached over and wrapped my hand around his, and they relaxed and intertwined with mine.

"That was… not what I expected." He cleared his throat.

"Yeah. It was very heartfelt, huh?"

"It was," he said, glancing out the window at the water.

"Do you feel better now that you've heard what he had to say?"

He turned back to look at me, and his green eyes were filled with a mixture of empathy and pain, and it took my breath away.

"I don't honestly know what I feel. I want to say that I don't care because he wasn't there for me. But hearing those words, I don't know, maybe there was more there than I'd thought there was."

"That's very fair."

"I wish he'd owned up before he died so we could have had a chance to meet face-to-face and have this talk. It's sort of one-sided, where he got to say his piece, and I didn't. But maybe it's better that way."

"Maybe all that was meant to come out of this was your relationship with Romeo and Tia."

"Yeah. And if I hadn't met Romeo in this way, I don't think I would have been open to meeting them on my own. And now Tia is blowing up my phone every day, and I don't even mind it. So maybe something good really did come out of all of this."

I moved to my feet and climbed onto his lap, wrapping my arms around his neck. "Something good did come out of it."

"Yeah? So, we read the letter. Are you ready to pay up?" he teased, his thumb tracing along my bottom lip.

"I always pay up, Captain."

Without warning he was on his feet with me in his arms. He carried me to the bathroom and set me on the counter before leaning over and placing a hand on each side of my face. "Thank you for making me read that letter."

"Thank you for letting me be there with you."

"Now I'm going to rock your fucking world," he said against my ear before nipping at my neck.

"I'm counting on that," I said, as he tugged my tank top over my head.

I kept my arms up as he pulled off my sports bra, as well, and then he dropped to his knees and reached for the band of my running shorts. I pushed up just enough for him to tug them down my legs. My fingers tangled in his hair, and he groaned.

"Goddamn, sweetheart. I love your fucking body so much. I can't get enough." And he pushed my legs apart and buried his face there.

My head fell back against the mirror as he licked and sucked my most sensitive area. He wrapped my legs over his shoulders and tugged me forward, giving him better access.

My fingers gripped the countertop as I bucked against him. His tongue slipped inside, and it was more than I could bear. I was already exhausted from our run, and my body surrendered to him.

Panting and gasping.

Tugging at his hair as his thumb found my clit, knowing exactly what I needed.

I nearly came off the white marble as bright lights sparked beneath my eyelids, and my body trembled.

"Lincoln," I cried out as he moved faster, sending me right into oblivion.

Every muscle, every bone, every inch of my body completely shattered.

He stayed right there, waiting for me to ride out every last bit of pleasure.

I couldn't speak. My body was spent, and he stood up and shoved his shorts down his strong thighs before tugging his tank top over his head.

His cock sprang free and pointed directly at me, and he chuckled. "He loves you as much as I do."

"The feeling is mutual," I whispered.

He stroked my cheek. "You okay?"

"Yeah, just trying to keep up with the GOAT of the NFL on a run and then get my world rocked right here on the counter." I chuckled.

He studied me before turning on the shower and then scooping me up and carrying me in with him. He set me on my feet, and I reached down to stroke him. He grabbed my wrists and lifted my hands to his lips. "Not right now. That can wait."

And he spent the next twenty minutes gently washing my body, washing my hair, and kissing my neck. He wrapped me in a towel and dried my hair with the other towel sitting on the counter before wrapping it around his waist.

This man had a way of making me feel like I was the only woman in the world.

And I loved every second of it.

I didn't want this time to ever end.

We'd been existing in a bubble, and I wasn't in any hurry to leave it.

twenty-six

. . .

Lincoln

BRINKLEY'S ARTICLE about that asshole, Breen Lockhart, had gone to print today, so we'd celebrated with a lunch date at Cottonwood Café. Because who didn't want to be sexually harassed by an inappropriate woman on a Wednesday afternoon?

"You two sure do spend a lot of time together. You sure it's all work and no pleasure?" Mrs. Runither purred as she leaned over the table. One of her nipples was fully exposed when her low-cut dress flopped open. She clearly wasn't wearing a bra, and my taste for macaroni and cheese had just completely vanished. I looked at my girlfriend because I wanted to look anywhere but at the tit that was currently resting next to my menu.

These weren't the kind of knockers that you wanted displayed across your lunch table.

Brinkley glanced over at me with a wicked grin and then turned her attention back to the older woman. "He's a full-time job, Mrs. Runither. And you've got yourself a little situation or, er, a big situation going on."

The woman glanced down and chuckled. "Ahhh... maybe that's what you two need to get a little motivated."

"Definitely not," I grunted under my breath so only Brinkley could hear me.

"All work and no play makes Lincoln a very boring boy." Her tangerine lips were unusually large, and it wasn't a good look.

"Trust me, there's nothing boring going on here." I winked.

She clapped her hands together. "I'm sure there isn't. I'll get those orders right out."

"That woman would be green with envy to know that I woke up with your head buried between my legs this morning." Brinkley leaned close and whispered in my ear.

"I fucking love hearing you cry out my name before the sun comes up."

She smiled, cheeks pink and eyes hooded. She was the sexiest woman I'd ever known, and the thought of not waking up with her every day had me on edge. I was a selfish prick. I wanted her to take a job out in New York and move in with me. But at the same time, I wrestled with it, because seeing her happy was equally important to me. And if working for the magazine that was based in San Francisco was what she wanted, I wanted that for her, as well.

At least I was trying to.

I held up my glass of lemonade. "Congrats on the article, sweetheart."

"Yeah, thank you. They've been really great to work with."

"*Sport-X* has?"

"Yep. The editor is amazing and really positive. They sent someone out to shoot photos of Breen and sent them to me for approval. They just really include the journalist in the process, and that isn't always the case."

"And where are they located?"

She rolled her eyes and then smirked. "Funny you should ask. They're located in the Big Apple."

"Ah, New York City, huh?"

She chuckled. "Don't pretend you didn't know that. But they focus primarily on hockey, and I don't want to be stuck writing about one sport. I mean, if I was going to do that, it would be football. But everyone wants this story, and it makes me a more desirable package. So, hopefully, the three magazines I'm talking to make me a fair offer."

"Oh, you're desirable all right. And it has nothing to do with me." My hand found her thigh beneath the table.

"Hands to yourself, Captain." She raised a brow. "I won't be sad when we can be out in the open with our relationship. Although, I'm guessing everyone in Cottonwood Cove suspects something's going on with all the time we spend together."

"Good. I want every fucker out there to know that you're mine."

"So possessive," she purred.

Mrs. Runither approached the table and set our food down, and the way she paused and stared at me as she slowly licked her plump bottom lip made me shiver with discomfort. She chuckled and walked away.

"You are so dramatic." Brinkley swatted my shoulder, and then we both reached for our forks.

"What? She freaks me out. I can tell she's visualizing me naked while she's licking those sausage lips."

Brinkley laughed, and we spent the next hour talking about all her options. All the places that she'd applied to.

I didn't like that the future was unknown at this point. I knew where I was going, and I wanted to know where she was going.

She was currently writing the story about me since we'd finished the interview. Each night, she let me read what she'd written, and her talent was blatantly apparent in her words.

When we pulled up to my house, there was a dude

standing near the front door with an enormous floral arrangement.

"Oh, that's Jeremy Farmer. I used to babysit Jeremy when I was in high school." She chuckled as we both got out of the car.

"Brinkley, hey," the dude said as his gaze landed on me. "Oh, wow. It's really you. Everyone has seen you around town, but this is my first time. I'm a big fan."

"Nice to meet you, Jeremy." I extended my hand before taking the flowers from him.

"I, er, took them to your house, but then Janine told me to bring them over here, because you two work together a lot, I guess. We didn't want to leave them outside."

"Janine owns Cottonwood Blooms," Brinkley said to me because I didn't have a clue who she was. "Thanks for hunting me down, Jeremy."

Only in a small town do the delivery people forgo the address and just go find you themselves.

Brinkley gave him a quick hug, and we said goodbye, but the kid was still standing there, gaping at me.

"If you want to bring your jersey over later, I can have him sign it for you," she said as she waved, and he did a strange little jump and fist-pumped the sky.

"Thanks so much. I'll be back later today."

I laughed as we pushed inside because I was suddenly curious as fuck who was sending my girl flowers. I assumed it was *Sports-X*. I set the arrangement on the kitchen counter, and she plucked the card out of the flowers, and her smile dropped the slightest bit. Most people wouldn't have noticed, but I knew this woman well. She either didn't like who they were from, or she knew that I wouldn't like it.

I snatched the card from her and read it.

Brinkley, there's no one I'd rather have do me justice than you. I'll be in town this weekend, and I'd like to see you. XO, Breen

I tossed the card onto the counter and stared at her. "Why

the fuck is Breen Lockhart sending you flowers, and why does he want to see you?"

"I'm assuming the flowers are because the article went live today. It was probably just a friendly gesture. And I had no idea he was coming into town this weekend, but we're friends, so it's not odd to reach out."

"Don't be naïve," I hissed. "That fucker wants you, and we both know it."

"And I can take care of myself. I shut him down the first time, and I'll do it again this time, if necessary." She crossed her arms over her chest.

"Fuck that dude. You aren't meeting him anywhere alone."

She raised her brow. "Excuse me? Are you actually telling me what I can and cannot do?"

"Damn straight, I am. I don't trust him."

"You don't trust him, or you don't trust me?"

I walked to the refrigerator and pulled out a bottle of water, thinking over my words before I spoke. I was a hothead, and she was stubborn. That combo could be explosive.

"I don't trust him."

"Neither do I. So you have nothing to worry about," she said, her face hard and determined. "I know how to handle myself, Lincoln."

"I'm aware. But that doesn't stop me from wanting to protect you."

"I don't need protecting. I've been surviving in this big, bad world all on my own for a very long time."

"Are you going to meet with him?"

"I mean, he's a friend. How can I not go say hello?" She threw her arms in the air.

"Easy. You just tell him to fuck off."

"No, that's what you would tell him. I'm making a name for myself in this business, and interviewing athletes is my job. I can't have you freaking out every time I get together with someone."

"I wouldn't freak out about anyone else. This guy is different."

"Why? Because he fucked your ex-girlfriend? Maybe you're still hung up on her," she hissed, and I moved close to her, backing her up until her ass hit the counter of the island.

"Don't fucking twist this. I don't give two shits about her, and you know it. I don't like the guy; he's bad news. I don't want you alone with him. That's all I'm saying." My hand moved to her neck, and my thumb traced along her jaw.

Her gaze softened. "Fine. I'll agree to meet him out in a group and invite my siblings, and you can even be there. But do not go all caveman barbarian on me. He doesn't know we're together, and he doesn't need to. The first time I turned him down, I was single. I've got this handled."

"Fine. I can live with that."

She smiled. "Did we just work through our first disagreement? At least our first disagreement today."

I leaned forward and kissed her. I'd let this go for now, but I had every intention of watching that bastard like a hawk.

She had no idea what a piece of shit the guy was.

———

"Are you going to be a baby all night?" Brinkley asked as we drove to Garrity's, her family's bar that Hugh and Lila also ran.

Apparently, Breen was in town with a few friends, some of them being women. Of course, my girlfriend was thrilled to tell me it was more of a couple's trip. She loved proving me wrong, but I'd noticed the way he'd looked at her that first time he'd been in town, and that dude was not inviting her out as a friendly gesture.

"I'm not being a baby. I'm looking forward to seeing your

family." I'd been going to Sunday dinners for weeks now, and they'd all become friends of mine at this point. I played cards with all the guys last week, and they'd somehow convinced me to make our trip to Iowa for Lionel a full-blown boys' trip.

"Remember... he's a client, and I've got it handled. Don't be storming the castle if the guy says hello to me."

"I will let you handle it." I shrugged.

Unless he's inappropriate, which I know he's capable of because I've heard a lot of rumblings about the dude.

But I wouldn't go there right now.

When we arrived at the bar, everyone was already there. Maddox and his brother, Wyle, called me over to join in on a game of darts before Cage and Hugh came to join us, holding a bunch of beers. Finn was away filming final edits on his new show, and it was all everyone in town was talking about.

Brinkley walked over to meet her sister and Lila, who had drinks at the table, with a few different appetizers there, as well. There was no sign of the dickhead Lockhart, and a part of me hoped he wouldn't show up.

"You really don't like the guy, huh?" Hugh asked, keeping his voice low. He remembered how I'd warned him about Breen back when his sister still hated me.

"Just heard a lot of things. I don't like the idea of her being alone with him."

"Well, you've got all of us here, so there's nothing to worry about," Cage said, glancing at the door when a loud ruckus pulled our attention away.

In walked Breen, along with three dudes that looked somewhat familiar. They were most likely hockey players, but they definitely didn't play for the Lions because I knew all the players on that team. There were at least five women with them, and the whole group looked heavily intoxicated.

"There she is!" Breen shouted. "This girl right here did me right in her article!"

He wrapped an arm around Brinkley, and my hands fisted at my sides as we stood a good twenty feet away from them.

He stood behind her, his arm around her neck as he kissed her cheek.

"Easy, brother. Nothing's going to happen with all of us here," Maddox said, keeping his voice low. The dude was as cool as they come, and we'd grown close.

"I'm so down for a brawl," Wyle said. "I never mind a good bar fight."

"Well, it's not great for business, so let's hope it doesn't come to that. But we've got your back if necessary." Hugh sipped his beer, and his gaze moved from me to his sister.

Brinkley looked completely relaxed as she laughed and shook hands with each person in their group before introducing Lila and Georgia, as well. She was right. She could handle herself.

But it wasn't her that I was worried about.

I continued playing darts, my gaze moving over to their table every few minutes. Breen's group had pulled up a table beside them, and they were ordering shots and beers and having a good time.

We took a break and walked over to get some food. I stood beside Brinkley. Her hand found mine beneath the table, and she smiled up at me as if to say, *I was right. You were worried for nothing.*

"Well, if it isn't the fucking GOAT of the NFL. Lincoln fucking Hendrix, I didn't know you were still in town."

"I'm sure you're more than aware that I'm writing a story about Lincoln. It's public knowledge, and it would be hard to miss for anyone in the sports world," Brinkley said with a laugh, raising a brow as if she were challenging him.

"Isn't that coming out soon? I just figured that was long over. Can't imagine there's a whole lot to ask this guy. Seems like all he does is play football and fuck women." His words were slurred.

My shoulders stiffened. "You don't know shit about me. But you sure do seem to care, don't you?"

"I just don't get the hype. You're not all that great. You just steal all the thunder from every other athlete in the city." He tipped his head back and slammed another shot.

"Dude. He's called the GOAT because his stats are fucking incredible," one of the guys said before turning to me and extending his arm. "I'm Elliott Franks. I just signed with the Lions, and I'm a huge fan."

"Thank you. Nice to meet you." I glanced over at Breen, who was chugging his beer now and pouting. "I'm not even living in San Francisco anymore. The glory is all yours, brother. I'm sure you're more than aware that I'm moving on."

"Yeah, man. Did they kick your old ass to the curb?" His words were barely legible, and I glanced over to see Hugh, Cage, Maddox, and Wyle all squaring their shoulders like they were ready to teach this guy a lesson. My gaze locked with each one of them, and I held up a hand. I wasn't going to make a scene. He was an asshole, no doubt about it, but my girl was on a roll with her new career, and I wouldn't do anything to ruin that.

Breen was older than me, so I had no idea why he was calling out my age. The guys that were with him did not look impressed, but the girls were giggling and hanging all over him.

"Sure. Something like that, buddy." I reached for my beer and took a sip. Brinkley looked at me, and her lips turned up in the corners. She knew he was egging me on, and I was doing whatever I could not to react.

"You still pissed that your woman came to my bed while she was with you? She couldn't wait to fuck me when you failed to please her. Did you put that in your article, Brinks?" he said with a boisterous laugh. "Because I fucked your ex real good for you."

"Dude," Elliott said, looking appalled. "That was out of fucking line."

Hugh made a grunting noise beside me like he was dying to lay the guy out. Maddox, Wyle, and Cage were looking at me with pleading eyes, begging to give the go-ahead to throw down.

"I can assure you that he knows how to please a woman," Brinkley said, startling everyone when she spoke.

"I guess you didn't interview his ex then, did you?" Breen laughed, but no one was chuckling now. He'd gone low, just like he always did. I didn't join in this time, as much as it killed me to just let him insult me. I was taking the high road —for my woman.

"You know, you keep bringing her up, but I don't see her here with you. So, it must not have been all that good with you two, huh?" Brinkley winked, and Breen's brows cinched like he couldn't figure out if she was playing or being serious.

"Well, it obviously wasn't good with them either." He looked like a petulant child, too drunk to talk his way out of his own mess.

"You know, I checked my sources pretty well and learned that Lincoln ended their relationship long before he knew you two had been sneaking around. But that's not really on him; that's on you and her, right?"

"And that's your big source for knowing the asshole can please a woman?" His laugh was loud and sloppy, and everyone around appeared to cringe a bit.

"No. My source is *me*. I've tested the goods, and I keep coming back for more," she purred before pushing to her feet and tugging my mouth down to hers. She kissed me like she wanted the whole world to know that I was hers.

And I fucking loved that she was done hiding it.

"Fuck me," Breen groaned under his breath, but we all heard him, and Brinkley pulled back to look at him.

"No, thank you. I'm a one-man-only kind of girl. And I'm keeping this one for as long as he'll have me."

Georgia and Lila both howled, and Cage shook his head with disgust, yet the dude couldn't wipe the smile off his face.

Hugh let Breen and his group know they were cut off, as the bar would be closing soon, and he wanted them out of there.

"Damn. Take care, Brinks." The asshole paused, and I squared my shoulders in warning. If he so much as touched her, I'd knock his head off his shoulders. He held his hands up. "I'm just giving you shit, Hendrix."

I nodded, happy to see his ass leave the bar. He held a hand up and stumbled out of the place with his entourage in tow.

"That was badass, baby," I whispered against her ear.

"I told you I can handle myself. I just needed you to trust me." She turned in my arms and pushed up on her tiptoes to kiss me.

Trust didn't come easy for me.

But I trusted this woman with everything I had.

twenty-seven

. . .

Brinkley

IT WAS a beautiful day for a wedding.

I couldn't believe it was finally here. I'd spent the last week finishing my article about Lincoln, and I'd never been so proud of anything that I'd written.

Maybe it was because I was madly in love with my client.

Maybe it was because he had such an interesting life.

Maybe it was because his stats were off-the-charts impressive.

I wasn't sure why this one felt so different. It was the article that was going to breathe new life into my career.

I was proud of the work we'd done together. Of the story he'd allowed me to tell.

Hell, maybe I was just emotional because the first Reynolds sibling was getting married today.

I was in the primary bathroom with all the girls, getting our hair and makeup done. We were at Georgia and Maddox's house, where the ceremony was taking place in the next hour. The guys were all gathered in Maddox's man cave, most likely having drinks and giving Hugh a pep talk. Lincoln was in there with them, as they'd all grown close.

Georgia and I were both bridesmaids. The maid of honor

was Lila's best friend, Del. Her mother was currently dating Lila's father, and the two were gushing about how cute their parents were together.

"Well, you two always wanted to be sisters. I didn't think it was possible, but at this point, who knows?" Sloane said with a laugh as she wrapped her hair around the barrel of the curling iron. She was a bridesmaid along with Rina, as the four of them had always been thick as thieves since they were kids.

"I think Tate and Bernadette make the cutest couple." Shay held her hands to her chest. She was married to Travis, Lila's brother, and she was also a bridesmaid.

"I'm guessing there's a lot of sex going on with them since they've both been single for so long," Sloane added.

"Ewwww," we all said in unison.

"Why do you always have to take it there?" Delilah rolled her eyes.

"Someone's got to take it to dirty town. You can count on me."

My mother helped Lila attach her veil to her long, dark waves that ran down her back. She looked so stunning that a huge lump formed in my throat.

"I wanted to give you these earrings that were my mother's," Mom said as she handed Lila the pair of pearl earrings. "This is your something old, sweetheart."

I glanced over to see Georgia smiling as two tears streamed down her face. Lila was like a sister to both of us, and Lila and my mom had a very close relationship.

"Thank you," Lila said as she fanned her face with both hands, trying hard not to cry.

"Don't you dare cry," Sloane said as she swiped at her own tears. "I just did your makeup perfectly."

We all wore strapless light pink gowns that ran down to the floor, aside from little Gracie, who wore an adorable white dress, and her hair fell down her back in dark spiral curls.

Everyone was sniffling when a knock came at the door. Georgia hurried to open it, just as all my cousins came flooding in. Some with babies in their arms and toddlers at their sides.

"Hey, happy wedding day," Dylan said as she sauntered in first. She was wearing a floral maxi dress, and her gorgeous hair was pulled back in a long ponytail. My eyes couldn't help but move to the small bulge in her stomach.

She turned to hug me as Lila pushed to her feet to greet each one of them. When Dylan pulled back, she smirked. "Yes. My hot husband put a baby in me. I was waiting to tell you when we were all together."

Georgia squealed, and my mom hurried over to hug Dylan.

"I thought you were waiting?" I asked.

"We were. But we've traveled so much this last year, and I don't know. We like being home. We finished the house we were building in Honey Mountain. And the thought of a little Wolf running around was suddenly all I could think of."

"I'm so happy for you."

"Thank you. We're really excited. Wolf's still pouting that it happened so quickly. He was looking forward to months of practice." She waggled her brows before turning to hug Lila. She gushed over the gorgeous princess-cut wedding dress with tulle for days.

I hugged Everly and bent down to give a squeeze to her adorable little toddler, Jackson. Her little girl, Emerson, was a perfect mix of both Everly and Hawk.

Ashlan's girls, Hadley and Paisley, were both wearing beautiful matching sundresses, with their hair tied up in little buns. They were holding on to their mother's hands and whispering about something.

"What's going on?" I whispered back. Both girls looked up at their mama with big smiles.

"Well, I'm going to say it if she won't." Dylan shrugged,

and Ashlan gave her the slightest nod. "This one got knocked up, too. We've been waiting to tell you today, but we were supposed to wait until after the wedding."

"Are you kidding? Hugh and I love babies, and we're both thrilled to hear you guys are growing your families. That's what today is all about, right? Family and love and all being together."

"Damn it, Lila Mae James. I mean Lila Mae Reynolds," Delilah said as she swiped at her face. "Why do you always have to make everything so sweet? Sloane, you need to fix my makeup."

"All right. Are there any more baby announcements before I clean up this mess?" Sloane said with her hands on her hips.

Charlotte chuckled. "Nothing to report over here. The twins keep me plenty busy." She glanced at the stroller with her two sleeping little angels.

"Hey, if I got lucky enough to have one of each on my first try, I think I'd be done," Sloane said before turning her attention back to her makeup sprawled on the counter.

"Um." Vivian winced. "I haven't even told my sisters yet because we literally found out yesterday. But baby number three is officially on board. I knew something was up when I was craving all those cupcakes these last few weeks."

There was lots of squealing and laughing and hugging going on.

"What in the world are they putting in that Honey Mountain water?" I teased, and we took turns hugging one another all over again.

It was exactly how it should be today.

The love in this room was impossible to miss.

Vivian, Dylan, Ashlan, Everly, and Charlotte all grabbed the little ones and made their way out the door. They wanted to go see Hugh before they found their seats.

We finished getting ready, and Lila stood up when her father knocked on the door.

Delilah shook out Lila's long train, and we got emotional at the sight of her.

"It's time," Sabrina, the wedding planner, said. "Let's get you all lined up."

Georgia and I kissed Lila's cheek as my mom whispered something in her ear and hugged her one last time. The three of us headed out first to go find Hugh.

Lincoln and Wyle were just walking outside to take their seats when he saw me. He tugged me close and kissed me. "You look fucking stunning."

"You look pretty good yourself, handsome."

He held on to my fingers before pulling away and winking. I watched him walk off in his black suit beside Maddox's brother.

I had a vision of this being me and Lincoln someday.

I'd never been the girl that sat around dreaming about my wedding day. I was always so focused on volleyball and school and then on my career. But lately, I thought about it.

This was the first man that I ever saw myself with long-term.

I wanted things I'd never wanted before.

And it was making it difficult to choose where I wanted to accept my next position. *Football Live* had interviewed me remotely, and they'd offered me a great job. I'd be focusing primarily on football if I signed with them, and they'd come with a very impressive package.

But now, Audrey from *Stride Forward* was also in the mix, and I'd had such an amazing experience working for her when I was in college.

Sports Today was the holy grail in the world of sports. I'd dreamed of working for them someday and never thought in a million years that it would happen this quickly. They were having me come to the city next week for an interview. It was the place every sports journalist wanted to work. I wasn't as certain about the package, as the man I'd been in touch with was very focused on the story I'd written about Lincoln, but he insisted it would be wrapped in a full-time offer.

Well, I'd know soon enough where I'd be living for the next few years.

I turned my attention to my brother as he and all the guys walked out.

Hugh looked so handsome in his black tuxedo, his long hair wavy and resting on his shoulders, just like it always did. Lila wasn't the type of bride to demand he cut it off for the wedding or pull it back in an elastic band. She loved my brother exactly as he was, and he loved her just as fiercely in return.

Cage was Hugh's best man, and then Finn, Lila's brother Travis, Brax, Dylan's husband Wolf, and Maddox were his groomsmen.

Hugh walked over to me and Georgia as Wolf strode beside him. We took turns hugging and turned our attention back to our brother. "You both look gorgeous. Did you see the girls? We've got more babies coming into the family."

"Yes. We're so excited," I said, squeezing Wolf's hand.

"Congrats." Georgia beamed.

"Thank you. I couldn't be happier." Wolf nodded.

"Did Dylan tell you what they're naming the baby?"

"No," we both said at the same time, looking from our brother to Wolf.

Hugh reached into his tuxedo pocket and pulled out a onesie. "They gave me an early wedding gift."

He held it up, and it read: *I'm named after my Uncle Hugh!*

"Oh my gosh. Two Hughs, huh?" Georgia clapped her hands together. "That's amazing."

"He's a pretty cool dude to be named after," Wolf said with a nod. "And Dylan said she liked the idea of having a Wolf and a Bear in the house."

We all shared a laugh.

"Pretty special," Hugh said, and he used the back of his knuckle to dab his eye as if something were in it. But we knew better than that.

"That's an honor. Your name lives on." I pushed up to kiss his cheek. "Happy wedding day, brother."

"Thank you. And thanks for standing up beside Lila. She loves you both like you're her own sisters."

"We feel the same," I said, with no hesitation.

"Okay, Mama. I'm going to walk you down to sit with Dad." Hugh wrapped his arms around our mother before offering his arm for her to hold on to, and he led her out the door to where everyone was seated.

There were rows of chairs with a walkway between them. The views of the water were breathtaking, and a gorgeous arch wrapped in pink and white flowers with greenery threaded all around it sat at the end of the aisle.

Once Hugh returned, he nodded at their wedding planner.

"All right. Let's do this," Sabrina said as the violinist started to play.

One by one, we each walked down the aisle.

Georgia and Maddox.

Me and Brax.

Rina and Wolf.

Shay and Travis.

Sloane and Finn.

Delilah and Cage.

Gracie made her way down the aisle, dropping flower petals along the way and looking like a little princess. She took her seat beside my parents, and my mom pulled her onto her lap.

Every time I looked over at Hugh, he'd smile at me, and I was unable to hold back the tears. My brother was one of my best friends, and seeing him find his happily ever after did something to me. He was the first of the five of us to get married, and he'd found his forever in Lila.

They were made for one another.

I searched the crowd and found Lincoln and Wyle sitting with my cousins. And Lincoln's gaze locked with mine.

Just like it always did.

The wedding song began to play, and I pulled my gaze from him as Lila made her way down the aisle. She looked like a princess, with her dress swooshing around her.

The sun was just going down behind the clouds, and the sky was a mix of yellow and orange. A slight breeze moved around us, and it was a perfect evening for an outdoor wedding. I glanced over at the ocean in the distance. The cove was a special place for all of us.

My attention returned to the gorgeous woman making her way toward my brother.

Hugh moved to stand in front of her as he shook hands with Tate James, Lila's father, and smiled down at Lila. Tears were streaming down her face, and he used his thumbs to swipe them away.

"They're happy tears, Bear," she croaked.

"I know, baby."

They moved to stand in front of Father Davis, who was marrying them today. They said their vows, and Ever and Hawk's son, Jackson, waddled down the aisle with a pillow holding the rings.

They were pronounced husband and wife, and everyone cheered.

My gaze found Lincoln's once again, and in that moment, I knew that this man was not only my right now... he was my forever.

twenty-eight

. . .

Lincoln

I COULDN'T BELIEVE it was almost time to head to New York for official training camp. I had a realtor looking for homes not too far from our training facility, and my mother had already found a house not far from the city, and she'd be making the move next month.

I'd worked my ass off as far as my workouts had gone this summer, and I was definitely in the best shape of my life. I was ready to make this change and play for the Thunderbirds. There was only one thing that wasn't clear, and that was what would happen with me and Brinkley and where we'd live. She didn't know where she was going to be, and I was determined to show her that it really didn't matter.

Our addresses had very little to do with our relationship, in my mind.

So, I'd taken her away for a few days before our worlds were completely turned upside down.

We'd left for Cabo San Lucas, Mexico, last night, and I'd just woken up and stepped outside onto our private patio. I knew she was exhausted, and a few days away would be a good way to unplug and relax a little bit before life got crazy again.

I took in the ocean and breathed in the salty air.

"Hey," she said as she opened the sliding glass door and stepped outside. "How long have you been awake?"

I was stretched out on a lounge chair, and I opened my arms so she could slip in right between my legs, and I wrapped my arms around her.

"About an hour. I wanted to let you catch up on sleep."

"Well, I slept really well. This place is gorgeous. I can't believe we have our own villa. You're full of surprises, Captain." She chuckled.

The waves crashed against the shore, and I kissed the top of her head. "I think we could both use a little downtime. It's hard to unplug when you're at home."

"That's very true. And we have a lot going on between the two of us."

"We do. That's what I wanted to talk to you about." I stroked her hair, and she turned a bit, resting her chest on mine so she could look at me.

"Ahhh… the talk. I know we've been putting that off."

"We've agreed that we'll stay together and figure things out. But I want to talk about some options."

"Okay." She smiled, tucking her dark hair behind her ear. "Let me hear these options."

"I've shown you some of the places my realtor sent over, but I'd like you to be more involved in the process."

"But we don't know where I'll be based."

"Regardless of where we live, we want to be together, right?"

"Yes. Absolutely."

"Good. If we were going to be living in the same place, which we very well might be—I'd ask you to live with me. So, I'd like you to help pick the home that we live in."

Her eyes widened. "You want to live together?"

"Fuck yeah, I do. We already do. We spend every night

together. Every day together, and I was fucking miserable being away from you when I took Lionel to meet Coach Hardin. I mean, I'm glad the kid is going to be playing there, but I didn't like being away from you."

Her teeth sank into her plump bottom lip. "I didn't like it either. But that was really sweet of you. And you're giving him this amazing opportunity with the scholarship you gave him."

Coach Hardin couldn't offer Lionel any money this year, but he agreed to have him walk on to the team, which would fulfill this kid's dream. But I didn't want him to start his life off buried in debt with student loans, so I'd agreed to cover his school and living expenses as long as he was working hard and attending classes.

"Yeah. Everyone needs a break sometimes. Lionel's a really good kid."

"He is. And you're a really good guy, Lincoln Hendrix."

"So, does that mean you'll move in with me?"

"Of course, I want to live with you. But what if *Sports Today* or *Football Live* offer me a job that I can't turn down?"

"Then we'll have a place in San Francisco and a place in New York. But it'll be together."

"Okay. I like the sound of that. It'll be hard living on opposite coasts, but we'll make it work. And if one of them do hire me, I can work there for a year and prove myself, and then hopefully, they'll let me work remotely after that."

"It'll all work out, sweetheart." My thumb traced over her bottom lip. "I'm hoping to play out the rest of my career in New York. I'm not big on change, and we've got a really strong team and a great coaching staff. But you just never know, so we'll do whatever it takes, right?"

"I'm all in." Her teeth sank into her bottom lip.

"Yeah? Did seeing your brother get married give you any thoughts about your own wedding?"

"It's funny, I never used to think about that. I'd never been in a relationship where I saw things going that way. But I'm not going to lie, it's different with you."

"How so?" I asked as I pulled her up farther so her mouth was right in front of mine.

"I think about it. I think about our future. How about you?"

"I never thought I'd want to be married. Never thought I'd have children. I was serious when I told my mother that she'd probably never have more than a bunch of footballs from me. But little Gracie has me wanting to put a whole lot of babies in you."

Her head fell back in laughter. "She's the cutest little girl on the planet. I kind of always imagined I'd be a great aunt and that would be it. But I think about babies now. I mean, not *right* now. We both have things we want to accomplish first. But I see them in our future."

"A fucking little girl with your dark eyes and hair. She'll own me, just like you do."

"Oh, I own you, do I?" She chuckled.

"You own this, Brinkley Reynolds." I pressed her hand to my heart.

"And you own mine."

"So, no getting scared and running, okay? We both know it's going to be a bumpy couple of weeks while we figure all of this out. But we want the same things in the future, and we'll work hard to get there."

She nodded. "I'm in."

I kissed her hard before pulling away. "Okay, let's eat and then go for a swim."

"I thought we weren't working out for the next three days. Isn't this supposed to be a vacation?" she asked, raising a brow.

"Well, fucking you in the turquoise water feels like a vacation to me."

"I like the way you think." She jumped up and hurried into the room.

We ordered room service and sat outside, looking at the photos of new home listings my realtor sent over while we ate pancakes and bacon.

There were two homes that we both really liked from the photos online, and we agreed to go see them after Brinkley's interview in San Francisco.

Things were coming together.

We had a plan.

I pulled on my swim trunks just as my girl came around the corner wearing a white bikini and a white cowboy hat on her head. Her tan skin glistened, and I wanted to kiss every inch of her gorgeous body.

We walked down the few steps to the private beach beside our villa. Brinkley dipped her toe in the water. "Oh, it's a little chilly."

I picked her up and flipped her over my shoulder because I was not waiting one more minute. She squealed and tossed her hat onto the shore as I ran us out to deeper water, dunking us both beneath the surface.

When we came up, my hands were on her waist, and she was laughing and swiping at her eyes before pushing her long hair away from her face.

"I guess that's one way to get used to the water." She gripped my shoulders and wrapped her legs around my waist.

"You're so fucking beautiful," I said as I nipped at her mouth. "Fuck. I didn't bring a condom. I had big plans of what I was going to do to you out here."

She smiled as she ground up against my erection. "I told you that I went on the pill. I've never been with anyone without a condom before. You'd be my first."

"I haven't either." I ran my tongue down her neck, and her head fell back. "I'd love to feel you with nothing between us."

"Me, too," she whispered, her hands in my hair as she pulled my mouth to hers.

I was standing chest-deep in the dark turquoise sea, the sun shining down on us, and this gorgeous woman wrapped in my arms.

Our tongues tangled, and I moaned into her mouth as she continued grinding up against me. My cock swelled, and we continued making out for what felt like hours but was probably more like minutes. My hand moved between us, pushing her swimsuit bottoms to the side and stroking her a few times before shoving my trunks low enough to free my eager dick.

"Is this what you want, baby?" I purred into her mouth as I teased her with my tip.

"Yes." She pulled back to look at me as I positioned her above me, and she slowly slid down, taking me in, inch by glorious fucking inch.

"Holy fuck," I hissed. She was wet and tight and everything I'd ever wanted.

Her hooded eyes closed, her head fell back, and she took me all the way in. Her breaths were labored, and I gripped her hips and moved her up slowly at first.

We found our rhythm, and I pumped in and out of her as she rode me like a fucking stallion.

I tangled my hands in her hair, tugging her mouth back down to mine, and kissed her hard.

Desire built.

Faster.

Harder.

With a need I'd only ever experienced with this woman.

My woman.

My hand moved between us, and I circled her clit because I knew she was close. Her nails dug into my shoulders, and she tightened around me, and I couldn't hold on another second. She shattered right before my eyes, and I went right over the edge with her.

My entire body quaked as a guttural sound escaped my lips.

She rode out every last bit of pleasure, and I continued thrusting into her.

When our breaths slowed and her gaze found mine, she smiled. "That was amazing."

"You're fucking amazing."

She chuckled. "Let's do that again soon."

"Any time, sweetheart."

———

Cabo had been exactly what we needed, but now we were back to reality, and the pressure was getting to both of us. This looming timeline that I'd be leaving in a few days, and so much was still up in the air with her. She'd flown out to interview with *NFL Today*, and she really liked them; however, she didn't want to be pigeonholed to only one sport. But she was keeping them on the back burner.

"So, you're going to be in New York. That's so far away," Tia said as Brinkley and I shared a FaceTime screen with her. We'd made a day trip to meet her in person when we got back from Cabo, and she liked to FaceTime often, so we'd been talking daily ever since.

"Yeah, but you'll come to a game, and we'll keep talking as much as we can, okay?"

I spoke to Romeo often now, too, and the two of them had become family in a matter of a few weeks.

"That sounds like a plan. Brinkley, you've got your big interview coming up, right?"

"Yep. And Lincoln is coming with me, so that will make it less stressful for me, having him there."

"He gets to go into the interview with you?" she asked.

"He does." Brinkley chuckled. "I have that story I wrote about him, and they want to print it, as well as offer me a long-term position. But I think with the story being about Lincoln, they requested that he be there, too."

I had red flags going off that they'd asked me to come along. It was not the norm, and as far as I knew, they didn't know we were a couple. The one thing Breen fucking Lockhart hadn't done was expose our relationship, which I was grateful for. Not because I didn't want it out there, but because I wouldn't want to do anything to hurt her career. So, in my opinion, it was odd that they'd asked her to bring me along to the interview. Brinkley had a one-track mind, and *Sports Today* was what she considered the gold standard of her profession, and she wanted it. She wasn't going to question anything they asked of her, but I sure as fuck would.

"I know you want to work there, but I think it will be hard for you guys to live so far apart," Tia said as she tucked her hair behind her ear.

"We'll do whatever we need to do," Brinkley said.

"Oh, man, you guys are so freaking cute. Well, big news. I broke up with Leo. He never makes time for me."

I raised a brow. Teenage dating advice was not really my strong suit, and it was the last thing I wanted to talk about.

"How's the weather?" I asked, and they both laughed.

"We'll talk about Leo later, when it's just us," my girlfriend said. I loved that she'd made such an effort to get to know Romeo and Tia. It meant a lot to me.

"Perfect. Call me later." She blew us a kiss and ended the call.

"She reminds me so much of myself at that age," Brinkley said.

"Damn, baby. I would have been all over you when I was a horny teenage boy."

She moved toward me, standing between my legs as I sat at the kitchen table. "And now you're just a horny man, huh?"

I laughed. "Only for you."
And that was the damn truth.

twenty-nine

. . .

Brinkley

"I NEED THIS TO GO WELL," I whispered as we rode the elevator up to the top floor. We'd stayed at Lincoln's penthouse apartment in the city last night. He said he wasn't going to put it on the market until we knew where I'd be living. If I took the job here, I'd stay at his place, and we'd travel back and forth.

"You have nothing to worry about. You have a story they want. A writing style that they've already said they were impressed by. You already have a great offer from *Football Live*, and you have another interview coming up. The ball is in your court. You don't need them, baby. They'd be lucky to have you."

"I know, but I want this one. I've dreamed of working here since I was a teenager."

He nodded. "Just hear them out, and don't settle for less than you deserve."

"You'd like them to make me a crappy offer, wouldn't you?" My voice was all tease, but I could tell it had rubbed him wrong.

"I want this for you, as long as it's right. I've told you that we'll make it work, no matter what happens."

"I was kidding. But obviously, it would be easier for you if I just came to New York with you." I shrugged. "I wish they were located out there."

"Whatever it is, you know that I support you."

"I know." I remained a few feet from him in the elevator. "We have to keep things professional right now, but I'll be kissing you real hard in an hour."

"Don't tease me, sweetheart." He raised a brow just as the doors opened, and he motioned for me to step off first.

I wore my favorite black pencil skirt, a white blouse, and a black suit coat. My hair was pulled into a neat chignon, and I'd changed shoes three times because I wanted everything to be perfect. I'd settled on nude stilettos. I wanted this so badly I could taste it.

I didn't know why they'd asked Lincoln to come. I didn't want to make it a big deal because he'd seemed uncomfortable when I'd told him. But I had written a story about him, and they wanted it. That was part of the deal. I'd never worked with a magazine of this caliber, so as far as I knew, this could be perfectly standard to bring a client along.

"You must be Brinkley Reynolds." The receptionist was in her mid-thirties, tall with blonde hair, and she had a friendly smile. Her eyes moved to the handsome man beside me. "And you're Lincoln Hendrix. I'm a huge fan."

I chuckled when Lincoln scowled before quickly forcing a smile. He didn't want the attention to be on himself today because he knew how much this day meant to me. The woman led us down a hallway and knocked on the door before we stepped into a large conference room.

There were three men in suits who came around the table and approached Lincoln first. They all shook his hand and stood there gaping at him. I sensed his discomfort immediately. I shook it off. They ran a sports magazine, and he was an icon on the field. It was fair that they were excited to meet him.

I wasn't going to let anything ruin this day.

"This is the star of the show, Brinkley Reynolds," he said, holding his hand out to me.

They shifted their attention my way and made introductions. Lou Colson was the president and the man I'd been negotiating with. Darrel Fisher was their chief legal, and Steve Monty was the managing editor. We settled around the big table with all three men on one side and Lincoln and me on another.

"The story you wrote was one of the best I've read in a very long time," Lou said, and my heart raced. He was a very powerful man in the industry, so a compliment from him was as good as it gets in my world.

"Thank you. That means so much to me," I said, trying to keep my tone even as the nerves were setting in.

You've got this. Shake it off.

Lincoln glanced at me, and I saw the pride there.

"And finally allowing fans to get to know a little more about you, Lincoln, is going to have the magazine selling off the racks." He turned his attention to my boyfriend. "Obviously, you know we want this story and any future stories that you're willing to let Ms. Reynolds write about you."

Future stories? We had never discussed any articles with Lincoln in the future.

Lincoln squared his shoulders. "This is the story. She'll be moving on to other athletes, I presume."

I could feel the tension radiating from him, and it was time to speak up. This was an interview, and I needed to sell myself.

"I wrote the article on Breen Lockhart that I forwarded to you, as well, and I'm open to any interviews that you would want to set up for me. I'm also open to getting out in the field and covering games and meeting athletes." I paused and sucked in a breath because I desperately wanted to prove that I could do this job. "I've wanted to work for this magazine for as long as I can remember. I'll do whatever it takes to be the best at my craft. I promise I won't let you down."

Lincoln's hand found my thigh beneath the table, and I knew he was trying to comfort me.

"That's great to hear, Bailey," Lou said. "We're interested in what Mr. Hendrix is willing to do beyond this current story that you've written. Maybe he'd agree to give you an exclusive interview once or twice a season?"

What the hell? Did he really just call me by the wrong name?

"Her name is Brinkley, not Bailey," Lincoln hissed, and I knew that he was pissed off with the direction this was going. I needed to turn this around.

"Right. Please forgive me," he said. "We'd be willing to buy whatever articles *Brinkley* writes about you moving forward, and we can look into a permanent position down the road."

Why were they only talking to him? This was my interview. My hands fisted on the table, digging my nails into my palms to remind myself to keep it together.

"I thought you were interviewing me for a full-time position today? That's what we spoke about on the phone and in our emails," I said, raising a brow as I looked Lou Colson right in the eyes.

"Correct. It's a conversation that we're starting, pending what Mr. Hendrix has planned regarding future articles with you."

"Come on, gentlemen, what exactly are we here for? Let's shoot it straight because, at this point, you've wasted her fucking time and mine."

"Lincoln," I said under my breath as I met his gaze. "I've got this."

Because we both knew what we were here for now.

They were using me to get to him.

They had no interest in me.

"So, what exactly is this? You just wanted to get Lincoln here?"

"She has a gift, no doubt about it. We're interested in offering her a future position pending what you can commit to. This story will put her on the map, and that's because it's about you." He directed his answer to my boyfriend, speaking as if I wasn't sitting right here. As if I hadn't just spoken.

My mind was spinning. This was a complete disaster.

You will not get pushed around by a bunch of pretentious pricks.

"Is there a job beyond interviewing Lincoln Hendrix?" That was the million-dollar question at this point.

"We'd like to focus on Lincoln for now."

"Fuck this. You're yanking her fucking chain, and it's a shitty thing to do." Lincoln pushed to his feet and turned to face me. "Come on. This isn't happening."

My blood was boiling because these men were assholes, but I could handle them. I didn't need my boyfriend to speak for me.

"I've got this." I gave him a hard look, but the truth was... I *didn't* have this. It had gone from bad to worse.

"No, sweetheart. There's nothing to work out here. They're using you to get to me. And I won't allow it." He offered me his hand, and I took it. My chest was pounding so hard I could hear my pulse in my ears.

"Mr. Hendrix, I assure you that we're interested in offering her a position down the road."

Lincoln didn't respond, and they made no attempt to speak to me.

I whipped around, feeling a lump form in my throat, but thankfully, my anger won out over the sadness threatening to erupt. I pointed my finger right at Lou Colson. "You should be ashamed of yourself. Calling me here when you had no interest in hiring me."

"That's not the case. Why don't we talk this over?" he said, but Lincoln and I were moving already.

He led me down the hallway to the elevator and ushered me inside. He hit the button to the lobby, and I just stared at him in disbelief.

How had this gone so wrong?

Lincoln moved closer, but I put my hands up.

"Don't," I said as I covered my mouth with my hand to hold back the sobs. The tears were so heavy that I blinked several times, desperate to keep it together. I didn't want him to comfort me right now. I couldn't think straight at the moment, and if he touched me, I'd fall apart. When the doors opened, I held my head high and walked through the lobby.

We made our way to the parking garage, not saying a word. He opened the passenger door, and I slipped inside.

We'd planned to stay in the city tonight, as he was flying out to New York in the morning. We were going to celebrate over dinner and come up with a plan.

I'd assumed I'd be thinking over the job offer and meeting with them again tomorrow to sign my contract.

Lou Colson had made it clear in our phone calls and emails that they would be offering me a contract to coincide with me allowing them to print the story about Lincoln.

This was supposed to be the day I'd dreamt about for years, but instead, it was a complete nightmare.

I was mortified and humiliated.

They had completely used me. They weren't interested in hiring me at all.

Lincoln pulled into the underground parking beneath his building. "Look at me."

I turned to face him. The tears had been falling since we'd gotten in the car, and I was sure my eyes were red and swollen by now. I wasn't big on falling apart, but the disappointment had set in, and there was no stopping it.

"Baby, don't let this get you down. They're a bunch of assholes."

Don't let this get me down?

I was well beyond being down.

It had been a complete disaster.

I used the back of my hand to swipe beneath my eyes. "That was a disaster. I wish you hadn't been there to see that."

"I'm fucking glad I was there. I wouldn't have wanted you to be there alone with those assholes."

"I can take care of myself, Lincoln," I said, tipping up my chin. "You didn't need to step in."

I didn't know how to handle all these emotions. The disappointment and the anger were at war with one another.

"I will always protect you."

"Well, I'm sure a part of you is relieved that this job is off the table. Less of a chance of me staying here." It wasn't a fair thing to say. I was just spewing venom at this point.

He reached beneath my chin. "I'm not going to lie. I'd be fucking happy to have you beside me. But I did not want today to go this way. I know how much you wanted this, and I wanted it for you. It fucking pisses me off that they pulled this shit with you."

"Well, it really pisses me off that I've worked really fucking hard, Lincoln." My voice trembled as I cried through my words. "I've tried to prove myself. And all they cared about today was you. That's how it's going to be, isn't it? I'll just be the reporter that wrote Lincoln Hendrix's story, and then when news breaks that we're dating, I'll just be your girlfriend."

We both knew there was a lot of truth in that statement.

People put athletes on pedestals. It was part of the reason that Lincoln had been so apprehensive to share his story. He liked keeping his life private.

"It's not how I'll ever see you."

I nodded because I knew that he meant it. "I know. And I know you can't help that you're famous and that you're amazing and the greatest of all time—but I need to shine, too. You get that, right? I need my own thing. I don't just want to be someone's girlfriend."

He looked at me like I'd just punched him in the gut. But the reality was setting in that once we went public with our relationship, my job would be greatly affected.

My profession. What I'd worked so hard for.

No one would take me seriously.

"Have I ever treated you like you were anything but amazing? I have been cheering you on since the minute we started working together. You have other offers, baby."

"Right. But do they only want me because they want that story?" I asked as I looked out the window. Was everyone just after the story?

"You are so fucking talented. You know it, and I know it. I will not let anyone dim your light. Do you hear me?" He didn't answer the question because he couldn't answer it.

I knew my worth.

Hell, I'd always known that I could do anything I set my mind to. But today had thrown me. I hadn't thought that they would have called me in just to get to him.

His gaze searched mine, and I knew that he saw it there.

The real question.

Would I ever shine on my own if we were together?

I'd never been that girl that worried about shining. Worried that someone would dim my light. I'd always been confident in my capabilities. But Lincoln's fame was bigger than anything I'd ever dealt with.

He pushed out of the car and opened my door. We made our way upstairs, neither of us speaking.

There wasn't much more to say.

The reality was setting in.

I didn't know what to do or how to handle all of this.

It was our first day out of the bubble. Our first real obstacle and it was already a shitstorm.

I walked into the bathroom and shut the door before turning on the faucet in the bathtub.

I needed space.

I tied my hair up and slipped into the water, letting myself cry all the tears until there was nothing left.

This day had been an eye-opener regarding my future.

For the first time in my adult life, I was doubting myself. Wondering if anyone was genuinely considering hiring me based on my writing skills.

How would Lincoln look at me if I didn't have anything of my own to be proud of? If my entire life was wrapped up solely around him.

That was not how relationships were supposed to work. There was supposed to be balance.

I may not be the GOAT of the NFL, but I was proud of the work that I did out in the field. Of the interviews that I'd conducted over the years and the way I could use my words to present people to the world in the best light.

But would anyone even consider that when they looked at me now? Once word got out that I was dating Lincoln Hendrix? Hell, Lou Colson didn't even know we were a couple. Just the fact that Lincoln had awarded me with the story of a lifetime had been the reason he'd shown any interest in me.

It was never about me or my writing ability.

They wanted Lincoln.

This was all new to me, and my head was spinning.

I knew if I stayed here right now that Lincoln would try to fix this for me.

But just like he needed time to figure out where he wanted to play all those months ago, I needed to figure out my future, too.

I dried off and got dressed, throwing my clothes into my bag and dragging my suitcase out.

Lincoln was just closing the front door, and he held up a bag of food from our favorite restaurant in the city.

But I wasn't in the mood to eat or to celebrate.

His gaze moved to my suitcase. "The first sign of trouble, and you're already running?"

"I'm not running, Lincoln. I'm going home. I need to think. I need to see how this works. I need to know where I fit."

"You fit right fucking here," he said, his hand pounding on his chest. "If you don't know that, then you don't know me the way that I thought you did."

I cleared my throat and tipped up my chin. "I know you. I know you'll just try to fix this and tell me everything will be fine. But I need to figure out my stuff, and I can't do that when I'm with you."

"Why the fuck not?"

"Because I love you. And I want to make you happy. But I need to make sure I don't smother myself in the process. Can you just give me this time?"

"It doesn't sound like I have a choice." He wrapped his arms around me. "But you don't need to leave. I fly out tomorrow. This is your home."

"I need to think, Lincoln. I do that best at home, sitting on the shore." I pushed up on my tiptoes and kissed his cheek.

It felt like goodbye.

But neither of us was willing to say those words.

thirty

· · ·

Lincoln

"THAT WAS AN IMPRESSIVE FIRST DAY, LINC," Coach Balboa said. "You're exactly what this team needs. I think we're going to take it the whole way this year."

"Yeah. It's a great group of guys. We're going to work well together."

"You're at the hotel for now, right? You going to check out a few houses this week?" he asked as we walked toward the locker room.

I nodded, but my gut was in knots today. I hadn't slept well the last two nights because I missed my girl something fierce. We'd barely spoken, but I'd called to check on her a few times. I was trying to respect her space, but it was fucking killing me.

"Yep. I have a few homes lined up to tour later in the week."

"When is Brinkley coming out?" he asked. He knew we were together, as did Brett and Lenny. Hell, they'd all seen it the first time they'd met her before we were even together. I think they probably knew before I did.

I scrubbed a hand down the back of my neck and let out a breath. "Not sure. She's going through some shit. You know,

274

dating me isn't easy, especially if you're trying to make a name for yourself as a sports journalist."

He came to a stop. "How so?"

"You don't need to waste your time on this shit. You've got a team to coach."

"Lincoln, you're a member of this team. That means we're family. Your problems are my problems. Tell me what's going on. I've been married for thirty-five years, and I have three daughters. I know a thing or two about women." I smiled. This was what I hadn't had on my last team. Balboa actually cared about his players, and we weren't just dollar signs to him.

"She had an interview with *Sports Today* the day before I flew out. They asked that she bring me along to the interview."

"It's not public knowledge that you're a couple yet, right? Why'd they want you there?"

"She wrote that story about me, and she's been shopping it around. Obviously, they want it. So, they were going to make her an offer for a full-time position, along with her agreeing to give them the story. But when we got there, they didn't do that. They basically just wanted me to agree to as many interviews as they wanted as leverage to give her a job. They treated her pretty shitty, and I got her the hell out of there."

"That's just fucking wrong. I'm guessing she doesn't want to give them the story or work there now."

"She was mad but also really disappointed. She'd really wanted it. Then she was questioning if a part of me was happy because it meant that was one less potential position that would keep her out west. And sure, I'd like her to be living here with me; I can't deny that. But I didn't want that shit to happen. And then you add in the element that now, she doesn't know if anyone will hire her for the right reasons, and she doesn't want to just be known as my girlfriend, or some shit like that. Hell, I get it. She was mad I jumped in, but I wasn't about to sit there any longer after the way they were treating her. I don't know." I scrubbed a hand down my face. "She wants some time to figure out where she fits into my world and how this will work."

He nodded. "I get that. It's a lot. Relationships are tough on their own, but bringing in the element of fame, and her wanting to find her own way with her career, complicates things. But the greatest advice I can give you is that this is not about you, Lincoln. She's trying to prove herself, and I'm guessing it's not easy to be in a relationship with someone who doesn't need to prove himself anymore. She's a strong woman. It sounds like she doesn't want to just exist in your world; she wants to create her own and share it with you. Hell, it's refreshing. Think about how many women out there want to be with you for the wrong reasons. You've found the one that isn't in it for the fame or for what you can do for her. She wants to make her own way. I fucking respect the hell out of that."

"I agree. But I don't know how to fix it."

"Well, I think she told you how to fix it. By giving her space to deal with it herself. You could try just listening to what she asked of you. Respecting her wishes."

"Fuck. Patience is not my strength. She's not calling much, just short little texts. I'm freaking the fuck out."

"Take it from a man who has lived with four women… you'll get better over time. She doesn't want you to interfere. She wants you to trust her to handle it. It's pretty simple, actually."

"And what if she goes to work for some asshole like Lou Colson? Am I just supposed to stand by and do nothing?"

"Absolutely. That's exactly what you do until she asks for your help. She's a strong woman. Do you really think she's going to put up with a guy like Lou for long? You've got to trust her, Linc. It won't work if you don't. She's fighting for that independence right now. Let her have it."

"Fuck. You make a good point." I shrugged. "I'll give her space. I'm going to catch a shower and head out."

"All right. Call me if you need anything. Good job today. I'll see you tomorrow."

I thought about what he'd said as I showered, and after I dried off and got dressed, I made my way back to the hotel.

My phone dinged with a text from my girl right when I got to my room.

Brinkley

I hope your first day of practice went well. I love you. Thanks for giving me time to think. <heart emoji>

There isn't anything I wouldn't do for you.

She didn't respond. I fucking hated this. I wanted her here, but Coach Balboa was right—this wasn't about me.

Patience wasn't my strong suit. I wanted this shit behind us.

But I'd put my head down and focus on what I could do right now, which was training hard for the new season.

And that was exactly what I did.

———

Three fucking long, painful days had passed.

I'd barely slept because now that I'd grown used to having her in my bed, I couldn't sleep without her.

So, I ran harder. Lifted more. Pushed out on the field like I was playing in the fucking Super Bowl every damn day.

"Jesus, dude. You're a fucking superhero. I need a break. Water. Maybe a goddamn banana. I can't go this hard in the heat without a breather," Brett said, as he clapped me on the shoulder.

"You don't win Super Bowls by taking breaks every five minutes," I hissed.

"Uh, I hate to be the one to tell you this, asshole, but we've been going hard for over five hours. And Brett's right. But I don't think you're a superhero. I think you're a grumpy dick," Lenny said.

"I've been called worse."

I've also been called better. A rude gentleman.

I'd spent most of my life not allowing myself to be vulnerable. Not getting attached to anyone outside of my mother.

I'd put my guard down with Brinkley, and I was paying for it now.

Because I missed her. I didn't know what to do with that. How to fix it. And I wasn't used to not being in control. Not being able to figure shit out.

Tia had lectured me last night when we'd FaceTimed about respecting Brinkley's space. Apparently, she talked to my girlfriend a lot more than I did right now. She'd gone on and on about how women need to have their own identity, and Romeo had popped in and rolled his eyes, which earned him an elbow to the side.

My texts with Brinkley were brief.

She basically just wanted to know that I was surviving training camp.

Hell, I was begging to be challenged physically right now, because that was the best way that I knew how to numb myself. Working so hard that I couldn't think about anything else.

But it wasn't fucking working.

"Sorry. Just want to have a good season."

"Bullshit, brother." Brett wrapped an arm around my shoulder and led us to the locker room. "It's about Brinkley, you pussy-whipped motherfucker."

"It's always about a girl." Lenny barked out a laugh. "Our boy has got it bad."

"Fuck you." I rolled my eyes.

"It's only been a few days. You need to chill. She'll come around." Lenny dropped his bag onto the bench, and I opened my locker.

I didn't know if she was going on more interviews or what was happening. She'd tell me when she was ready.

Her brothers and brother-in-law were texting me often, but they were tight-lipped about Brinkley. I'd tried to ask a few questions, and Cage had called me out and said they knew better than to speak for her.

I nodded. "I'm fine. You pussies just can't keep up with me. That's on you."

Brett barked out a laugh. "You want to go grab some beers tonight? Blow off some steam?"

"Maybe tomorrow. My mom moved into her new house yesterday, so I'm going to head over there and help her unpack for a few hours."

"I love Mama Hendrix. Tell her as soon as she's settled, I'll be expecting an invitation to come over for her famous chili," Brett said.

"Mama Hendrix is hot, just like her chili," Lenny sang out, and I reached for my towel and snapped him on the side. He howled, and everyone laughed.

"Do not call my mother hot," I grumped.

More laughter.

This was the team I was meant to play with.

We were going to do big things together, but I couldn't get excited about it just yet.

Because nothing worked when she wasn't here.

thirty-one

. . .

Brinkley

I'D ARRIVED in New York late last night. I hadn't told Lincoln that I was coming. I wanted to share everything with him after I took care of business.

I'd taken the bull by the horns after that dick weasel, Lou Colson, had called me back. The man had completely changed his tune. He'd basically offered me whatever I wanted but still continued to call me by the wrong name.

Bailey.

He'd just been desperate to get that story. But if he were the last man on this earth with the only sports magazine out there, I'd keep the story to myself.

Fool me once, shame on you.

Fool me twice… I will hold a grudge until the end of time.

Is that the saying?

Oh, right—fool me twice, shame on me.

That wasn't happening. No one would fool me twice.

These last few days had been exactly what I'd needed.

I'd figured out a few important things.

First off, I was an independent woman. And no one could take that away from me. Not the president of a big magazine who couldn't get my name right.

Not anyone.

I decide my worth.

My fate.

Who I am and what I will accomplish.

Secondly, if one door closes, another one always opens. Being let go from my job months ago was not as terrible as I'd originally thought. It was the best thing that had ever happened to me. And now, there were more doors waiting for me than I'd realized.

Thirdly, just because we want something, doesn't mean it's good for us. I mean, I spent years eating every sour gummy worm I could get my hands on. And what did that give me? Canker sores and belly aches.

Just because you want it, doesn't mean it's right.

Sports Today was not the place for me. They'd shown me who they were. They'd only called me back because they thought I was desperate enough to go work there after they'd treated me horribly. The reporter in me didn't even have to reach far to get him to talk. He'd offered me the job in exchange for the article, and he'd said I would only need to interview Lincoln once a season. The man really didn't get it. The first time I'd said no, he'd offered me a corner office and top billing.

Yet he still didn't know my name.

I didn't want what he was offering.

There were only two things that I wanted.

Lincoln Hendrix and a job that challenged me.

And I lived in a time where I could have both. I could work hard and take what I wanted in this world because I was worthy.

I'd never just be someone's girlfriend.

I knew it, and Lincoln knew it.

And damn, had I enjoyed telling Lou Colson to take his offer and *shove it where the sun don't shine.* He'd sputtered and panicked when I'd made it clear that he wouldn't be getting the story I'd written about Lincoln or any future interviews with him, either.

Because Lincoln Hendrix was my boyfriend, and sometimes, I was the boss.

I'd arrived at *Strive Forward* magazine a few minutes early. This time, I wasn't nervous. There was a peace that I'd found back home as I processed everything. After I'd sulked and let the rejection sink in and then realized it wasn't me being rejected. It was just some guy who wanted Lincoln's story. That had very little to do with me when I broke it all down.

I was damn good at my job, and I knew it.

So, the next job that came along could take me or leave me.

Because a job would not define me. A man would not define me.

I was my own woman. My career was a bonus. Something that would challenge and fulfill me.

And Lincoln—he owned my heart.

He made my life better. He loved me in a way I'd never known was even possible. And I loved him just as fiercely.

He didn't define me. He completed me.

I was going to be okay no matter what happened today.

I'd find the right company to work for eventually.

I didn't recognize the woman behind the counter, as it had been several years since I'd worked here.

"Ms. Reynolds, Audrey Andrews is ready to see you," the receptionist said.

"Thank you," I said as I followed her back to the conference room.

Audrey was waiting for me when the receptionist pushed open the door. There was a woman that stood beside her when my mentor pulled me into her arms.

"I'm so happy that you agreed to interview here. This is Marie Hardy, our chief legal."

The receptionist smiled before closing the door as I shook hands with the woman beside Audrey, and we all took our seats.

"It's a pleasure. I've heard a lot about you. We're thrilled that you agreed to come out here and that you're considering working with us," Marie said.

"Thank you for having me. I'm really excited about this opportunity."

Audrey passed out water bottles to each of us before taking the seat across from me.

We spent the next forty-five minutes with Audrey praising me and referencing every article I'd ever written. It felt good to be recognized for my work, and it didn't hurt that they both continually got my name right.

"I do want to put something out there right away, just in case you have an issue with it." I cleared my throat.

"Please. The floor is yours," Audrey said, her brows cinched as if she was anxious to hear what I had to say.

"The article that I've written about Lincoln Hendrix is not on the table as part of this negotiation. I've agreed to commission that story to *Football Live*, as they specifically cover football, and I feel it's the best place for it." I reached for my bottle of water and took a sip, waiting to hear if they were going to end the conversation here.

"You know that I read it after you submitted it to me. Obviously, I thought it was very well written. You've got a gift for getting the right information from the people you interview. There's no fluff. It's one of my favorite things about your work." Audrey smiled. "And I agree that *Football Live* is the best place for that particular piece. You know that we don't specifically cover one sport. We focus on athletes. Men *and* women. All sports are on the table."

I nodded. "It's what I liked most when I interned here. I want to be very upfront so that there are no secrets between us. I am also in a romantic relationship with Lincoln Hendrix. I won't be conducting any further interviews with him moving forward. We have a personal relationship, and I want to protect that. So, if that is an issue at all, there is nothing further to discuss."

They glanced at one another and smiled.

"I like your fire. And dating a professional athlete is not easy. Marie can vouch for that." She smirked.

"My husband is Mike Cabo," Marie said.

"The basketball player with the most points scored last season?"

"The one and only. I use my maiden name at the office, and I understand what it means to prioritize your relationship. I respect that more than you know."

"So, this just means that we now don't cover the GOAT of the NFL, nor the MVP of the basketball courts." Audrey chuckled. "Lucky for you both that I like human stories and so do our readers. We want to find the underdog who overcame a lot to make the team. The athlete who never gave up and found success in a sport where no one thought they would. Does that still appeal to you, Brinkley?"

"Very much so," I said.

"I was worried you wouldn't want to relocate out here, but seeing as Lincoln is living here, I think we actually may have a chance with you." She smiled.

We spent the next three and a half hours talking about our love of sports and the athletes that have inspired us. Audrey and I took turns trading stories about our favorite articles to date.

I knew I'd found my new workplace home when I left the office.

It felt right.

I'd met several of the people who worked there, a few that I'd known from years ago, and others that had joined the team since I'd left.

They made me a wonderful offer. I'd taken the contract with me to look it over and agreed to come back the following day to sign and make it official.

Audrey and Marie both hugged me goodbye, as they really didn't stand on ceremony here.

It was my kind of place.

I knew I'd thrive here, and that was exactly what I was looking for.

And it didn't hurt that it was based in the city where the man that I loved happened to live now.

I took the elevator downstairs and dropped to sit on the bench in the large lobby. I pulled up the family group chat and sent a message.

> It couldn't have gone better. They were amazing. It's exactly what I was looking for.

GEORGIA

I knew it! You just needed to find the right place, Brinks. Did you sign with them?

> I wanted to play a little hard to get. I said I'd bring it back tomorrow.

HUGH

Atta girl. Kicking butt and taking names. Proud of you. Have you told Lincoln yet?

> He's my next stop. I want to tell him in person.

CAGE

Fix things with him. The season starts soon.

CAGE

Oh, congrats on the job. I knew you'd find the right place.

Laura Pavlov

> Did you just ask me to fix things before the
> season starts BEFORE you congratulated
> me? <middle finger emoji>

CAGE

I'm sorry. I've got real issues over here. Mr.
Wigglestein has knocked up another bitch in
Cottonwood Cove, and everyone is up in
arms over here. I'm hiding in my office and
taking a breather.

GEORGIA

Damn. Mr. Wigglestein pulls the ladies!

FINN

Have you seen him? The dude's balls hang
down to the ground.

HUGH

Cage's balls? What did I miss?

I laughed as I called my Uber.

GEORGIA

OMG! We are talking about Mr. Wigglestein's
balls.

HUGH

What is your obsession with this dog's
genitalia?

CAGE

That is not what we're talking about. That
was all Finn. The dude has a premiere next
week, and he's talking about a dog's balls!

FINN

Keeping it humble, brother.

> The world is going to go crazy for you, Finny.
> Life will never be the same.

FINN

Was that supposed to make me feel good?

Keeping it real while I wait for my Uber.

GEORGIA

Maddox is on the same page as Cage. He wants you to fix things with Lincoln, and he said to tell you that he refuses to take sides this time. Apparently, he gave his heart to me, but he gave a little bit of it to Lincoln.

HUGH

Lincoln has a big piece of my heart, too. I'm not going to lie.

CAGE

He's much nicer to me than you are, Brinks.

Hey! I never said anyone had to pick sides this time. We didn't break up. I just needed to figure out my life.

FINN

Good. I got us BFF bracelets to wear to my premiere.

CAGE

I just vomited in my mouth.

FINN

Because you were looking at Mr. Wigglestein's oversized testicles?

CAGE

No. Because you are a suck-up.

My Uber is here. I'll text you jackasses later.

CAGE

Make things right. We need him to put a ring on it and seal the deal.

GEORGIA

Go get your man, Brinks!

I chuckled and tucked my phone into my purse before sliding into the Uber. The drive to the swanky hotel was quick, and I knew Lincoln would be out of practice by now, and I wanted to surprise him.

Otherwise, I'd be sitting out in the hallway, waiting for him until he returned.

"Thank you," I said to the driver as I hopped out of the car after he pulled beside the curb. Butterflies fluttered in my belly.

I'd barely slept, barely eaten, and barely functioned during our time apart. I'd thought about what I wanted in life, and it always came back to him.

After I'd allowed myself some time to sulk about my dream job being an enormous joke, everything became clear.

I'm my own person. I didn't need to fear being overshadowed by my boyfriend's fame, because only I could allow that to happen.

And I wasn't that girl.

Not now. Not ever.

I was confident in who I was, and I wouldn't allow my insecurities to get in the way of my happiness.

And he'd given me the time that I needed.

But now that I was here, I had no patience. I wanted to be with him right now.

I hurried to the front desk, admiring how nice the place was. There were crystal chandeliers hanging above. Black velvet couches with white floral arrangements were placed around the impressive lobby.

My hotel, where I'd left all my stuff this morning, was a few blocks away and not nearly as decadent as this place.

"Hello," a woman greeted me. Her black hair was pulled back in a tight bun, and her red lips were perfectly lined.

"Hi. I'm Mrs. Jack Sparrow, and I'm here to check in. My

husband arrived a few days ago," I said, remembering that he'd booked the room under Mr. and Mrs. Jack Sparrow.

She raised a brow. "Do you have an ID?"

I went to pull out my driver's license and realized it wouldn't have the correct name on it. "I actually don't have it with me."

"Let me call up to the room," she said.

"No!" I yelled, not meaning to say it quite as loud as it came out. The woman startled.

"Excuse me?"

"Sorry. I'm surprising my husband."

"Okay." She raised a brow. "Do you have a credit card or any sort of identification with your name on it, *Mrs. Jack Sparrow?*"

The way she said my name sounded very snarky, and I did not appreciate it.

"Let me ask you something," I said, pausing to read her name tag. And wouldn't you know, it was the name that Lou had called me one too many times. "*Bailey.*"

"Yes, Mrs. Sparrow?"

"Did you ask *Mr. Jack Sparrow* for his identification?"

"Well, I wasn't working when he checked in. But I'm sure someone did. It's hotel policy."

"I actually doubt that. And let me tell you what my problem is with this situation," I said, flailing my hands around. "Haven't women been held to a different set of rules than men for long enough? Come on. Let's join forces and agree to say: No more! Power of the woman, Bailey!" I shouted.

"Ma'am, I wouldn't care if you were a man, a woman, or a turtle. If you want to check in to this hotel, you need to have identification."

"Fine. Call the room. But just be aware that you have failed not only me but all women far and wide." I raised a brow as I sulked at the counter.

"I can live with that."

Damn. This was not going as planned.

But I didn't even care.

I just wanted to see him.

And I didn't want to wait another minute.

thirty-two

· · ·

Lincoln

I STROLLED into the hotel after going to grab a late lunch down the street with the guys, and the finest ass I'd ever laid eyes on beckoned me from the front desk.

A pull so strong that my head whipped in her direction.

I'd know that perfect peach-shaped backside anywhere.

I'd also recognize that voice, which was currently expressing her displeasure with the woman standing in front of her. She was yelling about women being held to different standards and going on and on about the injustice in the world.

The corners of my lips turned up.

"Mr. Jack Sparrow is going to be furious that you wouldn't give me a room key," Brinkley hissed.

"She's correct about that. Mrs. Jack Sparrow is listed on my room reservation." I stepped up behind Brinkley and wrapped my arms around her. My chin rested on her shoulder as I breathed her in.

Lavender and honey.

I nipped at her earlobe.

"I'm so sorry about that, Mr. Sparrow. I'll give her a key now."

"Hey. Aren't you going to ask for his identification?" Brinkley asked as she turned around to face me, wrapping her arms around my neck with a wicked grin on her face.

"I, um, oh my gosh. You are…" the front desk lady sputtered as recognition set in, and she whispered. "Lincoln Hendrix."

I reached into my back pocket and pulled out my wallet, handing her my fake ID. "Captain Jack Sparrow, ma'am."

Brinkley gaped, and I handed her the other ID. She looked down at it.

"Sweetheart Sparrow?" she said over a fit of laughter.

"You left before I was able to give it to you." I winked as the woman behind the front desk handed me back my ID, along with the room key for Brinkley.

"I'm sorry about all that," she said, winking at my girl. "Power of the woman, Mrs. Sparrow."

"That's Sweetheart to you, Bailey." Brinkley chuckled, and I intertwined my fingers with hers and led her down a hallway a few feet away.

I pressed her up against the wall. "I missed you, Mrs. Sparrow."

"I missed you, too."

My hand found the side of her neck, my thumb tracing along her jaw. "You here to stay this time?"

"I am." A tear ran down her cheek. "I'm sorry for leaving. I just needed some time to figure everything out. I was embarrassed and humiliated by what you saw that day. But I shouldn't have run."

"Nothing to be embarrassed about, baby. I love everything about you, aside from your stubborn ass."

"This ass?" she asked, pointing toward her backside.

"That's the one."

She tugged me down, and my mouth covered hers. Her lips parted in invitation, and my tongue slipped in.

Goddamn, I missed everything about her.

Our breaths were coming hard and fast, and I pulled back, my forehead resting against hers.

"Come on. I want you to tell me everything. Let's go upstairs."

Easier said than done. We were alone in the elevator, and my mouth was on hers once again. Once I got her into the room, I pulled her onto my lap as I sat down on the couch.

"Wow. This room is much nicer than mine," she said as her gaze moved around the large suite.

"You have a fucking room here?"

"Well, I flew in late last night. I'm staying at a dump up the street. But it's my dump, and I like it." She raised a brow. "Not really. I hate it. I was trying to be independent. I had things I needed to do before I came here today."

"Tell me."

"Well, for starters, that dick weasel, Lou Colson, called me —well, he called *Bailey Reynolds*." She rolled her eyes. "He had a change of heart and was suddenly willing to do what-ever it took to hire me. It was all a ploy to get to you. I shut that guy down so fast. I shouldn't have taken out my frustra-tion on you."

I wrapped my arms around her as she told me everything. How she'd spent the last few days on the shore, figuring out what she wanted out of life. How she went to the interview today and killed it. How she'd sold my story to *Football Live* because it was the right fit for that story but not for her. *Strive Forward* magazine felt right. She'd made her own rules, and they'd respected them. And then she told me about the rules she'd laid out for them.

"Wait. So, you aren't ever going to interview me again?" I pouted as she ran her fingers through my hair.

"Nope. And I also spoke on your behalf and told *Sports Today* that you would never do an interview with them again." She shrugged; she was so fucking adorable. "You see, I really am the boss sometimes, Captain."

"Yeah? I mean, you are Mrs. Sparrow. Obviously, you're a badass."

Her teeth sank into her bottom lip. "Yep. So, I want to go over the contract with you tonight."

"What? You want my opinion on the situation? That won't be hurting your womanhood?" I teased.

"The only thing hurting my womanhood at the moment is the fact that I've been away from you for days."

"Me, too, baby. And I'd love to look over your contract with you. Does this mean you're going to be based here?"

"Yep. You and me in the Big Apple, Captain."

"Fuck. I love the sound of that."

"Me, too. Did you go see those houses?" she asked as her head settled in the crook of my neck.

"Hell no. I was not about to speak for you. I knew you'd figure out your shit. You just had to torture me in the interim. I told Jay that I'd call him when you were ready to schedule a tour. I want the house that we choose to be everything you want."

"Damn, that was smooth, Mr. Sparrow."

"Not as smooth as the feel of your pussy against my cock," I whispered in her ear.

"Oh, my. I see the dirty talk is still on par." She rotated so she was straddling me. "How about you have your way with me in this fancy room, and then you take me back to mine so we can grab my things?"

"If I can have you right now, I'll do just about anything."

"Good, because I'm here, and I'm all yours."

"Damn straight, sweetheart. You've been mine since the day I met you." I pushed to my feet, and her legs wrapped around my waist.

"Well, not the very first day. That day you were a jackass, and I wouldn't have agreed to be yours if you'd begged me."

"I'm never above begging, sweetheart."

"That's Sweetheart Sparrow to you." Her head fell back in laughter as I dropped her onto the large bed.

I took a minute to look at her.

My girl.

Everything felt right in this moment, and I couldn't wait to start our lives together out here.

Out of the bubble.

Just me and her.

———

"Wow. It's pretty, but it's a lot of house, don't you think?" she asked as she walked from the kitchen to the dining room.

"You'll grow into it," Jay said.

"Can you give us a minute?" I asked our realtor. We'd toured several houses over the last few days, and this was the last one on our list.

"Of course. I'll meet you outside."

"Is this one not in the running?" I asked.

"Honestly, the only one that feels right is the one we saw yesterday morning. It's not too far from your mom's house, and it's close to both the training field for you and my work," Brinkley said.

"It was the smallest one we've seen. You don't want to find something we can grow into?" I teased.

She moved closer to me. "I grew up with four siblings and two parents, and we always had a dog, a cat, or a turtle. That home is half the size of the one we saw yesterday, and there was plenty of room for all of us. We aren't the type of couple to be in different rooms. I like having just one great room where we would hang out. When I'm at home, I want to be with you. And when we have kids, they'll want to be with us. We don't need a cold mansion. We need a home."

I loved that she knew what she wanted. That she had a plan for us, and I wanted every part of it.

"Yeah? You don't want a room you can run to when I aggravate you? You think you're done being bothered by me, huh?"

"Oh, don't get cocky. You aggravate me all the time. But I love it because I love you." She pushed up on her tiptoes and kissed me. "Did you like the house that we saw yesterday?"

"I've lived in a high-rise for years, so all of these homes have been appealing to me. I like the idea of having a big yard. But all that matters to me is that I come home to you. That's the house that I want."

"I can see us there. I can picture you mowing the lawn and me working in the garden. I picture myself in that gorgeous kitchen, wearing your jersey with nothing beneath and cooking dinner for us."

"Sold," I said as I leaned down and kissed her.

"Let's tell Jay and go write up an offer. We need to get back to the hotel to pack. Finn has texted me no less than a dozen times." We were flying out right after my practice in the morning to make it to his premiere in Los Angeles and be there to support him. His production company was throwing a big party for him.

"He is so happy that you were able to sneak away to attend this event for him. He got you and all the guys some friendship bracelets." She chuckled. "I don't know if he's ready for what's about to happen to his life."

"I don't think anyone can prepare for it. He'll be fine. He was born to shine, just like you were." She tugged my head down again and kissed me hard.

"I love you. Now let's go buy us a house."

And that was exactly what we did.

We wrote up the offer, and they accepted it immediately.

Brinkley fought me about being on the deed, but I wasn't buying this home without her.

It was me and her.

I'd start with the house, but I'd be putting a ring on that finger real soon.

One thing at a time.

thirty-three

· · ·

Brinkley

WE'D ARRIVED in Los Angeles just in time to get changed and make it over to the theatre where they were premiering *Big Sky Ranch*.

This show had been publicized like crazy, and everyone was talking about Finn Reynolds.

The internet.

Social media.

He'd be going on tour to promote the show real soon, and tonight was just the start.

CAGE

Mom's already crying. You know I can't handle this kind of emotion. Even Dad is teary-eyed. Where is everyone?

HUGH

Lila and I are here. Come to the lobby where Finn said to meet him.

Lincoln and I just pulled around back. We'll be right there.

GEORGIA

Maddox, Wyle, and I are almost to the lobby.
Finny, this is your day. I can't stop crying
either.

I dabbed at my eyes for the hundredth time in the last hour. My brother was a movie star. I'd already known it, but the rest of the world was about to find out.

"You okay?" Lincoln asked as the man Finn had told us would be waiting for us out back, opened the door and led us inside.

"Yes. I'm just really happy for him."

"Did you call Tia and Romeo? Are they here?" I asked as we headed toward the lobby. Yes, we'd invited them to the premiere because Tia had nearly fainted when she realized that Finn Reynolds was my brother, and I was scoring serious points as the coolest girlfriend by inviting her. Romeo acted unfazed but agreed to come to hang out with me and Lincoln. But I'd seen the way his eyes had widened when I'd told them I could score them two tickets. They didn't live too far from LA, so they'd used their mom's car and made the trip here. Lincoln had gotten them a room next door to ours tonight, and we'd all spend the day together tomorrow before we headed back to New York and they went home.

"Yep. Apparently, they just found Georgia," he said, as he glanced down at his phone.

GEORGIA

I'm with Romeo and Tia. We are already
practically best friends.

CAGE

Where the fuck are you people? Mom just stopped to pee for the ninth time since we left the hotel. Apparently, she's nervous and has the bladder of a Labrador puppy. And Dad is talking to every stranger we see like they're old friends. They all know that Finn is his son.

> Let them take this in. It's a big deal. How about you check your grumpy attitude at the door?

CAGE

I'm sorry that my attitude is hindering you, Brinks. You've got your man, you've got a new house, a new job, and now you aren't sulking like a big baby anymore, so now you're the attitude police?

> Bite me, Cage. I've always been the attitude police. Don't be a hater.

FINN

Hey, no fighting today. Let Mom pee as much as her bladder requires. I'm heading to the lobby now to meet you.

When we got to the lobby, it was like a Reynolds family reunion. Everyone was there, aside from Gracie, who'd stayed back at home and was having a sleepover at her best friend Piper's house.

Jenny and Grant Murphy were here. They were my parents' closest friends, and their daughter, Reese and Finn had been best friends since they took their first steps. I knew Finn had been pretty miserable with Reese living in London, as they'd always been inseparable. He'd been bummed that she'd be missing his big premiere, but she was swamped with work, and it was a long way to travel for one night.

We all hugged, and I made introductions as I took Tia and Romeo around to meet everyone.

"I can't believe I'm going to my first premiere ever," Tia said as she gushed to my superstar brother.

"Well, I'm honored that you came," Finn said to her before wrapping an arm around me and hugging me tight before doing the same to Lincoln. He then pulled out some kind of bracelet and tied it around Lincoln's wrist. I glanced around to see Cage, Hugh, Maddox, and Wyle wearing them, as well, which made me laugh.

"Is that Finnegan Charles Reynolds, a.k.a. the movie star?" a voice called out, and we all gasped to see Reese standing there.

"Holy shit. I can't believe you're here!" Finn yelled before scooping her up and spinning her around, her feet leaving the floor.

They had always just been Finn and Reese. They were Cottonwood Cove's favorite besties because they got into endless antics together and were always laughing and having a good time. I knew there had been tension with Reese's ex-fiancé because he and Finn had never really gotten along, and it had been a bone of contention for years.

"Who's that?" Tia asked, her eyes wide as she watched them gushing over one another.

"Damn, Tia, it's none of your business." Romeo shook his head and shot a look at Lincoln that basically said, *welcome to my life.*

"It's okay to be curious about people. Is that his girlfriend? She's gorgeous." She glared at her brother.

"Well, thank you. That beautiful girl is my daughter," Jenny said, as she and my mom walked up behind us. They both pulled out their phones and stood there, taking photos of them hugging. "And boy, do we wish they were dating."

My mom chuckled. "We always thought it would happen, but they never crossed the line. But they sure are cute together. They've always been one another's biggest cheer-leaders."

"It's stupid. They should get a room and do the deed." Cage raised a brow and crossed his arms over his chest.

"I'm going to pretend I didn't hear that," Grant said as he and Dad snuck up on us, and we all laughed at the warning look that he shot Cage.

"You all knew she was coming, didn't you?" I asked.

My mom and Jenny nodded and spoke at the same time. "We did."

"Are you kidding? These two always know what's going on. I wasn't told until ten minutes ago," my father said. "Apparently, they thought I would slip and tell everyone."

"You're a little loose-lipped." Hugh chuckled. "If I want to know anything, you're the one I go to."

"What? I'm a vault." My father held his hands up in defense.

"Dad, you're a vault with a broken lock. But I'm grateful. I never know who the fuck is pissed at me and what I did. I can always get you to tell me."

"Well, there's a strategy there. I'm a peacekeeper." My father winked at my mother.

"A very handsome peacekeeper." Mom waggled her brows, and Cage rolled his eyes.

We were all chuckling and having a good time.

"Who the fuck is this?" someone hissed, and I whipped around to see Jessica Carson in a black-sequined gown that hugged her curves all the way down to the ground. I imagined the woman couldn't eat so much as a single pistachio wearing that dress. Her breasts looked painfully lifted, and her strides were short due to the mermaid-style fitted gown, but it was clear she was on a mission. Her makeup gave her an airbrushed look, and even though she had the features of a gorgeous woman, she looked a bit scary at the moment.

Angry.

Enraged.

A little off-kilter.

"Oh my God. It's Jessica Carson," Tia whispered with her eyes wide as saucers. "She was the lead in my favorite Disney show a few years ago."

"She doesn't look like a Disney character right now. She looks kind of terrifying." Lincoln leaned in and kept his voice low.

"Like *boil-a-bunny-in-the-pot* type of unhinged, right?" Cage said. "This is why you don't dunk your pen in the company ink."

My parents and the Murphys weren't listening to us; they were too busy watching the scene unfold in front of us.

In the middle of the lobby of the most popular theatre in Los Angeles.

We were early, and Finn would have to step back outside and walk the red carpet soon. He'd just met us here before everything got started.

"He slept with her?" Lincoln asked, keeping his voice low.

Hugh leaned in. "He technically didn't sleep with her. They hooked up one time. He got some red flags and backed way off."

"Well, there's a little bit of a gray area there," Cage reminded him, and we all grew quiet when she stopped in front of them, and Finn set Reese's feet on the ground.

"This is my best friend, Reese Murphy. And you need to pull yourself together. This is a big day for both of us. Let's tone down the outbursts, yeah?" Finn said, which, for my brother, was about as harsh as he got.

He usually let things roll off his shoulders. But he'd always been different when it came to Reese.

"Hey, Jessica. Congrats on the show. I know it's going to be a huge hit. I can't wait to see it." Reese extended her arm.

Jessica looked down and glared at her hand before Reese pulled it back to her side. "Listen, *bestie*. He and I are walking the red carpet together. *Because we're together*. So, there will be no public hugging and carrying on amongst you two. You got it?" she seethed.

"I wish I had some popcorn right now," Cage whispered, and Lila swatted him in the chest.

"She definitely gets right to the point," Maddox said, and his brother barked out a laugh.

"That's one way of saying it." Wyle smirked. "She's fucking unhinged."

"What the hell are you doing, Jessica? You don't get to speak to her that way. You are completely out of control. I'll meet you in the back to walk out together, and we can continue the conversation there. Not here, in front of my family and friends." Finn's voice was colder than I'd ever heard it, and Jessica's head snapped up and moved in our direction.

She walked toward us, and I squeezed Lincoln's hand, unsure of what she was going to do.

"Hey, y'all. You must be Finn's family. I'm his better half, Jessica."

She'd completely transformed her tone and was acting sugary sweet. None of us said a word as she'd basically just been a complete asshole to Reese.

And Reese was part of the family. She was also one of the nicest people I'd ever known.

"Well, we will definitely have to catch up later. It was so great to meet y'all. I'll see you in a bit." She had a wide smile on her face and waved before turning on her heels and marching away.

Reese walked toward us, eyes wide as she winced. "Well, that didn't go so well."

I opened my arms and hugged her before introducing her to Lincoln and his siblings. She made her way around the group.

"Do you see what I'm dealing with?" Finn said, rubbing

his temples. My parents and the Murphys were taking turns hugging and fussing over Reese.

"I warned you, brother." Cage raised a brow.

"I didn't sleep with her," Finn said through gritted teeth, glancing at my parents to make sure they weren't listening.

"I think there's some confusion there," Hugh said over his laughter.

"How is one confused about whether or not they slept with a woman?" Lincoln asked, his brows cinched together.

"Well, it's sort of a *tip thing*." Georgia burst out in laughter as the words left her mouth.

"Oh my gosh, are we back to the tip debate?" Reese said as she stepped into our little huddle. "I told you not to go there, Finny."

My brothers, Georgia, and Reese were all laughing hysterically, and everyone else looked completely confused.

"He dipped the tip of the, er, *company pen* into the *wanton ink*. Just the tip, though." Cage smirked. Everyone fell back in laughter.

Yes. Finn had shared his little escapade that had gone awry with us, and apparently, he'd told Reese what happened, as well.

"It's not funny," Finn hissed. "She was all over me. I'm human. Things got heated, and she was on top of me." He glanced around nervously.

"And?" Maddox asked, looking between us.

"Well, we sort of started, I mean, just the slightest bit." He shrugged.

"He's trying to say that the tip made contact…" Hugh covered his mouth with his hand to hide his smile.

"And then she fucking bit me. Hard. I still have a scar." He shivered dramatically as he rubbed his shoulder. "I called it off. There were some major red flags. Like the fact that she gouged me with her nails and drew blood right before she sank her teeth into me like a fucking vampire. I got the hell out of there, but she wouldn't accept the fact that I didn't want to take things further. And we work together, so I've just sort of ignored it. Now, she's acting like we're together. Nothing has happened since."

"Since you bumped her with the tip of your dick?" Cage said dryly.

"Well, yes. That is exactly what happened. And look at how she just acted. Thank God she didn't get the whole package." He waggled his brows. "Let's just say that my agent is not pleased about the situation."

"It'll be fine. You'll have some space between filming now, so it will all blow over." Reese bumped him with her shoulder, and I watched as all the tension left his face. "This is your big night. And I'm here, so…"

"I'm so fucking happy you're here." He kissed the top of her head.

"Finn, they're calling you," my mother said, hurrying over to straighten his bow tie. "Get out there. We'll see you inside."

"Okay. Find Angelique. She'll take you to your seats. Dylan just texted that they were all pulling up now. Angelique has a row reserved for them, too." Angelique was Finn's agent.

He hurried off just as Angelique came walking our way. I'd met her a few times when I'd visited Finn on set. She ushered us inside the theatre and whispered in my ear.

"It's a real shitshow with this Jessica Carson situation. I warned him to be careful. It's no secret that the woman is always in the midst of a lot of drama. And I've heard she's got it bad for Finn."

"Oh, I think you are spot on. I just witnessed a bit of a meltdown." I chuckled.

She shook her head. "Never a dull moment. You guys enjoy. This row is yours. Your cousins have the row behind you."

We all shuffled around and found our seats just as Uncle

Jack waved at us, and they all made their way over to their assigned seats.

Lincoln was beside me, and he leaned close, whispering in my ear. "All that sex talk has me ready to haul your ass back to the hotel."

My teeth sank into my bottom lip as I turned to look at him. "You're insatiable."

"Only with you, sweetheart."

I wouldn't have it any other way.

epilogue

. . .

Lincoln

IT WAS OUR SEASON OPENER, and I was champing at the bit to get out on the field. I'd always loved football. It was a part of who I was. But it was different this time, as I stood on the sidelines waiting for the coin toss, wearing number sixty-nine proudly.

It had always been only my mother out in the stands, cheering me on all these years. But my circle had grown.

My family had grown.

My mother was sitting in the midst of all the Reynolds chaos, and Romeo and Tia were right there with her. It was as if they'd always been a part of my life.

At least that was how it felt.

Bradford and Alana were sitting beside my mother. Tia was next to Georgia and Lila, while Romeo managed to squeeze between Maddox and Wyle. Hugh, Finn, and Cage were sitting beside them. Little Gracie was sitting on her Uncle Hugh's lap, wearing a gigantic pair of pink head-phones because Brinkley had worried that the noise would overwhelm her.

These were my people.

My teammates in life.

They supported me, and I'd walk through fire for any one of them.

We'd won the coin toss, and I slipped my helmet on as the crowd roared. I glanced over to see Brinkley several feet away on the field. She'd gotten a press pass and was covering the game, but she would not be interviewing me.

It was something she felt strongly about, and I fucking respected the hell out of it. Her career was important to her, but there was nothing more important than our relationship —for either of us.

I winked at her, and she just stood there smiling at me.

My girl.

I couldn't wait to put a ring on her finger. We'd moved into our new home, and we'd gone to Paris for Maddox and Georgia's wedding, and life had been busy. I wanted to do something really special for her, but I hadn't thought of what it was just yet.

A smack on the side of my head had me whipping around, and Brett Jacobs stood there with his eyes bugging out of his head. "Uh, we got a game to play, asshole. You want to stop staring at your girl and pull your shit together?"

"Wipe that goofy-ass look off your face," I said over my laughter when I realized the crowd had picked up on what was going on, and cheers and laughter bellowed around the field.

We'd gone public with our relationship, and we were both fine with it. We didn't flaunt it and preferred quiet nights at home, but we didn't hide it when we were out together.

I returned my focus to the game.

We got in the huddle, and I called the first play.

Everything about my life felt lighter now. When I was on the field, I wanted to do everything I could to score points and win games. But when I was off the field, I had a whole life going on.

And it felt damn good.

There was a lot more to play for now.

But whether or not we won this game—I still went home a winner. No doubt about it.

The whistle blew, and the ball was hiked.

I ran back, hyperfocused, as I gazed down the field. We wanted to come out the gate strong. Make a statement.

And there was Brett. He'd juked the dude covering him and was exactly where I needed him. I pulled back and released the ball.

Putting it right in his hands, just as he was tackled to the ground.

But I'd take a sixty-two-yard pass for our opening play all day long.

I high-fived the guys who'd covered me and given me the time to get that ball into Brett's hands.

The next play was a pass to Terry Langley, and he rushed for ten more yards.

The crowd was going crazy, and it felt damn good to be back out here, doing what I loved.

With the people that I loved out here supporting me.

It didn't get any better.

We battled for the next several hours. It was hot as hell outside, and we pushed as hard as we could to bring home the win. And that was exactly what we did.

We'd won by ten points, and Coach Balboa was proud as hell as we all gathered in the locker room and celebrated.

After we'd showered and changed, I made my way out of the locker room to a slew of reporters. I answered a few questions that they fired off, and Brett and Lenny were right there with me.

And that was when I saw her.

My gaze locked with Brinkley's, and I couldn't get out of there fast enough.

"Listen, these guys are here to answer whatever else you

want to know. I've got a date with my girl, and frankly, she smells a lot better than all of you."

There was a lot of laughter, and I made my way through the crowd as my teammates took over answering their questions.

"Great game, Captain."

"Thanks. I thought you'd be stuck here running interviews." My fingers interlocked with hers.

"I got what I needed, and my sexy boyfriend played a great game, so I'd like to get out of here with him."

"That sounds good to me, sweetheart."

"Lincoln, when are you going to put a ring on it?" someone shouted from behind us, and I'd normally ignore them. But not today. That was a question that I didn't mind answering.

"I'm working on it!" I held up my hand and heard the laughter behind us.

Brinkley's cheeks were a little pink, and I fucking loved it.

"Does that scare you?" I teased.

"I don't scare easy. I'm ready when you are." She smiled as we walked down the hall.

"Good to know."

We were meeting everyone at our place and having dinner catered. When we pulled up, they'd all beaten us there, and there were cars parked all along the large circular driveway. I opened the garage door, and we saw Finn standing in the garage on the phone, and he didn't look happy.

"Is he all right? I'm guessing this shit is getting to him, huh?"

"Yeah. Maybe you could talk to him? You know a thing or two about the press, right?" Brinkley said. Her tone was light, but I heard the concern beneath it.

Big Sky Ranch had become the number one streaming show out there at the moment. Sometimes, everything comes together, and a show just has that magic.

Finn happened to be the star of the show, and his popularity had soared overnight. Unfortunately, his costar was enjoying the fame and was doing a bunch of interviews, bad-mouthing Finn for breaking her heart. He was taking a lot of heat at the moment, and he'd yet to speak out about it.

We stepped out of the car, and Brinkley gave me a kiss before jogging toward her brother. "I'll meet you guys inside."

"You all right?" I asked after he ended the call.

"Yeah. Great game, by the way."

"Hey, we're talking about you. I'm sure this shit is getting to you."

"You know, it's a weird mix of a lot of things. I've waited so long to find a show that would sort of launch my career, you know?" He glanced out at the street before looking back at me. "And now there's this woman spreading all these lies about me, and it's not what I want to be known for."

"What does Angelique say?"

"Well, we just thought it would all blow over at first. But now, Jessica's going on these talk shows and saying we discussed marriage and having a family together, and none of that is true. We never even went out on a date. We don't chat on the phone either. I don't know much about her outside of our professional situation. We hooked up that one time, and I've been honest about what happened, as much as everyone wants to joke about it. I did stop things because I knew something wasn't right. I've kept my head down for months since. I haven't been going out, haven't been with any women. I don't want to fuck up my career." He scrubbed a hand down his face.

"You've got the truth on your side, brother. It will eventually die down. Has Angelique tried talking to her or her team?"

He nodded. "Yep. Jessica just keeps saying that all press is good press, and it's helping the show. She loves it. But it's making people fucking pissed, and I'm getting these aggressive messages on social media. People want us together now. It's a fucking nightmare."

"Fuck. I'm sorry you're going through this. Just stay the course, Finn. She'll talk herself into a corner."

"That's what Angelique thinks. She said I just need to keep a low profile. If I end up dating someone down the road, we'll present me as a relationship guy and not some womanizer, I guess."

"It's good you have this downtime between seasons. I'm excited to see the house you bought. Brinkley said it's right on the water and not too far from town."

"Yeah. That's been a good thing. I've been able to throw myself into working on the new place and taking the boat out on the water. And I'm not going to lie, being home helps. No one bothers me there."

"Cottonwood Cove, man. It's hard to beat. The people are nosy as shit but protective to the core. They've got your back, and so do we."

"I know you do, and it means a lot."

"You know I'm here if you want to talk. And you're welcome to stay out here with us for as long as you want. We've got plenty of room."

"Thanks. I've had a lot of fun out here. I'll be back for as many games as I can swing, pending my filming schedule."

"Good. We love having you all here."

And I meant it.

I followed him inside, and the house was buzzing. My mom and Alana were helping the caterer get all the chafing dishes set up. Maddox and Georgia were standing with Wyle, who was playing bartender. Hugh and Lila were out in the backyard with Gracie, and Tia was out there playing with them. Cage, Romeo, and Bradford were talking about the game, and Finn went over to join them.

"Hey," Brinkley said as she slid up beside me. She'd

changed into a pair of denim cut-off shorts and a white tee. "How'd it go with Finn?"

"He's going to be fine, baby. Your brother has a good head on his shoulders. I think he probably needs to find himself a woman and let everyone see that he's the stable guy that he is. Jessica will blow herself up eventually."

"Well, you know firsthand just how great life can be when you've got yourself a good woman," she said, her voice teasing.

"Damn straight. I used to come home alone after games to a quiet house. And look at this. Look what we've created together." I wrapped an arm around her shoulder and pulled her close.

"A three-ring circus?" she said over her laughter.

"A family, sweetheart."

Her eyes softened, and she studied me. "So, are you really going to make an honest woman out of me?"

"Been dreaming about it for months. But don't pull your reporter shit and start trying to figure it out. I'd like to actually surprise you."

"Good luck. I'm hard to surprise." She tapped her finger against her temple. "I'm always one step ahead of my opponent."

I barked out a laugh. "Do you mean your lover?"

"I do love you something fierce, Lincoln Hendrix."

"Good. Because you're stuck with me for life. No turning back now." I leaned down and kissed her. "I love you."

"Oh, for God's sake. Get a room, people," Cage groaned, and everyone laughed.

And if I spent the rest of my life right here, I'd be the luckiest man alive.

As long as this woman was beside me—I'd found my home.

THE END

Do you want to see Lincoln's big surprise for Brinkley? Click here for an exclusive BONUS SCENE!
https://dl.bookfunnel.com/bkpskbniwj

Are you excited for Finn Reynolds and Reese Murphy to get out of the friendship zone in this small town, friends-to-lovers, fake dating romance? BEFORE THE SUNSET is available for pre-order now!
https://geni.us/beforethesunset

Do you want to know more about Lincoln's brother, Roman Knight? He will have his own book in the upcoming Magnolia Falls Series, book 1, Loving Romeo.
Pre-Order now!
https://geni.us/lovingromeo

acknowledgments

Greg, Thank you for supporting me every single day on this journey. For cheering me on, for believing in me and for giving me endless romantic inspiration!! LOL! Thirty three years with the love of my life gives me lots to write about! I love you forever!

Chase & Hannah… I feel like the luckiest person in the world that I get to be your mama! It's like hitting the jackpot every single day. You are the reason that I work hard, and the reason that I chase my dreams, because you both inspire me more than you know! I love you to the moon and back!

Willow, I am forever grateful for that first day that we met, and for every day since. Your friendship means the world to me. I don't know how I ever existed without you! I love you so much and am so grateful to have you in my life!

Catherine, thank you for your endless love and support. I love talking all things with you… from kaftans to dog stories to book events! Thankful to be on this journey with you. Love you!

Kandi, I am so thankful for you! For your friendship, your wisdom, your encouragement and all the laughs in between (and your fabulous style and decor tips). I look forward to our chats each day and love being on this journey with you. Love you forever my sweet friend!

Pathi, I can't put into words how thankful I am for YOU! Thank you for being such an amazing friend!! Thank you for believing in me and encouraging me to chase my dreams!! I love and appreciate you more than I can say!! Love you FOREVER!

Nat, I am so thrilled that you are on this journey with me (and Willow) now!! We are so lucky to have you and I'm thrilled to be working with you every day again!! So grateful for you! Love you!

Nina, I don't know how I ever made a decision without you. Thank you for always being there for me. From the little things to the big things. Thank you for encouraging me in every way! I am forever grateful for your friendship and to be on this journey with you! Cheers to many more years together! Love you!!

Valentine Grinstead, I absolutely adore you! You are such a bright light and I am so thankful for YOU! I'm thrilled that I get to see you lots this year! Love you!

Kim Cermak, You complete me. LOL! I'd truly be lost without you! Thank you for all that you do for me every single day!! I absolutely adore you!!

Christine Miller, I am so grateful for you! Thank you for making my life so much easier and for all that you do for me!! I am SO THANKFUL for you!

Sarah Norris, thank you for the gorgeous graphics, for all of your support and for always being willing to help even when I remember things at the last minute! LOL! l am incredibly grateful for YOU!

Meagan, Oh how I adore you! I love working with you and am so excited about creating the book box for this book with you! Thank you for being an amazing beta reader and for creating the most beautiful reels and TikToks and for helping to get my books out there! Your support means the world to me!! Thank you so much!!

Kelley Beckham, thank you for setting up all the "lives" with people who have now become forever friends! Thank you so much for all that you do to help me get my books out there! Thank you for letting me send you eight million cookies and being so kind and supportive in every way! I am truly so grateful!

Amy Dindia, You are the absolute sweetest and I'm so thankful for you. Thank you for creating absolutely perfect reels and TikToks for me. I am endlessly grateful for you!

Maren, Kat & the amazing Slack girls… thank you for the sprints, the laughs and the friendship!

Doo, Abi, Meagan, Annette, Jennifer, Pathi, Natalie, and Caroline, thank you for being the BEST beta readers EVER! Your feedback means the world to me. I am so thankful for you!!

Madison, Thank you for taking these gorgeous photos for the Cottonwood Cove Series. I am in love with this cover! Thank you so much!! Xo

Emily, thank you for creating these gorgeous special edition covers! I love them! So thankful for YOU! Xo

Sue Grimshaw (Edits by Sue), I would be completely lost without you and I am so grateful to be on this journey with you. Thank you for being the voice I rely on so much! Thank you for moving things around and doing what ever is needed to make the timeline work. I am FOREVER grateful for YOU!

Ellie (My Brothers Editor), So thankful for your friendship! Your friendship means the world to me! Thank you for always making time for me no matter how challenging the timeline is! Love you!

Julie Deaton, thank you for helping me to put the best books out there possible. I am so grateful for you!

Jamie Ryter, I am so thankful for your feedback! Your comments are endlessly entertaining and they give me life when I need it most!! But this book took the cake! BEST COMMENTS EVER!! I am so thankful for you!!

Christine Estevez, thank you for all that you do to support me! I love when I get to work with you on projects. Your friendship truly means the world to me! Love you!

Crystal Eacker, I am so thankful for you! Thank you for

doing whatever is needed! For making forms, beta audio reading, taking photos and making graphics!! You are such an amazing support and I'm forever grateful!

Jennifer, thank you for being an endless support system. For rallying readers, posting, reviewing and doing whatever is needed for each release. Your friendship means the world to me! Love you!

Paige, Thank you for your endless support! Your dancing videos are my favorite! But I'm most grateful that I have found such an amazing friend! Thank you for always making time for my books and for helping to get them out there in the world! I am so incredibly thankful for YOU! Love you!

Rachel Parker, Ah....I am so thankful for you my sweet friend! I love that I get to chat with you on every release day! I will keep Charlotte's swag coming for many years! Love you!

Sarah Sentz, thank you for always being so supportive and for making time to chat with me on every release! Thank you for helping spread the word about my books. I am forever grateful for you!!

Ashley Anastasio, I am forever grateful for your support and friendship! Thank you for sharing my books and making the most gorgeous edits and reels and TikTok's and book-marks ever!! So thankful for you!!

Kayla Compton, I am so grateful for your endless support! I love that you and I share a love for our favorite lake!! Thank you for spreading the word about my books and all that you do to support me!

Mom, thank you for loving Brinkley and Lincoln so much and for cheering me on every step of the way! I am so thankful that we share this love of books with one another! Ride or die!! Love you!

Dad, you really are the reason that I keep chasing my dreams!! Thank you for teaching me to never give up. Love you!

Sandy, thank you for reading and supporting me throughout this journey! Love you!

Sammi, I am so thankful for your support and your friendship!! Love you!

Marni, I love you forever and I am endlessly thankful for your friendship!! Xo

A huge shoutout to the Romance Readers Retreat for including On the Shore as one of your selected books!! Brinkley and Lincoln are honored…and so am I!! It means the world to me!! Xo

To the JKL WILLOWS… I am forever grateful to you for your support and encouragement, my sweet friends!! I can't wait for us to all be together this year!! Love you!

To all the bloggers, bookstagrammers and ARC readers who have posted, shared, and supported me—I can't begin to tell you how much it means to me. I love seeing the graphics that you make and the gorgeous posts that you share. I am forever grateful for your support!

To all the readers who take the time to pick up my books and take a chance on my words…THANK YOU for helping to make my dreams come true!!

keep up on new releases

Linktree Laurapavlovauthor
Newsletter laurapavlov.com

other books by laura pavlov

Cottonwood Cove Series
Into the Tide
Under the Stars
On the Shore
Before the Sunset
After the Storm

Honey Mountain Series
Always Mine
Ever Mine
Make You Mine
Simply Mine
Only Mine

The Willow Springs Series
Frayed
Tangled
Charmed
Sealed
Claimed

Montgomery Brothers Series
Legacy
Peacekeeper
Rebel

A Love You More Rock Star Romance
More Jade
More of You
More of Us

The Shine Design Series
Beautifully Damaged
Beautifully Flawed

The G.D. Taylors Series with Willow Aster
Wanted Wed or Alive
The Bold and the Bullheaded
Another Motherfaker
Don't Cry Spilled MILF
Friends with Benefactors

follow me...

Website laurapavlov.com
Goodreads @laurapavlov
Instagram @laurapavlovauthor
Facebook @laurapavlovauthor
Pav-Love's Readers @pav-love's readers
Amazon @laurapavlov
BookBub @laurapavlov
TikTok @laurapavlovauthor